I0633317

The Lady Pirates

Robert Cort

Published by Clink Street Publishing 2024

Copyright © 2024

First edition.

The author asserts the moral right under the Copyright, Designs and Patents Act 1988 to be identified as the author of this work.

All rights reserved. No part of this publication may be reproduced, stored in a retrieval system or transmitted, in any form or by any means without the prior consent of the author, nor be otherwise circulated in any form of binding or cover other than that with which it is published and without a similar condition being imposed on the subsequent purchaser.

ISBN:
978-1-915785-51-0 - paperback
978-1-915785-52-7 - ebook

ALSO WRITTEN BY ROBERT CORT

THE IAN CAXTON THRILLER SERIES

www.robertcort.net

"In honest service, there are commonly low wages and hard labour, but being a pirate there's plenty of food, drink, pleasure and ease, liberty and power. A merry life and a short one, that's my motto."

Bartholomew Roberts ('Black Bart'),
pirate captain, 1722.

CHAPTER 1

In the 17th and 18th centuries there were many pirates who sailed the Atlantic Ocean and the Caribbean Sea, but two women, Mary Read and Anne Bonny, were said to be more ruthless than most of the male buccaneers at sea. Indeed, they would probably cut the throats of any person who disagreed.

They dressed in men's clothing and committed unspeakable atrocities, all to demonstrate their power and to obtain large hoards of gold, silver and jewels. Their adventures have been written into history, but their hidden treasure may have never been found.

Eventually captured by the British authorities, Mary and Anne were tried at the court in Spanish Town, Jamaica. There, in front of a packed public gallery, their cases were heard. To be convicted of piracy, the result would always be... the sentence of death!

Hauled from the court, all convicted pirates would be taken back to their cell and await their destiny... the announced date of their public execution! Their futures now certain, their lives would soon end... whilst 'dancing the hempen jig'.

When Mary and Anne were brought into court, there was a gasp from the crowd in the public gallery. Despite being scruffily dressed, it was obvious to everyone that both were 'with child'. Chained by their ankles and wrists, Mary, aged 34, and Anne, just 23, were terrified and alone. Both just stared downwards, despairingly, resigned to their ultimate fate.

Their case was heard in the crumbling old wooden court building, which had certainly seen better days. Situated in the heart of old Spanish Town, some said the sultry courtroom smelled of death and decaying bodies, others said it was the gateway to Hell. For both Mary and Anne, it was the end of the road, the end of their plunderings galore.

The prosecution made its presentation, listing the many crimes both women had committed. Both Mary and Anne listened but offered little defence. The court suddenly fell silent and all eyes were fixed on 'his honour'.

The judge sat aloft, his aged and hollow-cheeked face was wrinkled and grey. His merciless dark brown eyes glared all around the courtroom and then he fixed his stare on the two bedraggled women. He adjusted his long white wig, clasped his wizened hands together and made the following pronouncement:

"Ye and both of ye are adjudged and found guilty of piracy. You are sentenced to death. You will be taken back to the place from whence you came. From there you'll be taken to a place of execution where you'll be hanged by the neck until all breathing has ceased… or until your neck is irreparably snapped."

This decision immediately brought an outcry from the gallery. "No woman in their expectant state should ever be punished by death," the crowd yelled. They stamped their feet and three women waved their fists at the judge.

Mary and Anne stared at each other in total disbelief. Mary immediately pleaded leniency… due to 'the belly'.

The judge hit his gavel several times to try to recover some semblance of order. Gradually the occupants of the public gallery quietened. The judge reminded everyone that this was a court of law. He stared back towards Anne and Mary for a few seconds and everyone held their breath. He then announced he'd changed his conviction decision. Both punishments were commuted from hanging… to a whole life sentence in the Spanish Town prison!

Prison life in Spanish Town was harsh and often very cruel, and the two women suffered more than most men. Mary Read's young child died at birth, but there are no consistent records of what became of Mary. One historical report says she died of a fever, another suggested she was eventually hanged!

Of the outcome of Anne Bonny, or indeed her child, again nothing for certain is known. Some reports say she died in prison, not long after her daughter was born. Another says her father purchased her release. The one thing that is absolutely true is that both women's names subsequently disappeared from all historical records. Nobody knows for certain what really happened to them.

That is… **until now**!

The two women's backgrounds couldn't have been more different. Anne was born near the town of Cork in Ireland. She was the illegitimate daughter of local lawyer William Cormac and his maid, Mary Brennan. When Anne was born in 1697, Cormac was worried and panicked. He decided to dress Anne as a boy and tried to pass off this 'boy' to the Cork community as the son of a relative. Cormac also tried to gain credit when he announced he'd volunteered to raise the 'boy' in his legal practice. Unfortunately, his efforts to hide Anne's true gender, and keep his indiscretion a secret from his wife, suddenly backfired. When young Anne was old enough to speak, she innocently told a visitor she was a girl! Cormac's reputation and career were both shattered overnight. He could no longer make a living in his town and made the decision to move away, taking with him both Anne and Mary Brennan. He decided to take his new family to the New World and when they arrived in Charles Town, South Carolina, Anne was dressed as their daughter. Anne Cormac grew up as a strong and often outspoken woman. She told Mary Read, later in life, that when she was aged 15, she so violently beat a man who had tried to rape her that she'd almost murdered him!

Anne became very difficult for her father to handle and after she'd married without his consent, she was thrown out of the family's South Carolina home. At just 16 years of age, she had married James Bonny, a sailor, who was described as lazy, useless and a general good-for-nothing. Anne was not in love with Bonny, she just saw him as her chance to escape from her tyrannical father and his repressive world. Bonny took his new wife to Nassau, on the island of New Providence. Just one of the cluster of islands that make up the Bahamas archipelago. Nassau, had a menacing reputation as a tough human settlement… a haven for marauding pirates!

'Calico' Jack Rackham, previously a pirate under Captain Charles Vane on the ship *Ranger*, had now become the captain of his own pirate ship, *Revenge*. Rackham got the nickname of Calico Jack because of the multi-coloured clothes he wore. However, following the 1717 Royal Proclamation by King George, which promised an 'Act of Grace' for any pirate who volunteered to give up their life of piracy, Jack Rackham, now aged 37, decided to take up the king's offer. Jack 'retired' in Nassau and was living off his ill-gotten gains. Then in 1719, he met Anne. She told him she was desperate to leave her lazy and persistently philandering husband. The local authorities said a divorce would not be allowed and Anne was threatened with prison if she didn't return to her husband and their family home. She had no intention of suffering either of these fates so she and Rackham returned to his ship, *Revenge*. Rackham collected together a number of his old crew and they sailed away from Nassau. Captain Calico Jack Rackham was returning to his former life... as a cut-throat pirate.

On board *Revenge*, Anne initially dressed as a man. Women found aboard a ship were deemed to be 'bad luck', so only Jack knew her true sex.

Anne knew that to be accepted as a man by the rest of the crew, she would need to be a pirate as well. This suited her as she wanted a new and exciting life, to seek the same adventures and wealth that Rackham had acquired. He regularly recounted colourful tales and stories about his previous pirate life... and all his exhilarating experiences!

Living in England, Mary Read's mother was previously married to a sailor to whom she had borne a son. However, some months after her husband's disappearance at sea, she became pregnant again, this time by a man she hardly knew. In order to hide her shame from her in-laws, she and her son moved to the countryside, where she planned to have the illegitimate baby in the home of a friend. However, at about the same time as the birth of baby Mary, her son suddenly died. Mary and her mother continued to live in the countryside alone until they ran out of money. Left penniless and desperate, her mother initially decided to dress Mary in her brother's clothes in an attempt to convince her mother-in-law that Mary was actually her grandson. She pleaded with her mother-in-law for money to help support her grandchild. The mother-in-law agreed and Mary grew up wearing only boy's clothes. That arrangement continued until the mother-in-law died. By now Mary had become a teenager and once again the family's income had dried up. Mary was sent out to work and found employment as a foot-boy for a French woman in a local town. Mary, however, had her own dreams. Dreams of adventures, wealth and a family. So, when Mary outgrew this foot-boy's position, she joined the army and became a successful soldier. She then joined a cavalry regiment where she fell in love with one of her fellow soldiers, a man named Tommy. While sharing a tent with Tommy, Mary decided to disclose her true sex. Tommy was ecstatic and their relationship subsequently bloomed. During the next lull in the war, they both obtained permission to leave the army camp. With several of the regiment's fellow soldiers in attendance, they were duly married.

After successfully being discharged from the army the couple started a new career. They chose to work together at an inn. Unfortunately, the marriage didn't last long because Tommy died of a fever. Mary was distraught, her heart broken. Downcast and disillusioned with her life, she eventually stowed away on the merchant ship, *Tusk*. It was heading for the New World. Unfortunately, during the journey across the Atlantic, the *Tusk* was captured by pirates who were sailing the infamous ship, *Adventure*.

With no definite plans, or employment lined up in the New World, Mary dressed again in men's clothes. She changed her name to Mark Read and decided to join the pirate crew. She was given a short-barrelled flintlock pistol, knife and a cutlass sword and was told to practise their use every day. She became very proficient at wielding the sword and fought bravely in battles and conflicts against her opponents.

Several months later, the *Adventure* arrived in Nassau and Mary went ashore. After a brief stay on the island, she decided to join a group of privateers, who'd all been hired by the latest Bahamas governor, Woodes Rogers. These privateers were no more than legal mercenaries who'd been given a licence from the British government to loot any merchant ship owned by an enemy of Britain.

Not long after the privateers' ship had set sail the crew decided to mutiny against the captain and become a band of pirates. Mary now found herself on yet another pirate ship and was once again enjoying the pirate life and realising new financial rewards. However, she quickly realised that whilst the mutineers were enjoying their new adventures as pirates at sea, they were not sufficiently organised, brave or skilled enough to win many serious fights. Indeed, they easily lost their fourth encounter, their first serious battle, when only six of their crew survived. Mary had fought bravely and, still dressed in men's clothes, she was recognised by the vanquishing captain for her courage and skills with the sword. She and the remaining five survivors were all taken aboard the victorious ship. It was on this new vessel where Mary's life would change… forever. She had joined the crew of Calico Jack's infamous pirate ship, *Revenge*.

Over the coming months the *Revenge* successfully attacked many merchant ships and Spanish galleons carrying gold, silver and jewels. Mary had become a serious fighter and fought like the most bloodthirsty of men. She was brave, skilful and fearless. Killing became a habit and she was rewarded with wealth beyond her wildest dreams!

It was in the summer of 1720 that the two female pirates finally spoke to each other for the first time. Mary, dressed, as usual, as a male sailor, was now 33 years of age. However, she looked like a much younger 'man'. On one quiet evening, whilst she was patrolling the poop deck and fulfilling her 'watch' duties, Anne approached her. She was also dressed as a male sailor but still had her own female desires. They chatted and Anne tried to seduce the sailor she knew as Mark Read. She was convinced 'he' was a young and attractive male. It was at this point that Mary was forced to share her secret in order to avoid an awkward sexual encounter. Anne burst out laughing and decided to admit to her own gender. Afterwards, the two females became firm friends and Anne was the only person aboard the *Revenge* who knew of Mary's secret. However, Rackham became both jealous and angry, due to the amount of time 'his woman', Anne, was spending with this 'male', Mark Read. At one point he even threatened to kill this 'man'! It was only when Anne finally came clean and told Jack of Mary's true sex, that Mary managed to survive.

On August 22nd, 1720, Calico Jack and his crew stole the prized ship, *William.* It was one of the fastest ships sailing in the Caribbean Sea. The crew had attacked and boarded the ship, looting it of all its treasure. Mary and Anne were exceedingly brave and, with the skilful use of daggers and swords, they maimed or killed a number of the male opposition. The *William* was a serious prize and became part of Rackham's fleet. Its shallow draft hull was favoured by pirates in the Bahamas because the waters were too shallow for the larger man-of-war British Navy ships. Jack sailed the ship with pride as he could now fully employ the fleet's hit-and-run tactics to full effect. They attacked and looted many merchant ships crossing the Caribbean Sea.

Although the two women pirates had little in common growing up, they'd now ended up on the same ship… and decided to share their plundered treasure together. Whilst neither were wholeheartedly keen on killing, or maiming their fellow human beings, they knew they existed in a world of 'kill or be killed'! Survival, and the ultimate financial gains, depended on their commitment and skills whilst using their knives and swords. Indeed, they constantly felt they needed to demonstrate to the rest of the crew that they were neither lacking in confidence, nor competence, when it came to fighting the enemy.

Over subsequent months, both women continued to prove they were extremely capable fighters. It was the men in their crew who were always the casualties during the skirmishes and conflicts. Mary and Anne repeatedly overcame all opponents, managing to survive with just the odd cut or bruise.

To show his appreciation of Mary's and Anne's skilled use of the sword, Calico Jack decided to honour the ladies by designing a new flag for his ship. The traditional plain black flag, indicating the presence of a pirate ship, was amended and a white skull with two crossed swords was added and now appeared in the centre of the flag.

As a result of their continued survival and successes, Mary and Anne had accumulated huge quantities of gold, silver and jewels. Most of this treasure they decided to hide, burying them in two secret places on an islet close to Nassau: a coral cay called Hog Island!

Nassau, the capital of the Bahamas, had a notorious reputation. It was one of many pirate sanctuaries in the Caribbean. From 1706 to 1718, Nassau was known as the 'Republic of Pirates' and was the stronghold of a loose confederacy run by privateers-turned-pirates. It was governed by an informal 'Code of the Pirates'. One of the codes introduced a form of democracy whereby crews of the Republic would vote on who was going to be the ship's captain and officers. It was also agreed that other pirate crews should always be treated with proper respect.

Pirate ships could often be found in or around Nassau. There they could collect both their supplies and any extra pirate crew they might need. Much of the plundered treasure was also hidden on the island and a proportion were used to help develop the thriving pirate town's community.

Because of the large volume of looted treasure known to exist and be traded in Nassau, the town attracted adventurers, villains, traders and wild women from afar. There were plenty of taverns and much gold and silver was traded for money. The money was then exchanged in the bars for drink, gambling and sex. It was often said that when a pirate slept, he never fantasised of going to heaven. Instead, his pre-eminent dream was to return to his forever paradise on earth… the fabulous port of Nassau!

Like most pirates, Mary and Anne recorded the locations of their buried treasure on handwritten maps, which they kept secretly hidden amongst their belongings. Copies of these maps were also buried at a separate special place on Hog Island. Calico Jack, being the captain, and a pirate for more years than he could remember, had accumulated a larger collection of treasure than any member of his crew. Most of his treasure had also been secretly buried on different Caribbean islands, such as New Providence, Heneagua and Cuba. However, he'd also hidden another significant haul under the floorboards of a room he occupied in the Star Inn. This tavern was owned by Jack's brother, and Jack and Anne sometimes stayed there when not on board ship. The tavern was located next to the harbour in Spanish Town, Jamaica.

What Jack didn't know, however, was that during one evening, after he'd drunk far too much rum and passed out, Anne had taken the opportunity to make copies of all his treasure maps. The details of the map showing where his fortune was hidden in the Star Inn, she had committed to memory.

After several more months of reckless piracy, Calico Jack, Anne Bonny, Mary Read and the rest of the crew, were eventually captured. They were easily apprehended by the British Navy when Rackham's crew were caught out whilst overindulging with wine and rum late one evening. The Navy quietly boarded the ship where only Mary and Anne were able to fight gallantly. The rest of the crew were just too drunk to help!

All Rackham's crew were rounded up and transported to Spanish Town, the capital of Jamaica. There they were thrown into gaol to await the date of their trial.

The fleet's officers were all tried together, found guilty of piracy and hanged on the 18th November 1720. For Calico Jack, however, just to be hanged was not seen as sufficient punishment. He was not only hanged but gibbeted and put on display on a small islet near the harbour entrance of Port Royal. Its message was simple and the intention very clear, a harsh public reminder to any person who decided to become a pirate, this would be your punishment… this would be your torturous end.

Before Calico Jack's execution, Anne Bonny was allowed into his cell to see and speak to him for one last time. There she told him, "I'm sorry to see you here, Jack, but if you'd fought like a man, you'd not now be hanged like a dog."

CHAPTER 2

Following the judge's revised conviction of life in prison due 'to the belly', Mary and Anne were dragged back in their chains to the court cell. They were neither elated nor relieved at the judge's decision. Both sat quietly on a hard wooden bench. Mary contemplated her uncertain future, incarcerated behind bars… until when? Probably until she had finally rotted and died! How many years would that take?

Anne, with her head bowed and buried in her hands, started to sob. Mary gently put her right arm around her young friend's shoulders, trying to comfort her in some small way. No words were said, none were needed. Both women now knew their own fate. They had both rejected honest employment, due to the low wages, hard labour, poor working conditions and the long hours endured at that time. Instead, they had freely entered into the world of piracy. Here they knew life could easily be cut short, but, conversely, it offered a new world of excitement, pleasure, liberty and wealth, plus lots of adventures and freedoms very few women would ever experience.

Yes, they'd been aware of all the risks. They'd even seen at first hand colleagues who'd had their lives cruelly curtailed or been seriously maimed for life. Such were the risks and rewards of a career as a 'gentleman o' fortune'… a pirate! For Mary and Anne it was the gold, silver and jewels they craved. But their buried treasure couldn't help them in prison. All their wealth, dreams and ambitions had disappeared. Their futures, for certain, would now be dominated by torment, cruelty and nightmares!

Mary looked at the stone walls surrounding them. Grey, depressing and dank. Parts were covered with green slime and mould, thriving after decades of constant high tropical humidity and the sweat and tears of former occupants. There were no windows or access to fresh air.

For the first time since she'd stowed away on the ship leaving Liverpool, Mary now felt homesick. She thought of the English green grass and the fresh country air. The birds and animals her only friends during a lonely childhood. She was never going to see them again.

Early the next morning, the old oak cell door suddenly crashed open and three burly guards marched in. Mary and Anne were immediately awake and were horrified as they gazed towards the door. What was going to happen now!?

The lead guard was rugged with long black hair. He stared at the two women, smiled and announced, "Well, ladies, time to go to a better place!"

The two other guards smiled and made tiny grunts. They certainly knew the Spanish Town prison was not going to be a 'better place'!

Mary and Anne's chains were removed and they were both pushed towards the doorway. The lead guard led the way along an underground passageway, the walls thick with accumulated grime. Anne followed barefoot, tripping and slipping on the wet cobblestones. One of the other guards followed Anne, with Mary close behind. The final guard brought up the rear.

At the end of the passageway they turned right and started to climb up a set of wooden stairs. At the top the lead guard opened a large door and walked out into a small courtyard. The rest of the group soon followed. They immediately experienced the harsh glare of the blazing hot sun. Waiting for the women was a prison carriage with metal bars fixed into two small side windows. Two chestnut-coloured horses were tethered at the front. The lead guard grabbed a padlock hanging on the side of the carriage, and pulled open the door.

"In 'ere, ladies," he shouted, standing back and keeping hold of the door.

Both women took deep breaths of fresh air. Anne shielded her eyes from the strong sunshine and looked around the courtyard for any possible route of escape. She quickly realised the courtyard was surrounded by high stone walls and a locked wooden gate.

The guard behind Anne pushed her forward and she reluctantly climbed aboard. Mary immediately followed and they both sat down on the hot, bare metal seats.

The lead guard slammed the door shut and secured it with the padlock. He climbed up onto the carriage and sat next to the driver. The two other guards stood on a platform at the rear of the carriage and clung on. The driver cracked his reins and the horses started to move. Another guard unlocked and opened the large wooden gate. The carriage was driven though the opening and out onto a narrow filthy lane. Shabby and decaying buildings were all the women could see from their windows. The stench of the excrement and urine thrown into the street was disgusting and nauseating.

The journey to Spanish Town's prison was hot and sweaty. After a few minutes, the carriage turned and passed along the harbourfront. Mary and Anne stared out of their windows and tried to breathe in the wonderful, fresh sea air.

They gazed longingly at cargo ships loading their goods from the quay. They didn't know where these ships were going, they didn't care… they just knew any one of them could sail them away from their punishment… to freedom.

People stopped walking when the black coach slowly passed by. They immediately recognised the distinctive prison carriage and wondered who the poor souls were on board. They could only see two women's sad and gloomy faces staring back at them. Who were these desolate and incarcerated people? What had they done that was so wrong?

Another few minutes and the carriage turned right and went down another narrow and foul thoroughfare. More chamber pots had been emptied from the nearby balconies onto the lane. Mary and Anne could, once again, smell the sickening stench. Halfway along the lane the carriage turned left and stopped outside two closed large wooden gates. Above the gates hung a painted sign announcing, *Spanish Town Prison*. This was the main entrance to the infamous gaol.

The lead guard jumped down from his seat and entered the gatehouse. Two minutes later the large wooden gates slowly opened inwards. The driver flicked the reins and the horses pulled the carriage through the open gateway, arriving in another small courtyard.

Mary took one last look out of the window and wondered if this would be her last view of the outside world… their last view of freedom. Anne buried her head in her hands again… and started to cry.

The driver stopped the horses outside a wooden doorway: access to the main prison building. Moments later, the lead guard stepped out through this door leaving it slightly ajar. He walked over to the carriage, unlocked the padlock and opened the carriage's door. The two other guards now stood at his side.

"Welcome to your new 'ome, ladies," said the lead guard, grinning through his thick, black beard. "Time to say goodbye to the outside world!" He waved his hand and pointed towards the building. "Welcome to a livin' 'ell!"

Mary leaned out of the carriage and looked around. One of the guards gripped her by the arm and pulled her down from the carriage. She immediately fell to the ground. Anne slowly stepped down from the carriage and helped Mary to stand up. They both stared and were terrified at their new surroundings, not that there was very much to see. The sun was now higher in the clear blue sky and they watched as the two wooden gates gradually closed behind them… and were locked. The rest of the enclosure was protected by high stone walls.

"This way," insisted the lead guard as he marched back towards the open door. After a push from the other two guards, Mary and Anne reluctantly followed.

They all entered a dark and dingy passageway, lit by just one burning candle. The air was slightly cooler but more humid and oppressive. They walked past a small office and several cells until the lead guard finally came to a stop. He looked through the tiny window of the cell door and shouted to the occupants to stand back. When he was happy with the result, he unlocked the door and pushed it open.

Mary and Anne were pushed forward. The lead guard stood back to give them room to enter the cell. Mary led the way with Anne following closely behind.

"Well, what we got 'ere then, boys?" said one of the inmates from the far side of the cell.

Mary and Anne were shocked and horror-struck. They looked back to the guard for help. Unfortunately, he just laughed and pulled the door closed. Seconds later they heard the key locking the door, and footsteps as the guards walked away.

The two women just stood and glared across the tiny cell. They were looking at three men! One was young, maybe the same age as Anne, with blond hair and dark-blue eyes. The other two were middle aged. Both had beards, long hair and were dressed in what could only be described as rags.

"Welcome to Shang-ri-la, ladies," said one of the older men, revealing a golden tooth. He looked at their swollen stomachs. "So nice to 'ave the pleasure of such lovely company. Ain't that right, Jimmy, me boy?"

"Sure is, Wally. Not seen such pretty wenches like these for a very long time. A very long time indeed!" Jimmy smiled and pointed to the young man. "This young scrag 'ere is Robbie. Want to tell us your names, dearies? Introduce yourselves to your new pals?"

Neither Mary nor Anne moved an inch, but then Mary decided to be friendly and not annoy the men. "I'm Mary and this is Anne," she said hesitantly, pointing at Anne, who was partly hidden behind her.

"Well, what pretty names they are, for sure," said Wally, flashing his golden tooth again. "I guess we're all goin' to be in 'ere for quite some time. Nice if we can all be good friends."

"Those two blankets in that corner, that's where you twos sleep," said Jimmy, pointing to the far corner. "Unless you want to cuddle up with us instead!"

All three men laughed. Anne squeezed closer to Mary.

"What are the chains for?" asked Mary, who had spotted two sets of chains fixed to the far wall.

"We all gets chained up at night by the guards," said Wally. "Stops us wandering off during the night and 'avin' our fun."

All three men laughed again.

Mary looked around the cell. Thick stone walls, cobbled floor, airless, oppressive and smelling of foul, dried sweat. A small barred window, above head height, was their only source of fresh air and respite from the awful stale stench. Five human beings incarcerated in a cramped and squalid room. What could be worse? she thought.

Mary walked across the cell towards the far corner. Anne tried to stay as tight to Mary as she could. Three pairs of eyes followed each step they made. Mary looked at the blankets, filthy, but at least they were dry.

"No feather mattress in 'ere, ladies," said Wally walking towards their corner. "Just cool cobblestones to lay on, under your blanket."

Anne sat down and pulled her knees close to her baby bulge. She leaned over and grabbed a blanket, pulling it over her bare legs. Mary looked at Wally and asked, "When do we get any food? We've not eaten today."

"Not till later, but don't 'old your breath. Pig swill t'is. No fine cooking in 'ere, me dear."

Mary closed her eyes and tried desperately to hold back her tears. Could this get any more hopeless, wretched or miserable? She opened her eyes again and looked at the three men. Suddenly she felt Anne's hand seizing her left leg. Looking down she saw Anne's face distorted in terror and panic. My God, she thought, what a horrible place… and, I dare say, it's all going to get a great deal worse!

CHAPTER 3

The minutes ticked into hours, then into days. Mary and Anne took it in turns to sleep and rest. They didn't trust these men, despite their friendly talk.

It was after the first week that things began to change… and started to get worse. The men's conversations became more explicit. Their hands took advantage of unguarded moments and then it was a full-on assault.

Wally and Robbie grabbed Mary and held her tight, whilst Jimmy used all his strength to rape Anne. The men laughed, whilst the women screamed, but nobody came to their rescue. Anne fought hard and scratched Jimmy's face, but his strength was too much for her.

Over the next few weeks – or was it months? It seemed like years to Mary and Anne – Jimmy, Wally and Robbie took it in turns to abuse both women. They laughed as the women screamed and fought back, but to no avail. The men were too strong. Mary wished she had a sword or a knife, but she and Anne had nothing, except their hands and bare feet.

Early one morning the inmates were suddenly awoken by Mary's startled scream. Blood was flowing from between her legs. Something's wrong with the baby, thought Anne and cried for help. Even the men saw Mary's distress and called the guard on duty in the corridor. The guard returned five minutes later with two colleagues, one male and one female. Wally, Jimmy and Robbie were taken out and moved temporarily into a neighbouring cell. This new cell was already occupied by five inmates, so it was a tight squeeze.

The prison governor lived on the prison premises with his wife. The governor's wife had a limited amount of nursing skills, so it was her, with Anne's assistance, who attended to Mary. It was about three hours later that the baby appeared, but there were no screams, shouts or wriggles. The baby was cold, still and dead. The nurse said the baby probably died some days before. Mary was washed and patched up as best as the nurse could manage.

The governor's wife was about to leave Mary in Anne's sole care, when Anne begged her for help to get her and Mary transferred to another cell. She was sympathetic, but told Anne it was not within her power. She promised she'd speak to her husband, but she already knew all the remaining cells were full.

After the governor's wife had left the cell it was another two hours before Wally, Jimmy and Robbie reappeared. Anne pleaded with the guard for her and Mary to be relocated to another cell, but the guard just waved his hand and pulled the door to. Seconds later, she heard the familiar click of the lock.

Anne stared at the three male inmates. Her face was a picture of loathing, bitterness and hatred. Slowly she crept back towards Mary, who was now fast asleep on her blanket.

The three men stood quietly and watched as Anne sat down next to her friend. They were genuinely feeling some remorse, but none of them apologised. They just sat down on the cobblestone floor and stared at Anne.

Two weeks later the governor's wife was called again. This time it was Anne's turn to produce her, and Calico Jack's, baby. This time a healthy girl was born. Within an hour, however, the baby was taken away and Anne never saw her daughter again.

Anne was distraught, but she knew the rules. Both she and Mary had been told when they'd first entered the prison that their babies would be taken away, unless Mary and Anne could name a family member who would be prepared to take care of them. They'd both said they didn't have any family members living close by.

It was four weeks later when a new prison guard called Jacob first appeared. From that moment onwards Anne and Mary's lives became slightly more bearable. Jacob, a 25-year-old giant of a man, with long black hair and matching beard, took pity on the women and became Anne's friend. He promised to protect both her and Mary and threatened all sorts of punishment to any male prisoner if either of the two women were harmed or touched again.

Wally decided to ignore Jacob's threat and tried his chances with Anne. In the middle of the night he crawled over and grabbed Anne's breasts. Anne was immediately awake and screamed out aloud. Immediately, Mary, Jimmy and Robbie were alarmed and awake. Jacob unlocked the door and smashed it back against the wall. He strode over to where Wally was lying and picked him up as though he was the weight of a straw doll. He threw him against the wall and Wally crashed to the ground. Jacob picked him up again, and, whilst he held him by his rags in his left hand, he hit him hard in the stomach with his right fist. Wally groaned, was dazed and was about to be sick when he felt Jacob's fist hit him again, this time on his jaw. Jacob threw him back onto the floor and went over to check on Anne.

The big man bent down and asked in a kindly voice, "Are you okay?"

Mary, now protecting Anne, had put her arms around her friend's shoulders.

"Yes. I'm okay. Thank you for helping," Anne replied.

Jacob smiled and stood up. He looked at the crumpled heap that was Wally and then to Jimmy and Robbie and said. "Let that be a lesson. Tell that bastard the next time he tries anything with either of these women, I won't be so lenient."

Jimmy and Robbie were terrified. They nodded and looked across at Wally. He was unconscious and both wondered if he was dead.

More weeks went by and the three male inmates kept as far away from Mary and Anne as possible. Wally's stomach still ached and he kept having severe pains in his head.

Mary and Anne became more relaxed, and after a long, quiet discussion, they formulated a plan. A scheme that, if fulfilled, would ultimately get them out of the prison for good!

Anne spoke to Jacob privately and said she would offer him 'favours' if, in return, he promised to continue to protect them and arrange for them to receive better food. This arrangement happened and Mary and Anne felt far more secure and comfortable in their cell. The food they received was also much more palatable. Their fellow inmates became jealous, but were afraid to complain.

Jacob had arranged with the prison's governor for Anne and Mary to be able to have time away from the cell and from the intimidation of their male inmates. This was just an excuse for Jacob and Anne to meet up for their sexual meetings in any empty cell available. The second part of the women's plans was to persuade Jacob to help them escape. It was after one of their 'encounters' that the next stage of the plan was proposed. Anne offered Jacob wealth beyond his wildest dreams, but only if he helped their escape.

Jacob considered the matter and thought it probably could be done, so he promised Anne he would think of a way. To help convince Jacob, she told him that all the gold and jewels she'd promised him were hidden in a building close to Spanish Town's harbour… not far from the prison.

Over the following two weeks a plan between Jacob and Anne was discussed and finally agreed.

It was 2am on a dark, but very warm, early January morning, when Jacob silently unlocked Anne and Mary's cell door. The three male prisoners were chained and fast asleep, but Mary and Anne were wide awake. Jacob quietly tip-toed over to where Anne and Mary were chained to the cell wall. Trying to avoid waking the other three sleeping prisoners, he carefully and gently released Anne and Mary from their shackles. All three then quietly left the cell and Jacob relocked the door.

Jacob led the way down a candlelit corridor. Anne and Mary followed closely behind. Their hearts were racing and perspiration dripped from their brows. They all stopped at a junction with another corridor. The far walls were grimy and dark, lit by a single burning candle. Jacob had rehearsed this escape route several times and now he felt he could almost follow it blindfolded. All was clear, so they progressed, anxious, hearts thumping and fingers crossed.

At the end of the corridor, they arrived at the most difficult part of the route. Jacob slowly eased his head forwards to look around the corner and down the next passageway. He knew two guards were always stationed just a few yards away. It was all quiet bar the usual snoring of prisoners.

Jacob could now see the two guards. They appeared to be asleep on their chairs. One had his head laid back and his mouth wide open. Jacob held up one hand, and with the other, placed his finger to his lips, indicating that the women should stand still and be quiet. Mary, sweating and her heart racing, noticed green mould growing on the wall close to where she was standing. She grimaced and quietly stepped away. Jacob turned his head and gazed along the other side of the dark passageway. Just one candle was burning to illuminate the corridor. All was still calm and quiet. There were no other noises or signs of more guards.

Jacob, Anne and Mary slowly tip-toed towards the sleeping guards. All held their breath and stared at the two snoozing bodies as they squeezed past and alongside the far wall. Suddenly one of the guards grunted and shifted his body, but still appeared to be asleep. Mary and Anne were frozen to the spot, eyes wide open. Jacob grabbed Anne's arm and, slowly, they moved on.

Eventually they arrived at the end of the corridor where it joined another passageway. Jacob, as quietly as possible, stepped across the cobblestones towards the far wall. This was one of the building's perimeter walls. Two more steps and he was standing in front of a thick oak door. An exit which would lead them outside and to freedom!

Anne and Mary anxiously watched as Jacob removed a key from his pocket and inserted it into the lock. Slowly twisting it, he suddenly stopped when he heard a low-squeaking sound coming from the lock. He stopped and waited, his heart pounding. The temperature was hot and the air heavy and humid. His clothes were now sticking to his body and he wiped the perspiration from his brow.

There was still no sign of any inquisitive guards. After a few moments he continued to slowly turn the key, this time praying the lock would yield without any further noise. Suddenly the lock clicked and he gently pushed on the door with his shoulder. He had earlier applied candle wax to the hinges so when the door moved there were no creaking sounds to be heard.

He looked through a small gap then pushed the door further ajar. The reflected soft glow of moonlight was illuminating part of the lane. Nearby buildings were casting shadows onto the lane's grimy surface. Jacob stepped outside and looked ahead. The cooler air immediately felt fresher on his face. At the far end of the lane, hidden in the shadows, he could see the silhouette of a stationary horse-drawn carriage; its driver waved a candlelit lantern. Illuminated by moonlight, Jacob waved back. The carriage slowly began to move forwards, pulled by a single horse.

Jacob turned around, checked the corridor once more, and then gestured for the two women to come across and join him. Mary grabbed Anne's hand and together they moved anxiously towards the doorway. Jacob pointed to the horse-drawn carriage slowly approaching. The women looked both ways and then made a dash over the mud and cobblestones towards it. Mary opened the door and they both clambered in. Jacob quietly closed and relocked the prison door, before he also darted towards the carriage. After climbing aboard he silently eased the door closed and sat down next to the two women. They were all breathing deeply and stared at each other, their faces conveying a mixture of shock and elation. Jacob looked through the window and back up the lane, pleased that nobody was following.

Anne's heart was still pounding. She couldn't believe they were free. Mary covered her face with her hands and gave a deep sigh of relief.

The carriage continued its slow pace in the direction of the harbour.

Ten minutes later, Anne leaned out of the carriage window and asked the driver to pull up outside the dark wooden building coming up on the right-hand side. A painted wooden sign, consisting of a white star on a black background, was hanging from a wooden frame above the entrance door. It was slowly rocking back and forth, due to the gentle sea breeze, making a low rhythmic creaking sound.

When the carriage came to a stop, Anne put her head out of the window again and looked up and down the lane. Once satisfied all was clear, she opened the carriage door, stepped down onto the muddy surface and walked down a narrow alleyway at the side of the inn. She stopped outside a small brown door, remembering this was not usually locked as it was access for lodging guests. Noting that all was still quiet, she slowly turned the door's handle. Relieved when the handle moved fully and the door opened without a sound, she quietly entered the building. Although the passageway was dark she could remember the route to the room that only she and Jack occupied.

Several minutes later, Anne exited through the same doorway, this time carrying two large, red velvet bags. She quietly closed the door and retraced her steps back towards the carriage. Mary, watching through the window, opened the door and let Anne quickly clamber back in. Anne returned to her seat and sat next to Mary. Jacob and Mary both anxiously stared at Anne and then to the two velvet bags. Anne smiled back and handed one of the bags to Mary. The second one she passed to Jacob.

Jacob slowly opened his bag and looked inside. His eyes lit up when he saw all the gold and glittering contents. He leaned across to Anne and gave her a heartfelt kiss and a hug. Then to Mary, another celebratory kiss. Finally, he leaned out of the carriage's window and whispered to the driver, "Lizzy, let's go home."

Lizzy, Jacob's wife, gently cracked the reins and the horse-drawn carriage slowly pulled away.

CHAPTER 4

After about another 15 minutes, the horse-drawn carriage drew up outside a two-storey, faded green wooden house. With a clay tiled roof, slatted wooden windows and a rusty first-floor balcony, it was typical of the properties in this area. Situated on the outskirts of Spanish Town, this house had been Jacob and Lizzy's rented home since they were married, two years ago.

Jacob, Anne and Mary stepped down from the carriage. Jacob quietly closed the door behind him.

Lizzy flicked the reins and the horse pulled the carriage down an alley at the side of the house. They headed towards an old timber stable.

"Let's get inside," whispered Jacob. He removed a key from his pocket and opened the front door. Anne and Mary followed him closely behind.

The front room was sparsely furnished and even after Jacob had lit a candle the room still didn't feel very lived in. They walked through another doorway, past the bottom of the stairs, and into the back room. Jacob lit two more candles and suddenly the back room had a warm and yellow glow. Here there was a small kitchen with an old wooden table, two dining chairs, two worn armchairs and a small cooking fireplace.

Both Mary and Anne walked over to stand closer to the unlit fireplace. Mary spotted two large boxes lying next to one of the dining chairs.

Jacob noticed what Mary was looking at. "We've already packed," he said, pointing his hand at the boxes. "At daybreak we're leaving. The house and furniture are both rented. All our personal possessions are in there."

"So, you goin' to make a fresh start too," said Mary. "What are your plans?"

Jacob raised his velvet bag. "With these, the world's our oyster! We're going to stay with Lizzy's mother in England for a while. After that I don't know. I need to get well away from

Spanish Town... especially the prison. Otherwise I might just end up back there – as a prisoner!"

The two women smiled. After all Jacob had done for them, they certainly didn't want that to happen.

Jacob continued. "We've got a cabin booked on the *Eagle*. It sails later this morning at 8.30. High tide."

They suddenly heard the front door open and close. A few seconds later Lizzy entered the room, wearing a long black coat, a large brimmed black hat and a thin black cotton scarf. The scarf covered her face, bar a small gap for her to see through. Jacob, Mary and Anne watched as she slowly disrobed. Once clear of all her outdoor clothes, Anne and Mary looked at a beautiful dark-haired young woman. Anne guessed she couldn't have been much older than 21 years of age.

"That's better, I was boiling in those clothes," said Lizzy, walking over to shake hands with Anne and Mary. "Hello, I'm Lizzy."

"I'm Mary, and this is Anne," said Mary, as the ladies shook hands.

"I've got a change of clothes for you both upstairs. Looks as though you're in need of a wash too. The clothes are second hand, I'm afraid. Jacob estimated your sizes for me. We've got to get you out of those rags!"

Jacob smiled quietly. He'd seen Anne 'in the flesh'... more than once, so he wanted to change the subject... and very quickly! "What are your plans, ladies?"

Anne and Mary looked at each other and then Anne replied, "We need to exchange some of this treasure for money." She held up her velvet bag. "And then head as far away from Spanish Town as possible. Change our names and make a new start... somewhere where nobody knows us."

"Have you got any family to go to?" asked Lizzy.

"Nobody in the Caribbean," replied Anne. "Even if we had, we wouldn't want to involve them with our problems."

There was an awkward pause, until Lizzy said, "I'll take you both upstairs. You can have a wash and see the clothes and wigs I've got for you. They should be okay, at least until you have an opportunity to buy some better clothes yourselves."

It was just after 7am when Mary and Anne left the house with Jacob and Lizzy. They were now wearing their new wigs and dressed in typical colourful Caribbean dresses. They looked so different from when they'd arrived at Jacob's house. Out of their prison rags, they hoped they'd naturally blend in alongside the local women.

After emotional goodbyes with Jacob and Lizzy at the harbourside, Anne suggested they spend the morning trying to find Lorenzo.

"Who's Lorenzo?" asked Mary.

Anne explained, "Jack said there'd been an illegal market in the Caribbean for trading gold, silver and jewellery for centuries, especially in the towns populated by pirates. So there's a small group of men specialising in exchanging customers' treasure for money, no questions asked. Lorenzo is one of them. He's been trading in Spanish Town for years and has a good reputation. Jack said he could be trusted and is usually fair. He's traded with him many times."

"'Ave you met this Lorenzo?"

"Yes. I met him about three months after I joined Jack's ship. Lorenzo's a nice old man, probably in his sixties now. He can usually be found in one of the harbour inns. That's where he carries out his business."

"Okay. Do you think you'll be able to remember what 'e looks like?"

"I think so. He probably won't remember me, especially in these clothes. Besides, he'll only be interested in what we've got to trade."

They eventually found Lorenzo propping up the bar in the King's Head. Anne showed him some of the contents of her red velvet bag. After some arguing and bartering, their negotiations were concluded. In exchange for five gold plates, a gold statue and some red rubies, the women left the inn clutching banknotes, bills of credit and various coins. All parties seemed happy with the financial transaction.

Armed with this money, they were able to buy some more fashionable clothes. Also, later that afternoon, they found overnight accommodation at the Ship Inn, located directly across the road from the harbour.

Anne was anxious to try on her new clothes and experience the feminine splendour of being dressed up and feeling like a proper woman again.

Mary, however, felt uncomfortable and couldn't remember the last time she'd worn such fine female fabrics. Nevertheless, she accepted the situation, at least for the time being. It was a new disguise because she was not dressed in men's pirate clothes! Who, after all, would imagine the notorious Mary Read wearing such female finery!?

That evening they'd bathed and cut each other's hair, swapped wigs and, in two newly purchased leather cases, packed all their new clothes, at least, all the clothes that were not required on their next journey. Having had little sleep the previous night, they slept deeply on a wonderful soft feather bed. It was sunrise when they finally awoke.

Eager to leave Spanish Town as quickly as possible, dressed as women of wealth, they strolled casually over towards the harbour to read the departure board that listed the timetable of all the ships due to depart over the next ten days. It also stated each ship's itinerary and final destination.

Anne, knowing Mary only had limited reading skills, looked at the timetable. "The next ship offering to carry passengers is the *Cutlass*. A merchant ship with four cabins. It's due to leave port in two days' time. Destinations are Madeira and Lisboa."

Mary whispered, "That's no good. We need to get away now."

"Mmm, I know. Have you any other suggestions?"

Mary stared at the two sailing ships being loaded and wondered whether to speak directly to the captains.

Anne also wondered if either of them might be their answer. After a few moments she gazed along the street, watching the people coming and going to the ships. Suddenly she spotted a black man hobbling in their direction. He only had one leg and was shuffling along with the aid of crutches. Anne recognised Pete immediately. After all, she thought, he did have some unique features.

As well as a haven for pirates, Spanish Town, and some other ports nearby, also became a safe refuge for escaped slaves from the nearby plantations. Some had also come from islands such as Cuba and Hispaniola. A few even went on to join pirate ships. Some, like 'Black Caesar', even rose to the rank of captain, before he later joined Captain Blackbeard's much larger fleet.

Several years ago, Pete, together with two other male slaves, Hob and Walt, all in their early 30s, had managed to escape from the Newson Sugar Plantation Estate, located about five miles from the town of Negril, on the west coast of Jamaica. They'd walked quickly along the edge of a neighbour's large sugar cane field and then had to run when they heard dogs barking in the distance behind them. After crossing a small river they continued to run for another 20 minutes until the barking noises decreased. As night-time set in, the men needed to rest. They found a stone sugar mill and hid there. Pete found a small wooden barrel of water and they all had a drink and a wash. The moon shone brightly so they decided to carry on. After about 30 minutes they could see, in the distance, the silhouette of the town of Negril.

It was about 2am when the men sneaked quietly into the town. They headed straight towards the harbour. Fortunately, it was all very quiet and when they arrived at the waterfront they found a small wooden longboat gently rocking in the water. It was tied to two posts. The boat was equipped with six oars and one small sailing mast. Pete told Hob to pull the boat towards deeper water whilst he and Walt went to try and find a supply of drinking water for their journey.

Hob untied the securing ropes and jumped into the water. It was cool and refreshing and came up to his knees. He slowly pulled the boat into deeper water and then clambered aboard. He used one of the oars to steady the boat against the gently pulling tide whilst he waited for his colleagues to return. About ten minutes later, Pete and Walt returned pushing a handcart containing two small casks of water. Thirty minutes later, the longboat and its three passengers were sailing on the Caribbean Sea. They used just two of the oars and swapped regularly. Two rowing and one resting. Initially they followed the northern coast. When the breeze became stronger, and they were satisfied they were out of sight from land, they raised the single mainsail and all three men rested. It was not long, however, before each of them had fallen fast asleep.

The sea was calm, but had a strong current, and a gentle breeze was pulling them further from the shore. When they awoke at daybreak, there was no land in sight… and they hadn't a clue where they were.

They began their journey with no plans as to where they were heading and had only about four days' drinking water. By the seventh day, Walt had died from a mixture of sunstroke and a fever. He was pushed overboard. On day eight, Pete and Hob began to hallucinate and argue. Eventually a fight started. Both men were weak and exhausted and Hob soon collapsed. He fell into the bottom of the boat and didn't move again. Pete began to cry and considered throwing himself overboard. When he next looked up, Pete thought he spotted a large sailing ship on the distant horizon. However, he was convinced he was hallucinating again and buried his head in his hands. Slowly the ship, with three masts in full sail, came closer and when Pete looked up again, it was close enough for him to see the men on board and the rows of guns at the ready. The ship was flying a plain black flag which, Pete knew, was the symbol of a pirate ship ready to attack!

Pete wasn't bothered. He just stood up and waved. The ship turned towards him and a longboat was lowered over the side.

The swell from the ship started to increase in size. Pete, still standing, began to lose his balance. As he was about to sit down, a larger wave hit the side of his boat and he fell into the sea. He frantically tried to grab the side of his boat as the other longboat approached. Suddenly a horrendous pain shot through his body, racing up from his right leg. The last thing he remembered was sinking – and everything went black.

It was three days later when Pete awoke. He thought he must be in Hell. But when he was able to focus properly he realised he was alive. He was lying in a bunk and on board a ship. He lay quietly, but then, when he tried to move, a pain shot through the top of his right leg. He screamed out loud and almost immediately a young woman came into the cabin. She rushed to his side and helped him to lie down on his back.

"Don't move," she ordered and wiped his moist brow. "You've lost most of your right leg. Shark bite from the look of the teeth marks."

Pete sighed. "Who're you?" he asked. The pain was beginning to ease.

"I'm Anne. You're on the *Revenge*. What's your name?"

"Pete. Is dis a pirate ship?!"

"Yes, and we've just saved your life!"

Over the following weeks Pete slowly recovered and helped out in the ship's galley. With the aid of a crutch, made by the ship's carpenter, he was able to move about. By the time the *Revenge* docked near Spanish Town harbour, to take on fresh supplies, Pete decided he'd had enough of travelling by ship. Anne gave him five of her 'acquired' ruby jewels and the crew helped him to get ashore.

The last words Pete had said to Anne were, "You saved me miserable life, Anne. I'll never forget you for dat."

CHAPTER 5

This same Pete continued to shuffle along the side of the street.

His black face was looking much older now, Anne thought, and his hair much longer and with streaks of grey.

"Hello, Pete," said Anne, as he tried to shuffle past her.

Pete suddenly stopped and stared across at Anne. "Do I know you, lady?" he asked, looking closer now at this attractive woman.

Anne smiled. "Don't you remember… the *Revenge?*"

Mary now joined her friend to see who she was talking to.

Suddenly Pete remembered and his face became a picture of shock. "Oh my God! Is it you, Anne? Really you!? I thought dey'd 'anged you!"

"No, we were the lucky ones," said Anne, pointing to Mary.

Pete took a closer look at Mary and then back to Anne. "Same voice, but you look different." He peered at Anne. "It's your clothes and 'air!"

Anne leaned a little nearer and whispered, "It's a wig. A disguise." She then told him about their escape from prison and their urgent need of transport.

Pete listened with interested attention. When Anne had finished, he rubbed his right hand across his weathered face and thought about their problem. After a few moments he said, "We can't have you just standing around 'ere. I'll take you back to me 'owse. I've got an idea."

It was a slow walk to Pete's home, which turned out to be a nice cottage in a respectable area of Spanish Town. Anne looked at Mary. They were impressed.

"You live here?" queried Anne, with a surprised tone to her voice.

"I've done alright for meself, since I've been 'ere, in Spanish Town. Those jewels you gave me, dey set me up. Billy, my partner, and me, we're moneylenders. Lucrative business. I do lots of me business with pirates. Dey always in need of money when ashore. Lots of drink and women, dat's what dey want! In return dey 'ave to leave some of dare treasure with me. Sort of guarantee! If dey don't come back, I keep dare loot – always worth more than de money I lent dem. Come on, let's get inside."

The two women looked at each other, smiled and then followed him up to the front door.

Twenty minutes later, Anne and Mary had seen most of the house and were impressed with the two bedrooms they were staying in. As they walked around the property, Anne told Mary the story and circumstances of how she had first encountered Pete.

When the women arrived in the kitchen, there was another man, a white man, younger than Pete, talking to him near the window. Anne and Mary had obviously entered during part of their conversation. The new arrival was explaining something. "…I'm tellin ya, Black Pete, they've been arrested. Caught by the British Navy. Bound to be 'anged, dey are now."

At this point the two men spotted Anne and Mary. Pete waved for them to come over. "Come and meet Billy. 'E's me friend and partner."

The two women walked across the room. Mary stared at Billy. Taller than Pete with brown curly hair. Probably about the same age as her, she thought.

Pete made the introductions. Billy smiled at the ladies and nodded his head.

"Billy called you, 'Black' Pete. Why's that?" asked Anne, staring at Pete.

"Dis brother's called Pete as well," explained Pete. "When I first met Billy, dat's what he called me, Black Pete. Said it would be less confusing." Billy smiled and nodded again. "Now dat's my name and most folks calls me dat. Other black men around 'ere, dare usually referred to as Black somethin' or other! It's all okay, we don't mind. Better than being a slave on a plantation."

"It's so good of you to let us stay, Pete," said Anne. "We need to get the rest of our clothes from the Ship Inn. We've paid our bill."

"I told Billy earlier. 'E'll collect dem when 'e leaves."

Anne said thank you to Billy, and Mary smiled.

"Now den, ladies," began Black Pete, shuffling over to the pantry door. "Let's get you a cool drink and I'll tell you me plan."

At this point, Billy decided to leave to collect the ladies' belongings. He'd already heard about the plan.

From the pantry, Black Pete collected three glasses and a large pewter jug containing beer. All three sat down next to a wooden table, close by was an open window. A refreshing breeze was blowing from outside and cooling the room. After pouring the beer Pete emptied his own glass in three gulps and topped it up again. The ladies sipped their beer.

Black Pete now began to explain his plan. "In 'bout three days' time, Captain 'Bluey', Ben Thomas, dat's 'is name, 'e's coming to Spanish Town in his frigate, *Empress*. This ship has 40 guns and carries about 100 pirates. It's big and powerful and de British Navy 'ave, so far, given it a miss, Dey prefers smaller fish! It was originally a British ship but de French stole it and used it to transport slaves to Guadeloupe, Martinique and Saint-Domingue. Bluey 'acquired it', should we say, from dem! Dose Frenchies, dey didn't really give 'im much of a fight."

Black Pete took another draught of his beer and continued, "Bluey trusts me. Goin' with 'im, ladies, will be much safer dan chancin' bein' a passenger on a merchant ship from dis port. The authorities will be looking for you dare. I keeps me ears to de ground and I lets Bluey know when de Navy's about. I also 'ear t'ings – 'bout merchant ships and dare plans. Spanish galleons and dare likes, moving treasure from New Spain and Mexico to Europe. I get well rewarded for all dis information. Nobody suspects me, Black Pete with just one leg. 'Pegleg Pete', some of 'em call me." Pete laughed. "Dey says 'e's 'armless, just a moneylender. Well, back in 1715, I told Bluey about dis particular French ship. I'd 'erd dat de French, after delivering dare slaves, were goin' to return with treasure from Mexico and Cuba. On the 24th November Bluey captured the ship, near de island of Saint Vincent. Again, I was well rewarded and Bluey, 'e got the big *Empress* ship."

Mary was impressed and wished she'd been there.

Anne had heard stories in the past about Captain Bluey from Calico Jack. She knew he was a serious and successful pirate.

"When 'e arrives I'll speak to 'im," said Black Pete, "and I'll get you both aboard."

CHAPTER 6

Black Pete and Billy stood on a headland looking out to sea. They were staring due south at the distant horizon. Although it was just daybreak, it was already hot and humid. Large black clouds were billowing up on the horizon and the warm sea breeze started to increase.

"Looks like a storm's a brewin'," said Billy, as they stared out to sea.

"Don't t'ink Bluey's comin' ashore with dis weather," replied Black Pete, adjusting his crutches on the uneven rocky ground.

"These women, Black Pete, they're both be 'tractive. Wha' d'ya think?" asked Billy, still staring out to sea.

"You leave 'em alone. Dare pretty, I agree, Billy boy, but killers and murderers dey are too! Cut your throat dey would. I've seen Anne in action. She'd rip you apart with 'er sword!"

Billy pondered on Black Pete's words. Maybe I'll stick with the local women, he thought. "Do you think Bluey will come now, or more likely tomorrow?"

"Don't t'ink 'e's comin' today. Let's get back and tell de women."

Billy helped Black Pete to walk back down the rugged slope. Large spots of rain started to land on their hats.

The following day Billy and Black Pete were back on the same headland and looking out to sea. The sun had just appeared over the horizon. It was another warm day, but not so humid. The sea looked refreshingly blue and calm.

"I reckon 'e'll be 'ere today," said Black Pete, placing his right hand across his forehead, shading his eyes from the sun. "Better get de longboat ready… and tell de women to pack."

Billy spotted what he thought might be a large ship on the horizon. He pointed. "Wha' d'ya reckon?"

"Not sure yet. Definitely a big ship," replied Black Pete. "Could be de British Navy, though. Let's wait a while."

The two men watched as the ship slowly advanced closer towards them.

Suddenly Black Pete exclaimed, "Dat's it. Dat's 'im!"

The two men retreated back down the slope. Things needed to be done.

Two hours later the large fighting frigate *Empress* had dropped anchor about a mile out from shore. All 40 guns were primed, just in case. A longboat had been lowered and was heading towards the harbour for supplies. It would probably take three or four trips to collect all the ship's requirements.

At the same time Billy and Black Pete were rowing their smaller longboat out towards the *Empress*. Also aboard were Anne, Mary and their two leather cases.

As the longboats passed each other, Black Pete waved. Quartermaster Richard Easter was standing in his boat with his flintlock pistol primed for action. However, recognising Black Pete, he tucked his gun back into his belt and waved back.

Black Pete started to explain to Anne and Mary what would happen when they arrived at the side of the ship: "I'll go aboard first 'cos Bluey, 'e'll be expectin' me. I've got some information for 'im. After dat I'll tell 'im 'bout you two. I'll explain who you are and mention Calico Jack. 'Opefully, dat will get you both aboard."

Mary and Anne listened and then looked at each other. Both had worried expressions on their faces. However, both then nodded to Black Pete. He smiled back and carried on rowing.

The two women watched as their boat got closer to the *Empress*. They stared in awe at the size of the ship.

As the two men rowed closer, a roped platform was being lowered on the ship's starboard side. On the platform stood three crew members. One was holding two loose ropes, the ends of which had been tied separately to the top of the ship's bulwark.

Black Pete's longboat sailed close to the platform, now hovering just above the water level. One of the crewmen stepped onto the longboat and he and Billy helped Black Pete move to the side. They then lifted him onto the platform and the two remaining crewmen held on to him. Billy threw Black Pete's crutches onto the platform and slowly he was hoisted up and over the side of the bulwark.

The crewman who had remained on the longboat handed one of the loose ropes to Billy. He held the other rope himself. The longboat was now able to hold its position on the choppy water, close to where the platform would eventually return.

After about 20 minutes, Anne looked up and noticed the platform being slowly lowered again. On board were the same two crewmen as before. She tapped Billy on the shoulder and pointed above. All four now watched as the platform slowly descended. Billy and the crewman gently loosened their grip on the ropes, enabling their longboat to drift slightly away from the ship. The platform again stopped just above the water. One of the crewmen waved for Anne and Mary to join them.

Billy and the crewman pulled on the loose ropes and the longboat floated back to the side of the platform. The ropes were handed to Mary and Anne whilst Billy and the crewman lifted the two cases onto the platform.

Anne was then ordered to step forward. She handed the loose rope back to Billy and stood up. Both men on the platform leaned across, grabbed her arms and pulled her onto the platform. Anne quickly snatched at one of the supporting ropes for balance. Mary was next to be waved over. Standing up gingerly, she too was then pulled onto the platform, grabbing at the rope Anne was holding. Slowly, the platform was hoisted back up.

The platform rose over the bulwark and was slowly lowered onto the ship's main deck. Anne and Mary gingerly stepped off. About 60 male faces were staring at them. Black Pete was standing next to a tall man with a black beard and long black hair tied at the back of his head. He was wearing a dark-blue coat and matching tricorn hat. Anne assumed this was Captain 'Bluey'... Ben Thomas!

Anne could remember some of the stories she'd heard of Bluey from Calico Jack. Although she'd never met him before, she had been told Bluey was a tall, strong and a well-mannered man. Well educated as a youngster, he had forsaken working for his wealthy merchant father, preferring the adventures of a pirate's life. He respected women and liked expensive clothes, especially dark-blue coats and similar coloured 'cocked hats'. His favourite weapons were two duelling flintlock pistols that he always carried in his sash. His rules were simple and democratic because, on a pirate's ship, there were neither members of the privileged class nor the strict ranking of the British Navy. Everybody had the same rights, and their roles and duties were appointed, according to their abilities and knowledge. On a ship full of murderers, bandits, and thieves, most decisions were determined by voting. Woe betide any captain who ignored the wishes and the voting of his crew. Captain Bluey was well respected by his crew and there were rarely any bad feelings towards him. Anne immediately found him very attractive.

"Welcome aboard, ladies," said Captain Bluey, as he stepped forward to greet them. He gently took hold of Anne's right hand and raised it to his lips. His dark-blue, almost black, eyes never wavered from looking directly into Anne's. Anne could feel a flush appearing on her face. After about five seconds, he released her hand and then did the same with Mary.

"Any friends of Calico Jack and Black Pete," announced Bluey, with a strong and authoritative voice, "are friends of mine. Great sailor and a true friend was Jack."

Both Anne and Mary felt a little overawed and just smiled back.

Black Pete then hobbled towards them and said, "Good luck, ladies. Dis's where I says me goodbyes. We may meet up again… who knows."

"Thank you for everything, Pete. You saved our lives." Anne leaned forward and kissed Black Pete on the cheek.

Mary then leaned forward. She also kissed him on the cheek and said, "It was nice meeting you, Black Pete. You'll always be our friend. We can never thank you enough."

Black Pete smiled and wiped his right eye. With the aid of his crutches he stepped sideways and then back onto the platform, where two crewmen stood at his side.

"You also saved me life, Anne," shouted Black Pete, as the platform started to rise. "I guess we're all quits now."

The platform rose higher and was gently eased over the side of the bulwark. Anne and Mary walked to the edge and watched as the platform descended. When it finally stopped, Black Pete was helped back into the longboat. Two crewmen remained with him as the platform rose again.

This time four oars were employed to row the small longboat back towards shore. The two crewmen would get a lift back to the *Empress* via one of the supply boats.

Anne and Mary waved and Billy and Black Pete waved back.

When Anne and Mary turned around and looked across the deck, their smiles quickly evaporated. They immediately noticed that none of the crew had moved and were all still staring at them. Anne shuddered and wondered what was going to happen next.

CHAPTER 7

"Haven't you lot got work to do!?" shouted Captain Bluey. "Haven't you seen pretty women before?"

The crew slowly dispersed, mumbling and grumbling as they went. Their fun was over… at least for the time being.

Captain Bluey walked over to join the ladies again. "I've arranged a cabin for you. It's small, but it's next to mine. Hammocks I'm afraid, but at least you'll be on your own – away from the men."

"Thank you," said Anne and she gave the captain a nervous, but flirting, smile.

"We don't want to be any trouble and would like to 'elp in any way we can," said Mary, looking around. "This is an amazin' ship."

Captain Bluey smiled. He then spotted a crewman walking in the background and shouted, "Dexter! Show these ladies to their cabin and get their baggage stowed away."

Dexter called on the help of two fellow crewmen and told them to bring the women's cases. He then walked on ahead to show Anne and Mary their new quarters.

Later that afternoon the *Empress* set sail. All the food and drink replenishments had been stored and the longboats securely stowed away. That evening, Anne and Mary were lying on their hammocks. They certainly felt more relaxed now they were finally sailing away from Spanish Town. They weren't bothered where the ship was heading, just pleased to be sailing away from Jamaica… away from their lifetime sentences in Spanish Town prison.

After their time in a prison cell, where their beds were cobblestone floors, the hammocks felt like luxury. Both started to reminisce about when they'd slept in hammocks aboard Calico Jack's ship, *Revenge*.

Suddenly Mary announced, "I think I want to be a pirate again!"

Anne was surprised and replied, "Really! What I want, more than anything else, is a normal life. Hopefully, one that includes a nice home, a husband and children, before I'm too old… and it's all too late."

"I saw you lookin' at our captain," said Mary, with a smug smile. She was thinking about their meeting with the captain earlier. She thought Anne had looked so young, pretty and seemingly so very innocent, blushing and eating up the object of her affections with her eyes. "You like 'im a lot don't you?"

Anne was lying on her back and staring at the wood-panelled ceiling above her. She watched the flickering shadows, created by candlelight and the motion of the ship. "My Jack used to tell me stories of pirates he'd met. Captains mainly. Lots of them, but the one that stuck in my mind was Captain Ben Thomas. Jack told me his nickname was Bluey, because he liked to wear dark-blue coats and hats. Now, meeting him for real, well, I think he's really handsome."

Mary laughed briefly and then in a more serious voice she replied, "I don't want to marry a pirate. I've loved once and lost me man. I've 'ad lots of thinkin' time in prison. All I want now is adventure, excitement and fortune. Lots of silver, gold and jewels. I've got lots of lost time to make up. Then I'll buy meself a big 'owse back in England. Way out in the countryside. Away from the sea and people. Share my life with the wildlife again. Ridin' 'orses. I kept dreaming of this sort of life while we were in prison."

Anne smiled and thought, being in control, free and wealthy seems to hold so much power over Mary. She wondered if it was because she had suffered such a poverty-stricken existence whilst growing up. "Are you going to ask for a change of dress? Back to the men's pirate clothes?"

"I want to be a pirate again, Anne. I can't be a pirate in lace and silk!"

Anne smiled. "Do you think this crew will accept you, fighting at their side?"

Mary leaned over to face Anne, causing her hammock to sway. "I know it's been a while since I 'ad a pistol, a knife and a sword, but I'll bet much silver I can still beat 'em all with me sword."

Anne turned towards her friend and her hammock started to sway gently as well. "Are you going to throw out a challenge?" she teased.

Mary thought about Anne's words and then replied, "It won't be long before someone'll be wanting to challenge me!"

Over the next two days Anne spent time talking to Captain Bluey and the first mate, Quartermaster Richard Easter. She explained that she and Mary wanted to get as far away as possible from Spanish Town and the British Navy. The New World, England, or back to her native Ireland. She didn't mind which… and would agree to whatever the officers finally decided.

Mary, meanwhile, had decided to visit the ship's stores. She wanted to try on some of the spare men's clothes. Pirate's clothes! Junkie, who was in charge of the stores, had seen it all before. He admitted to being 50 years of age, but Mary thought he was closer to 60!

Junkie laughed when he saw what clothes Mary had changed into, but she insisted they were what she preferred. Her attire consisted of an open-neck, white satin shirt, under a long black unfastened waistcoat, which fell to the side of her thighs. Dark-blue cotton trousers, secured by a scarlet red sash wrapped around her slim waist. The trousers were tucked into black knee-length leather boots. On top of her head she wore a matching red headscarf, folded and knotted in the nape of her neck. Her wig had been discarded and her light brown shoulder-length hair was drawn back and tied at the rear of her head.

"A nice lady like you shouldn't need them men's clothes," said Junkie. "They'll be for fighting men, not worn by good and pretty wenches like you."

It was Mary's turn to laugh. "Good, you say!? I've sailed the seas and seen both good and bad, better and worse, fair weather and foul. Knives and swords crashin', blood spillin', limbs and 'eads cut off. I've never seen any goodness in good! 'E who strikes out first is the victor. Dead men don't sting or bite!"

Junkie initially smiled, then stared long and hard at Mary, his eyes suddenly wide open. He'd never met a woman like this one before!

"Can you wield a sword?" asked Mary, leaning forward and staring into Junkie's face. "Or shoot a flintlock, or kill a man with a knife?"

Junkie's expression quickly changed. "I've been known to duel with a sword."

Mary looked around the room and saw a group of swords leaning against the panelling. "Pass me that cutlass." She pointed. "The one with the red 'andle. It matches me sash."

Junkie reached over and picked up the red-handled cutlass. He weighed it in his hand. "This was Barry Bodin's sword. Died 'bout a year ago, when we attacked a Spanish gal'yon. Didn't do 'im much good then. It'll be too 'eavy for a lady like you. Let me give you a much smaller and lighter one."

"No!" said Mary firmly.

Junkie passed her the selected weapon without further delay.

Mary looked at the blade closely, and carefully ran her finger along the sharp edge. She then practised some thrusts and blows, making sure it wasn't too heavy. "This is fine," she announced.

Junkie picked up his own broadside sword, spat into his hand, knitted his brow and walked over towards her. "Let's see what it's like in combat!"

He suddenly stepped back and made the blade sing through the air before taking a long slash towards her head. Mary easily parried his attack and stood back herself. Junkie came forward with two quick strikes, but Mary just flicked them away. Junkie tried again, this time with three lashes at speed. Mary defended herself and smiled at Junkie's frustration. Then it was Mary's turn to attack. In one swift motion she crashed her sword into his, pushing it away from his body. After touching his arm and right leg with the point of her sword, she then flicked his own sword completely out of his grasp. It crashed noisily onto the floor. Mary's sword was now just an inch from Junkie's throat!

Junkie was astonished and frightened. His eyes were wide open with fear. He'd never seen such skill. He quickly held his hands up high… in total surrender!

Junkie looked at his arm and then to his right leg, but there was no blood, just two gashes in the cloth of his garments.

"In a proper fight," said Mary, laying her sword down on the table, "you'd now be on the floor screamin'. I would 'ave removed your 'ead from your shoulders, with my very next blow!"

Junkie swallowed a lump in his throat and stepped back as far as he could. His eyes still wide open in shock. "Wow, lady, you're really good. Where'd you learn such skills?"

"Staying alive this long," said Mary. "I've been in quite a few fights over the years. No doubt I've got a lot more still to come!"

CHAPTER 8

The news travelled quickly. Junkie announced that 'this woman', Mary, could handle a sword like a man… better than most men he'd seen. Some of the crew said they wouldn't go near her, others decided they'd like to challenge her to a duel and see what she was really made of. The big question was, would Captain Bluey allow such a contest. After some debate it was decided to ask Quartermaster Richard Easter his advice.

As eight bells rang in the evening, Richard Easter walked into a room where 14 crewmen were eating their dinner. Their four-hour watch had just finished and it wasn't long before the conversation switched to Mary's alleged prowess with the sword. Richard's first reaction was not to believe Junkie's story. How could a woman be as good as a man!? Nevertheless, he did agree to raise the matter with the captain the next day.

Captain Bluey was surprised and decided to consult Anne on the matter. Anne simply said that Mary was the best sword fighter she'd ever seen… man or woman! He was intrigued and sent a message out to the rest of the crew asking for volunteers. Who would be prepared to step up for the challenge? Six names were put forward and Richard recommended Toby Spicer for the dare. He was chosen because he was a good swordsman, but not the best on the ship, a brave and confident fighter who had proved himself many times in battle.

Captain Bluey called Anne and Mary to his cabin and was surprised to see Mary dressed in her recently acquired pirate clothes.

Mary explained her reasons for the change of dress. She also wanted to be ready and an equal with every man on the ship.

Captain Bluey explained what the crew had been talking about – they wanted to see Mary in action… in a duel! He told her he was not entirely happy, but if she agreed, then he would reluctantly concur.

Mary looked at Anne, and gave her a knowing smile.

"Are you ready for this? asked Anne. She was worried about her good friend. "You've not had a serious fight with a sword for a long time. Some of these men will be tough. It's not going to be a poor swordsman who volunteers."

"Let's see then, should we?" replied Mary, in her usual confident mood. "It's important for me to get their respect. I can only do that if I'm better than their best."

Captain Bluey listened to the conversation. He had a slight smirk on his face. It would be extremely useful if Mary was as good as Junkie had reported. He always needed lots of good fighters, especially with the sword.

The contest was set for two days' time, at three bells in the afternoon.

Later that day, Anne decided she needed to be prepared and ready for the next attack on a merchant ship or a Spanish galleon. She visited the stores and selected her own sword and some appropriate fighting clothes. After his experience with Mary, Junkie did as he was told.

In the privacy of their own cabin, Anne helped Mary with her sword fighting practice. It was a small room, but that helped Mary with close contact and using her strength to push Anne away. She knew a man would be stronger, but she was confident her guile and skill would overcome the only advantage a man might possibly have.

The day of the contest arrived. Toby Spicer and Mary appeared separately on the main deck. The weather was favourable. No rain, but a calm, cooling sea breeze. As a result the ship was just motioning gently.

Mary looked across to where Toby was standing. He was smiling, confident and chatting to colleagues. He looked about Mary's age and of medium build. He also seemed reasonably fit and strong, but he didn't look across towards Mary. Mmm, she thought, maybe just a bit too confident! She started to feel annoyed!

There were about 50 members of the crew spread around the perimeter of the main deck. Most were talking, some pointed, but all were keen to see the fight begin. Several men were also standing on the poop deck and on the roof of the main aft cabins. A further eight were viewing from high up in the rigging.

Captain Bluey stepped forward and made his announcement: "This is not a fight to the death. It's just a test of strength and ability, until one party surrenders. I don't want any needless loss of life for any of my crew."

Both Mary and Toby nodded. They would abide by these rules.

Mary and Toby stepped forward until they were about two metres apart. Toby was still smiling. Mary didn't respond. They nodded and raised their swords to a vertical position. Now they were ready to fight.

There was excitement in the crowd. Cheers and groans began when the encounter finally commenced, The shouts were largely divided between loyalty to Toby and their admiration for Mary's self-belief.

Mary expected Toby to attack straight away and she was ready for his first lunge or leap. Her anticipation was correct and she easily parried him away. He lunged again and Mary smashed at his sword and then slashed a large gash in his shirt. Blood started to trickle and a red stain quickly appeared through the flimsy white cotton shirt.

The continuing crashing of metal on metal echoed around the hull of the ship. Toby pushed forward and Mary had to retreat. However, in her next movement she thrashed hard and Toby fell back and crashed into two barrels. Fortunately, these stopped him falling onto the deck. But whilst he was off-balance Mary lunged again. Toby was ready this time and ducked out of the way. They now stepped away from each other and both were taking deep breaths. More comments and encouragement were shouted from the baying crowd.

Mary tried to take this brief respite to wipe her forehead; however, Toby, sensing his opportunity, quickly rushed forwards, thrusting his sword in the direction of her chest. Mary quickly stepped aside and hit Toby on the back of his head with the handle of her sword. He fell onto the deck and lay on his back. His sword was on the floor next to his right hand. Mary immediately stepped forward and placed her right boot onto his groin, holding him down. Then leaning closer towards his body she pointed her sword to within an inch of his heart.

Toby closed his eyes in anguish due to the excruciating pain between his legs and his anticipation of an imminent and horrible death.

Suddenly, Mary pulled her sword away from her threatening position. She stood back and encouraged Toby to stand up. This was not a real battle, she reminded herself. To kill was not the object of today, it was solely to prove to everyone watching that she was dangerous, skilled and truly unrivalled when it came to wielding her sword.

From his supine position on the wooden deck, Toby paused and looked inquiringly at Bluey. The captain, however, just stood quietly with his arms folded and a broad smile on his face.

More comments and shouts were made from the watchers still circling around the perimeter. Toby picked up his sword and slowly got to feet. He was startled, dazed and knew he'd been beaten. Nevertheless, he decided to have one last final assault. He thrashed his sword across towards Mary's shirt, but missed her by inches as Mary easily stepped aside.

Seeing Toby was off-balance again, Mary swung her sword two-handed, with all her might. It crashed into his weapon and shattered the blade. Toby squealed and threw the remains of his sword onto the floor. He then backed away with his hands in the air. He'd had enough.

Cheers rang out from some of the audience. Junkie shouted, "See, I told you!"

Captain Bluey stepped forward, clapping his hands. "Well done, Mary. Very impressive. You've earned the honour of becoming a member of my crew."

Cheers rang out again and Mary's face turned a shade of crimson. Her next move, however, surprised everyone. She put down her sword and walked over to a still-somewhat-dazed Toby

Spicer and held out her hand. Toby looked at Mary's face and then her right hand. Finally he smiled and congratulated her, before finally shaking her hand. More cheers from the crowd erupted. Mary smiled, waved and walked away. She then spotted Anne, who had a large smile on her face and was frantically applauding. Mary smiled back and then returned to stand in front of Captain Bluey.

"Thank you, Captain, for those kind words. It's not Toby who's the enemy and I 'ope 'e and I can work, and fight, together in the future. 'E's a very brave man."

Later that evening, both ladies were back in their cabin. Mary was aching all over. She told Anne she thought she'd been using muscles she'd forgotten she still had!

Anne was relieved and pleased with the fight's outcome and gave Mary a big hug. "You were brilliant!" she said, after they'd unlocked their embrace. "I was so worried you wouldn't be ready for such an important fight."

Mary finished undressing and stepped into a wooden, cutdown half barrel, containing salty Caribbean sea water. She slowly eased her naked body downwards and into a cramped sitting position. The chilled sea water made her body tingle, but she was convinced her muscles would soon start to relax. She closed her eyes and her mind slowly drifted away.

Anne, in the meantime, was getting ready and pulling on her finest, and favourite, dark-blue dress. At the striking of three bells on the 'first dog watch', she was expected to join Captain Bluey for dinner!

CHAPTER 9

Whilst Mary continued to soak in her makeshift bath, Anne was eagerly awaiting the pealing of three bells. She was excited, but also apprehensive. After Jack, could she really have the same feelings again? She looked at Mary immersed in the water with her eyes closed. She appeared happy and content. Mary had told her of her simple wishes and now they'd partly been achieved. Anne was certain Mary would now be accepted as an equal, a pirate, with the rest of this crew.

Anne, however, hoped her own wishes were about to begin. Was this dinner going to be the beginning of another wonderful relationship? Suddenly, she thought of her first love, Calico Jack. Would he have approved or be jealous? What would she have done, or said, if the roles had been reversed and it was Jack who'd survived? Would she have been jealous of another woman?

Suddenly the peace and quiet was disturbed when, in the distance, the sound of the ship's bells began to ring. Anne counted… one… two… three!

"Good luck," muttered Mary, as Anne walked towards the door.

"Am I okay?" asked Anne, nervously touching her auburn, shoulder-length hair, but knowing all too well it was now too late to change her attire.

Mary sat up in her bath and looked across to Anne, standing next to the door. She rubbed her eyes with a nearby towel and said, "You look fabulous."

Anne smiled back, left their cabin and walked the short distance to the captain's quarters. When she arrived at the large oak-panelled door she hesitated, took a deep breath and finally knocked. After a few moments the door opened. "Hello, Anne, please come in." Bluey stood back to allow Anne to pass. The cabin spanned the full width of the ship's stern and had a large wall of small windows at the rear. Except in battle, the cabin was for the exclusive use of the captain… plus any of his invited guests!

The large cabin had the ability to be changed into either a day or a night cabin simply by operating the moveable wooden bulkheads. These could also be completely removed during battle, thus leaving the cabin clear for gunners to use to attack the opposition, or, more importantly, be able to defend the ship's own stern.

Anne walked into the candlelit room. She immediately spotted the bulkheads had been arranged in a night-time position. A large oak dining table, capable of seating ten people, was laid for just two settings. On the table were two carafes of red wine and four silver cloches hiding their meal.

Anne recalled many similar meals and liaisons she'd enjoyed with Calico Jack, but those were, she recalled, in a far less grandiose captain's cabin.

Bluey watched Anne as she walked across the room. She's a very attractive woman, he thought. Good looks and a nice figure. Although these assets appealed to him, he knew that, just from the few times they'd spoken together, he was also attracted to her intelligence and sense of adventure. All qualities he saw in himself.

Bluey had experienced several relationships during his 35 years of life, but no woman he'd met ever wanted a life at sea. They especially didn't see a long-term future with a man who was a pirate, a thief and a murderer!

Bluey closed the door and walked over to join Anne. As he stood in front of her his eyes roved from her face down the length of her dress. "You look wonderful in a blue dress. My favourite colour. It really suits you."

Anne was slightly embarrassed, but replied, "I hoped you'd like it. It's my favourite dress."

Bluey smiled. "Let me get you some wine." He picked up one of the carafes and poured red wine into two silver goblets then handed one to Anne. "Cheers." He held out his own goblet. "Here's to more successful adventures!"

Anne smiled and clinked her goblet with Bluey's. "And a happy future for us both."

They sipped their wine and then Bluey led Anne to the table. Anne knew which would be the captain's chair, so she deliberately headed for the opposite seat.

Bluey removed two of the four cloches covering their food. On the first platter were roasted sirloin of beef and buttered roasted potatoes. On the second, buttered carrots, 'pease' and green beans.

Bluey started to carve the meat whilst Anne helped herself to the vegetables. This was really a treat for Anne. So far she'd only eaten the food served to the crew. Nevertheless, she'd quickly discovered that Bluey's crew were very fussy when it came to their food. Most jobs on ship were heavy manual work, so they expected to be fed well… and they were.

Anne took two slices of meat, placed them next to her vegetables and started to eat. Bluey watched her with a smile on his face, before finally asking, "I hope the food is to your taste?"

"Oh, it's excellent, a real treat," said Anne. She was hungry and wanted to enjoy every morsel.

"Better than the Spanish Town prison food?"

Anne stopped eating, put down her cutlery and scowled at the captain. He hadn't touched any of his own meal so far. "Please don't remind me of those horrible days. I thought we were going to die there. We both nearly did!"

Bluey held his hands up in mock surrender. "I'm sorry, Anne, but I'm really pleased you're here now… with me."

Anne picked up her cutlery again and cut a small piece of beef. "So am I. We can't thank you enough for agreeing to let us come aboard."

Finally, Bluey started to eat his meal, but he hardly removed his eyes from staring at Anne. "Mary was impressive with her sword. She's going to be a great asset for my ship. Why does she want to be a pirate again? She's attractive and could easily find a nice man."

Anne sipped her wine and then explained. "She did have a nice man, once, sometime ago. Married a soldier. It's a long story; I'll tell you one day. But her husband died of a fever and it broke her heart."

Bluey picked up his own goblet and took a sip of his wine. "That's sad. You can see from her fierce fighting she's probably trying to overcome some sort of a grudge or grievance. She fights with great skill, but also with a ferocious spirit. Obviously trying to seek, maybe, revenge, or retaliation? Trying to escape from something horrible lurking in her past?"

Anne pondered on Bluey's analysis. However, after a few seconds she decided she didn't want to spend the evening solely talking about Mary, so she tried to change the subject. "Calico Jack used to speak fondly of you. Weren't you on a ship together?"

"Now, that's a long time ago. Yes we were, on the *Wild Dragon* – Captain Booth's ship. A great captain. Hard, but fair. There was never a need for mutiny under him. The crew all respected him. I learned a lot from him too, and we had a great time. But then we attacked a Spanish galleon, reputedly carrying lots of gold and silver. Booth got hit by a musket ball, straight into his right eye. He died immediately."

"But you and Jack survived unscathed."

"Yes. We boarded the galleon and robbed it of most of its silver and some of its gold. Once they'd been transferred to the *Wild Dragon*, Quartermaster Andrew Bates, who was now in charge, gave orders to sink the Spanish ship. But a number of us were still on board, so we quickly took charge and sailed away with the Spanish and the rest of their treasure. The Spanish were pleased and thankful for us saving their lives, so they took us to Nassau and dropped anchor about a mile from shore. They then lowered a longboat and gave us a chest of gold. The eight of us, abandoned by Bates, then rowed ashore. We shared out the gold and then Jack and I went our separate ways."

"Jack joined Captain Vane's ship, *Ranger*," said Anne. "But then he became captain of his own pirate ship, *Revenge*."

"I remember that. I joined Captain Oliver Lyle on his ship, *Shadow*. Two years later I had enough treasure to acquire my own ship. It was a nice ship, the *Shark*. But then Black Pete told me of a British ship that had been captured by the French. They were trafficking slaves around the Caribbean. We attacked it and took it over." Bluey spread his arms out wide. "This is it, the *Empress*. Been a great ship. Big, strong and powerful. Forty guns. The British Navy has left us alone… so far."

"Jack also told me you're an educated man from a wealthy family. Why did you decide to become a pirate?"

Bluey laughed. "Good question. Sometimes I ask the same question myself. Yes, I came from a privileged background. My father was, or hopefully still is, a wealthy merchant. I was sent to a good grammar school, where he paid for my education and everything was planned for me and my brother to join his business. But that was the point! I didn't have a real say in anything. My life was already planned out for the next 40 or 50 years. At 14 years of age I was introduced to a girl who was going to be my future wife!"

Anne looked at Bluey with a surprised look on her face. "So what did you do?"

"My best friend at school was a boy called James Hobson-Smythe. He was a bit of a rebel and after I'd told him I was unhappy with my family's plans for me, he suggested we run away together. Said he just wanted to have adventures and see the rest of the world. Suddenly, I had to make a decision – was that what I wanted to do?"

"Running away is one thing. I did that," said Anne, picking up her goblet of wine. "But I became a pirate to join the man I loved and escape a bad marriage. You had a wealthy future ahead of you, I didn't!"

"I know. But I didn't have my freedom! I also wanted adventures and to be able to stand on my own two feet. To be successful at something that *I'd* chosen. Not to have my life all planned out. In the end I decided to go with James. In the back of my mind I thought that if I failed, then, I could always go back home and live the life my family had already mapped out for me."

"But you didn't fail."

"Yes and no. James and I did run away and we stowed on board a ship heading for the Thirteen Colonies. We eventually arrived in Charles Town. That's in South Carolina."

Suddenly Anne burst out laughing.

"What's so funny?" asked Bluey, somewhat confused.

"I know where Charles Town is. That's where I grew up!"

This time it was Bluey who started to laugh. "Seriously! We might have unknowingly seen each other! Mind, James and I, we only stayed there for a couple of months, working in the docks. We then joined the crew of a merchant ship sailing to Jamaica. However, just before we arrived, we were attacked by a pirate ship. My first experience of that sort of an adventure. Fortunately it was the *Wild Dragon*, Captain Booth's ship! He wasn't as bloodthirsty as some and our merchant ship's crew weren't really fighters. So, anyway, the pirates stole what they wanted and then sent our ship on its way. James and I, however, both decided to try this new sort of adventure, it sounded like fun and a quick way to get rich. So we asked Captain Booth if we could join his crew. But before he agreed we both had to demonstrate our skills with a flintlock pistol, dagger and sword. James had grown up on a farm estate so he knew how to use a gun, and we both knew how to use a sword as we were taught sword fighting at school. So we were both accepted. Unfortunately for James, the next ship we met was a Spanish galleon and they were better equipped to defend themselves. James was killed when he lost his fight to a better Spanish swordsman."

"Oh dear. That's sad."

"One of the risks you take. We both knew that. Captain Booth explained all the dangers, but, I guess, we just thought we were invincible."

Over the next hour, they continued to talk about each other's lives. Bluey removed the remaining two cloches. One revealed cheeses and some 'ships biscuits'. The other contained washed, but unpeeled, bananas, oranges and mangoes.

After the meal ended, Anne was feeling full. She couldn't remember the last time she'd eaten such a big and enjoyable meal. She stood up, and, holding her replenished goblet of wine, she walked around the cabin. Bluey watched her every move.

Anne eventually arrived at his side of the table. She then reached out and clasped Bluey's right hand. She put her drink on the table and gently pulled his arm. He immediately stood up and followed Anne towards the bedroom area. They stopped next to the bed and Anne leaned upwards and gave Bluey a long and sensuous kiss.

Bluey then picked her up in his arms and gently laid her onto the bed.

Anne looked back as Bluey started to disrobe. She smiled and then commenced to unbutton the front of her favourite, 'lucky' blue dress.

CHAPTER 10

When Anne awoke the next morning, the sun was streaming through the stern windows, lighting up the far side of the captain's cabin. Anne rubbed her eyes and realised she was alone. She assumed Bluey had dressed and was already in his usual position commanding the ship.

As Anne started to get dressed, she could hear men running and a general commotion above on the poop deck. Bluey was shouting out commands. What's going on? she wondered.

Finally dressed, Anne left the captain's cabin, closing the door behind her. She walked along the corridor, up the stairs and onto the main deck. She stopped and stared as crewmen were shouting and running towards their stations. She spotted Mary looking over the bulwark and staring out to sea. She walked over to speak to her.

"What's going on?" asked Anne. She looked out into the Caribbean Sea but couldn't see anything other than the calm water and lots of blue sky.

Mary looked at her friend. "Good mornin'. I presume you 'ad a good evenin'?"

Anne smiled, but then changed her facial expression when she asked Mary the same question again.

"The boy in the crow's nest," replied Mary. "He shouted 'ship ahoy', a few minutes ago. Captain's given battle orders… just in case."

"Where's the ship?" Anne stared out across the sea. A small island was in view, but no ships.

"The boy pointed out this way, so we're all just lookin' and waitin'."

"I'd better get changed," said Anne, who then crossed the deck and disappeared down to their cabin.

Whilst Anne was changing into her sailor's clothes, she heard Bluey shouting again. This time he was calling for Johnny Hines, the ship's sailing master. He was the officer in charge of navigation and piloting. It was a difficult job because charts were generally inaccurate or nonexistent. Nevertheless, Johnny was a prize asset for Bluey as he'd created some of his own charts, which had proved reasonably accurate. He was good at calculating distances and locations after measuring angles utilising the position of the sun, moon and stars.

Bluey had mentioned to Anne, the previous evening, some details about the ship's officers. She knew Johnny Hines had been forced to join the crew two years ago. At the time he was the sailing master on a British merchant ship Bluey had captured. However, being young and single, Johnny found the life of a pirate far more exciting and rewarding, so he'd decided to stay aboard the *Empress* and become the ship's senior sailing master.

Anne heard more footsteps above and then the conversation between Bluey and Johnny Hines. Bluey said, "Johnny, Black Pete said there was a British Naval fleet in these waters. Not sure yet what Willy's seen. It could be that fleet. Just in case, work out a course for our nearest safe port."

"Should be Hispaniola, Captain. It's about a day's sailing from here, but I'll check."

Just then Anne heard Willy, the boy in the crow's nest, cry out again, but she couldn't make out exactly what he'd said.

"Okay, so it is the British Navy, with six ships in the fleet," she heard Bluey say. He continued, "Let's get moving... and quickly! They've probably already spotted us."

Anne heard more footsteps and then Bluey said calmly, "Turn about, Mr Godfrey, this is no place for us." Mr Godfrey was one of the helmsmen, responsible for steering the ship. After he'd turned the ship's wheel, the vessel commenced its new course.

Anne suddenly lurched when she felt the ship begin to turn towards starboard. She finished changing her clothes and then heard Johnny Hines tell Mr Godfrey the adjustments for the new direction to sail. She also heard the call for all sails to be unfurled.

Leaving her and Mary's cabin, Anne climbed back up the stairs and onto the deck. She was now dressed in her pirate's clothes, complete with her sword and pistol. The gunners, with their assistants, were all located at their battle stations. Everything was now much quieter and calmer, but everyone knew the danger was certainly not over... not yet!

The *Empress,* now in full sail, was swiftly heading in a south-easterly direction, picking up the trade winds. Willy was still perched in the crow's nest and scouring the horizon. He continued to shout down his observations until, finally, there were no ships in sight. He then climbed down the rigging and masts, passing by his replacement, 'young' Harry, whose turn it was in the crow's nest.

Anne walked over to Mary, who was still looking out to sea. "Hopefully, that was just a near miss," she said.

"Mmm," replied Mary. "I didn't really want us to tangle with six Navy ships!"

"It's made me think," said Anne, worrying about what would have happened if they'd been caught again. "I want to get off this ship. Not just this ship, any ship! I don't want to be a pirate anymore, I want a new life and to be many miles away from Spanish Town... and all the other islands in the Caribbean."

Mary looked at her friend. She was concerned and unsure what to say.

Anne continued, "Last night with Bluey, well it was wonderful. Just like the best nights I'd had with Jack. Jack was hanged and I don't want the same threat for Bluey, and my future."

Mary leaned back on the bulwark's rail, she was now facing towards the ship's main deck. "You think you've got a future with Bluey? Isn't 'e a career pirate... you know... for life?"

"I don't think so. We talked a lot last night. He said he'd like to retire, eventually... whatever that means."

"Isn't that what most pirates want? Obtain enough wealth and then settle down?" said Mary. "It rarely 'appens though."

"You don't want to, do you? You told me you still wanted the adventures and even more treasure than we've already got."

Mary took a deep breath. "I know, that's what I said."

Anne looked across at her friend. She had a surprised look on her face. "Have you changed your mind?"

Mary watched two gunners and their group tidy up and secure their gun into a safe sailing position. "Lying in my 'ammock last evening, it gave me time to think. I could 'ave killed Toby in that fight. It's not 'is fault I feel permanently angry. Fighting seems to give me a temporary release. I'm trying to kill all my demons, Anne. I still 'ave all those 'orrible nightmares."

"All the time I've known you," replied Anne. "You've seemed to be annoyed and seeking some sort of revenge. When you have a sword in your hand you fight with a frenzied look on your face."

Mary looked at her friend and smiled, "That's probably why I'm the best!"

"But do you really want a future like that? One day you'll get really hurt, if not killed!"

"Maybe that's the best future for me. A sword through me 'eart. Better than bein' 'ung by me neck!"

"I hope you don't mean that. What a waste that would be. Don't you want to be happy and settle down one day?"

"'appy!? What's that, Anne!? Me life so far 'as been mostly un'appy and painful. I never knew my father, as for my mother, she didn't love me. Just used me to survive. Made me dress up in boy's clothes. I didn't 'ave any friends or an education. I was lonely and 'ad nobody to talk to until I was about 13. I just played in the fields and talked to the birds and animals. I made friends with a farmer's 'orse and used to ride 'im a few times. Got quite good too. But I 'ad no real future, just a few dreams. When I joined the army I saw it as a big chance to escape. A chance for a better life, maybe to achieve some of me dreams. People spoke to me. I was able to have conversations and could channel me pain and anger into killin' the enemy. It worked for a while, I was one of the boys. But then I fell in love with a fellow soldier, Tommy, 'is name was. You should 'ave seen 'is face when I told 'im I was a woman and showed 'im me breasts!"

Anne laughed and Mary continued. "The army was surprised but was good about it, 'cos they knew I'd been a good soldier. We got married and I thought my luck 'ad finally changed. I really loved that man, Anne… me Tommy. But, of course, it didn't last. Nothin' nice lasts in my life. We weren't married a year and 'e died of the fever. The pain returned and so did me anger. I ran away, didn't know where to go. London, Manchester and then to Liverpool, that's where I went. Slept rough and with a few different men. The last one told me about a merchant ship that was leavin' the docks the next day. Goin' to the 'New World', 'e said. I didn't know anythin' of this new world so decided to stow away on board. I'd never seen the sea before. Brown, mucky water, as far as the eye could see. I was anxious, where was this new world? What would I find?"

Mary looked around the deck, not really seeking anything, just pausing to find her next words. "I'd been on that ship for a few days and was able to find food scraps and some rainwater. One evenin' our ship was attacked. I was 'iding in one of the small longboats. We were attacked by what I now know were pirates. They came aboard, shouting, swinging swords and shoot-ing pistols! I was really scared and 'id as best I could. Lots of people were killed. Gradually everything began to settle down and I listened to the pirates talking. They were looting the ship of food, wine, water and any treasure they could find. I 'eard one of the pirates say they were goin' to sink the ship, so I decided I'd better get off. Whilst the pirates loaded their ship, I sneaked out from my 'iding place and saw several dead men on the deck. One was about my size, so I took off my rags and dressed up in his clothes. At first it felt funny, but it quickly felt normal. After all, I'd spent more of my years dressed up in boys and men's clothes, than I 'ad in women's. I 'eard one passenger on our ship plead with the pirates. 'E said 'e wanted to be a pirate too. So 'e was dragged onto the pirate ship. I did the same and was pushed on behind 'im. Not long after that I 'eard a huge bang from a gun. The cannonball 'it our old merchant ship at water level. Very quickly it began to lean and take on water. The pirates cheered as the ship slowly sank. I could 'ear people, who were still alive on the merchant ship, shoutin' and screamin'. Some managed to get two of the small longboats into the water and climb in. It was 'orrible the people screamin'. The pirates didn't need to do that."

"So that was me," continued Mary. "Now a pirate meself. I was given a pistol, knife and a sword and told to practise every day. The flintlock pistol I didn't really like, but very quickly, I became quite good with a knife and the sword. Soon our ship, *Adventure*, was involved in more battles and our captain was pleased with me bravery and use of me sword. I quickly realised again that killing and maiming other people eased the pain and anger I'd felt all those years."

Anne didn't like what she was hearing, but she could understand her friend's pain.

Mary continued her story, "After that I was feeling a lot better with meself and practised really 'ard with the sword. On our way to Nassau, we met a Spanish galleon and the captain ordered us to attack. Both ships hit each other with gun fire. We sailed close and a lot of us jumped aboard the other ship. It was quite a battle. A lot of people were killed or maimed. I killed two young Spanish men. Not really proud of that, but they would 'ave killed me otherwise. Eventually the Spanish gave up and we looted their ship. I finished up with lots of gold doubloons and lovely jewels.

"When the *Adventure* eventually arrived in Nassau, I went ashore. I thought this was the 'New World' that people 'ad been talking about, but it didn't seem all that good to me. I got a job at an inn for a while. I'd worked in one before with Tommy, but I was missing me sword fighting and battles at sea… and, of course, collecting more treasure. So I joined a group of privateers and buccaneers, 'ired by Governor Rogers. It sounded like a lot of fun. 'Owever, not long after the ship had set sail, the crew mutinied against the captain and I found myself on another pirate ship. Initially it was fun and I got on well with one of the crew, Davy. Lovely young man. Looked a lot like me Tommy. I told 'im, and showed 'im that I was a woman. 'E promised to keep me secret if I let 'im 'ave 'is way. I agreed, but, unfortunately, that's when I became 'with child'. Davy got killed in our next conflict, shot in his left eye. After that you know the rest of me story, because that's when we were attacked by the *Revenge* and Calico Jack!"

"I remember that well," replied Anne. "I also remember when we first spoke to each other. I loved Jack, but when you arrived I thought you were a really attractive young man! Much younger than Jack. It was so embarrassing, but also so disappointing, when you told me you were a woman!"

Mary laughed. "Nobody else knew. It was our little secret."

"That is," said Anne, "until Jack became suspicious and jealous. I had to tell him the truth. He threatened to kill you."

Mary smiled. "'E didn't believe you, not until I'd shown 'im what I 'ad missing!"

"I didn't know that," said Anne, her eyes wide open and laughing. "You kept that a secret."

"I 'ad to. Jack said 'e would 'ave me flogged and thrown overboard, if I'd ever told you."

"You've been through a lot, Mary, and the horrors of that prison as well. I'm not surprised you're angry, but we've got a long life still to live… that is, if we can get off this ship somewhere safely."

Mary turned around and looked back across the sea to the horizon. There were no other ships to be seen. After a few seconds, she said, "What are you suggestin'?"

CHAPTER 11

The *Empress* continued to sail quickly. The trade wind had picked up and it was now in their favour. Captain Bluey gave orders saying the remaining sailors could relax and leave their battle stations. Where they were heading, he guessed, the British Navy wouldn't follow them. The Navy wouldn't find any friends there!

Johnny Hines, kept rechecking his calculations and reading his charts. Finally he told Captain Bluey that if this wind held they should see the coast of Hispaniola by daybreak tomorrow.

Later that evening, Captain Bluey and Quartermaster Richard Easter, were sitting at the table in the captain's cabin. They were discussing the plans for when the ship anchored in Saragoa Bay, opposite the pirate town of Léogâne. Easter explained that supplies were running low and needed to be replenished. He and Boatswain Archie Gillet had produced a long list of the ship's requirements.

Bluey, who normally left these sort of decisions to Easter and Gillet, said he was satisfied and agreed to their request.

Easter also told Bluey that three crewmen had requested leave but they'd only be short of one man… that is, if the two women were counted as crew.

Bluey smiled and glanced to the far side of his cabin. He could just see the corner of his bed behind the bulkhead. "What do you think, Richard? Do we include them as crew? Mary's certainly worthy."

"I'm not sure how long they're going to be on the ship," replied Richard. "Some of the men are still feeling uneasy about having women aboard. They think it'll lead to bad luck. I told them bad luck would only find them if they decided to challenge either woman to a fight!"

"I think Mary wants to stay on board indefinitely, but with Anne, I'm not so sure. Would one remain if the other decided to leave? Black Pete told me they were only desperate to get away from Spanish Town, not necessarily wanting to be pirates again."

"Women aren't my strong suit, Captain. I don't know how their brains work. Give me a man every time. You know where you stand with men."

Bluey leaned back in his chair and linked his hands together on the back of his neck. He was trying to think how he should respond. "Have a look tomorrow, when you go to Léogâne. See if there are any men who'd like to join us. I don't think we need more than three. Reckon we'll moor for about three days. Give some of the crew a chance to have a break. I'll have a word with Anne."

Easter stood and walked towards the door. He stopped and asked, "Are you going ashore this time, Captain?"

"Not sure yet, Richard. I'll let you know in the morning."

At this, Easter left the captain's cabin. Bluey sat still for a few minutes and pondered about Anne. He wondered what he would do, or say, if she did decide to leave the ship.

That same evening, Mary and Anne were in their cabin. Mary had just climbed into her hammock, but Anne wanted to talk.

"I'm going to speak to Bluey, tomorrow," said Anne. "I want to see his reaction when I tell him we both want to leave the ship in Léogâne."

"I'm still not sure what I want to do, Anne."

"I'm definitely sure, now," replied Anne, firmly. She sat down on her hammock and gently rocked back and forwards.

"I know. It's easier for you. You're much younger," said Mary, looking across at her friend.

"You're not old! You've got years ahead. That's if we can get away and set up a new life."

"Together!?" queried Mary, somewhat surprised.

"No. Not in the sense you're thinking about. I mean until we find somewhere safe. Change our names, a new identity. Make up a new history. Then see what happens. We might find two nice men to settle down with."

"Where do you want to go?"

"We could stay in Léogâne for a while and decide. The British Navy won't come there. It's a pirate town. Maybe we should think about South Carolina."

"What about our treasure? It's all in New Providence. We could go back there."

"I've been thinking about that," replied Anne, with a smile on her face. "I also know where Jack buried most of his treasure. The only problem is I've no longer got the maps I copied. Mind, I think I can still remember where his treasure is buried on Heneagua."

"'Ow are we going to get there?"

"I've not worked that out yet. We can decide between Heneagua, New Providence or South Carolina when we're in Léogâne."

Next morning, just after daybreak, the *Empress* glided slowly into Saragoa Bay. The perfect calm blue water sparkled as the ship dropped anchor. It was another warm and bright sunny day.

Two pirate ships were already moored close by. This area was a known pirate haven, a refuge where the pirates made all their own laws and rules. No fighting was tolerated here, not in this hidden corner of pirate paradise. So far the British Navy, and other official authorities, had ignored the town's existence, they preferred to pick off pirate ships in smaller numbers and out on the high seas.

Captain Bluey was watching as the longboat was slowly being lowered into the water. Richard Easter and his team were getting ready to go ashore, the first of several trips for more supplies. Anne strolled across the main deck to where Bluey was standing. She was wearing the same blue dress she'd worn when dining with Bluey, three nights ago. "Captain, can I speak to you, please?"

"My, we are formal this morning, Anne." He turned around to face her properly and left Easter to get on with his task. He rubbed his black beard and wondered what Anne was about to say.

"I've had enough of piracy, Bluey, and want to leave your ship... today."

"I see," said Bluey. He was not surprised at Anne's comment, but definitely sad. "That's a shame. I thought we were getting on well."

Anne smiled. "Yes we are, but I don't want to go back to that horrible prison. I don't want to be caught by the authorities again. I want a normal life."

Bluey looked down at his feet and wondered what to say. "I don't want to lose you, Anne."

"Then come with me."

"You know I can't do that. Not now, maybe soon, but not now."

"Then it's goodbye, Bluey. Mary and me, we want to be many miles away from the Caribbean. We want a new life. My life's been a mixture of sadness and adventure, now I want something more normal. I'd hoped it would be with you."

"It can be. Tell me where you want to go and I'll take you there."

Anne turned away and took a deep breath. "Then what, Bluey?"

"I don't know, Anne. But I want you to stay with me."

"That's not going to happen. You want your life on the seas. Chasing your dreams and adventures. More hunting for treasure. Me? None of that's important any more. It's not going to be my life. Somehow, and for some reason, I've been given a second chance. I'm not going to throw it away and be hanged on the gallows like Jack."

"So it's goodbye then, Anne. Is that what you really want?"

"No, Bluey, it's not what I want, but you've given me no choice." Anne moved closer towards him, stretched up and gave him a long, heartfelt kiss on his lips. She then turned away and walked over towards the aft cabins. She saw Mary standing at the top of the stairs, wearing a white cotton dress.

Anne followed Mary down the stairs and back to their cabin. Mary's bags were already packed. Anne sat down on her hammock, put her head in her hands and burst into tears. Mary leaned over and put her arm around her friend's shoulder. No words were needed, none were said.

CHAPTER 12

Mary, Anne and all their belongings were now in the longboat. The boat was returning to Léogâne for their next collection of supplies. As the longboat pulled away from the *Empress*, Anne didn't look back. She didn't see Bluey standing at the side of the hull, watching her sail away.

Mary did look back and wondered if she had made the right decision. Still, she had three days before it was finally too late.

The longboat, with its six oarsmen, cut through the water easily. It was in a sheltered bay and the sea was calm. Richard Easter was explaining to the ladies that Léogâne was a small town, but a sanctuary, a safe place for pirates to rest and take time away from the long days on the high seas. A place where they could exchange gold, silver and jewels for fun, drink, excitement and women. No questions asked. They were the rules.

Anne and Mary listened and watched ahead as the longboat pulled into the small harbour. Richard pointed to the inn opposite. "You should be okay staying there. I'll get my men to bring over your bags."

Anne and Mary were shown to their room, a spacious, airy and bright chamber, with two single beds. The window looked over the harbour and out into the bay. Anne stood by the window and gazed at the scene. In the distance she could see the *Empress* still stationary, anchored in the calm bay. One of the two pirate ships, moored when they'd first arrived, had now pulled up anchor and departed.

Five minutes later there was a knock on their door. Two of the crew from the longboat carried Mary and Anne's belongings into the room. The men wished them good luck and Mary said, "Thank you." After the men had left, Anne sat down on her bed and burst into tears.

Late in the afternoon a storm developed and it rained heavily for about an hour. Anne watched the harbour area gradually clear of people and the surface turn to puddles and mud. A large crash of thunder made both women jump as it rumbled and echoed around the surrounding hillside.

They had both unpacked all their clothes and Mary was looking out through the window. "Are you 'ungry?" she asked.

"No," replied Anne, in a sad tone. She was sitting on her bed. "Has it stopped raining?"

"Yes. There's activity back in the 'arbour again. D'you fancy a walk? Investigate this place, it shouldn't take too long."

Anne stood up and walked over to join Mary next to the window. The sun was shining again and the last of the black clouds were slowly disappearing over the hills. People had returned to the harbourside and were chatting and going about their usual business.

Anne stared out of the window and into the bay. The *Empress* was still there. "Let's get some fresh air; it'll soon be dark."

Mary looked at her sad friend and gave her a sympathetic smile. "Great idea. Let's go."

For the next two hours the two women walked around most of the town. Mary was right, it didn't take long. The lanes were narrow, just enough room for horses and carts. As the horses slowly passed by, strollers had to step well to the side to avoid being knocked over or splashed with the puddles and mud.

There were a number of bars and shops, clothiers and even a barber. All seemed busy and a number of the bars were noisy as well. There was lots of shouting and some music could be heard from at least two buildings away.

When they got back to their inn, Anne decided she now felt hungry, so they went to the bar area to see what they could find to eat.

The options were limited but both women found something they liked. They also ordered some white wine.

The wine arrived in a green glass jug. Mary poured two glasses and made a toast. "To our future!"

"Yes," replied Anne. "To our future and a new life... well away from the Caribbean Sea."

Anne was a little more cheerful now. "We've still got plenty of the gold and jewels I stole from the White Star, but we'll soon need to exchange some for more money."

"I've still got a lot of the money we obtained from Lorenzo. But, we don't want to run short. Also I've got these."

Mary removed a blue velvet pouch from her purse and placed it on the table.

Anne wondered what the pouch was for. It looked similar to a tobacco pouch. She looked at Mary with surprise and curiosity. "What's this?" she asked.

"'Look inside," said Mary, and pushed the small bag closer to Anne.

Anne slowly opened the pouch and looked inside. She then put her right hand inside and immediately felt the cold, hard feel of what she assumed were about 20 different sized small pebbles. She pulled out three of the stones and stared back at Mary. In her hand were two diamonds and a red ruby! She quickly placed them back into the pouch and looked around the room, making sure nobody else was watching her. "Where did these come from?" she whispered.

Mary leaned forward and whispered herself, "They're from Bluey. 'E gave me them, just before we left the ship. Told me to give them to you. You might need them on your travels, 'e said. A sort of goodbye present, I guess."

Anne gripped the pouch tightly and tears started to well up in her eyes. "I can't accept these!" She pushed the bag back across the table.

"Well you've got them now," said Mary. She pushed the bag back towards Anne and leaned back in her seat. "How you goin' to get them back to 'im?"

Anne bowed her head and sobbed. "Mary?" she said after a few seconds. "I'm doing the right thing... aren't I?"

Mary took a deep breath and looked around the room, thinking of what to say. Finally she leaned forward and said, "If you mean about Bluey, I don't know. I understand your reasons for wantin' to get away from the pirate life. Trying to get some sort of normality into your life, but you love this man don't you?"

Anne didn't raise her head, she just nodded. Eventually, she said, "I don't know what to do."

Mary covered Anne's right hand with her own, squeezing it gently.

Anne wiped her eyes with her free hand, but didn't look up. Suddenly the strained atmosphere changed when their ordered food was delivered to the table. Abruptly, Anne leaped up and ran out.

"Som'ing I said?" asked the woman, holding two plates of food.

"No, she's just upset," said Mary, surveying both meals.

The woman placed the food on the table and started to walk away. Suddenly, she stopped and spoke loudly over her shoulder. "Bet a silver shilling there's a man involved!"

When isn't there? Mary thought to herself and smiled.

CHAPTER 13

When Mary awoke the following morning, she noticed Anne was already dressed and staring out of the window. "You're up early this mornin'. Are you okay?"

Anne turned her head towards Mary's bed. "Yes, I'm fine. Woke up early and decided to get up. Just been watching the comings and goings in the harbour. It's really busy."

Mary sat up in her bed. "Is that all you've been lookin' at?"

"The *Empress* is still there, if that's what you mean."

"You 'ad any further thoughts?"

"Yes. I'm not going back on that ship, or any pirate ship anymore! It was you giving me Bluey's jewels that made me upset. Made me think maybe I'd made a mistake. But I know I've not. What about you? You've got one more day to decide."

"I know… and I don't know. We need to talk about the future. Where we goin' to go? 'Ow we goin' to get there? Decide if that's what I really want?"

Anne walked over and sat on the side of Mary's bed. She looked directly at Mary's face. "I don't want to force you to do something you don't want to do, but I don't want you to go back on that pirate ship."

"I know. But that's all I really know. A pirate's life, fightin', livin' with groups of men, sailin' the seas, collectin' treasure… and adventures. That's what I'll be givin' up."

"But what about your dreams? Moving back to England. Buying a house in the countryside. You might be captured and hanged. You won't have the same excuse next time."

"No. After all, who's goin' to want to make me pregnant at my age?"

Anne laughed. "I hope I look as good as you do when I get to your age. You make a very attractive young man!"

Both women laughed.

After a few seconds Anne became more serious. "I've been thinking. After the ship leaves tomorrow, nobody here will really know who we are. Nobody knows our names, I think we should change them."

Mary sat up and looked at Anne. She smiled and said, "Okay. What you goin' to call yourself?"

"I've been thinking about that too. My father's mother, I didn't really know her, had a nice-sounding name. An Irish name, Fiona."

Mary smiled back. "Yes, I like that. It's a nice name. What do you think I should be called… and don't say a man's name!"

They both laughed again.

Eventually, Anne said, "When I was growing up in South Carolina, my best friend was a girl… named Grace. I loved that name. Very innocent sounding. You're my best friend now, so what about the name Grace?"

Mary thought about it. "Sounds a bit religious."

"Even better," said Anne. "Nobody's going to associate a lady named Grace with a pirate called Mark or Mary Read."

"In that case we need to change our surnames too."

"Mmm, you're right. Common and simple names are probably the best. Makes it easier to write it down as well," said Anne. She tried to think of a suitable name. "I know. A common name in Ireland is Kelly. Yes, Fiona Kelly! Simple and easy to remember."

Mary pondered what surname she would like. "When I first joined the army, my sergeant was called John Pearson. 'E was really good to me, a really nice man. So I think I'll call meself Pearson, Grace Pearson. What do you think?"

"Sounds good to me. When are we going to start?"

"Right this minute!" said Mary emphatically.

"Okay, Grace, but if we bump into anyone from the *Empress,* we need to make sure to use our old names."

"That's it then, Fiona. It's Grace and Fiona from now on! Mary, Mark and Anne are gone forever, never to be mentioned… ever again!"

The two women didn't meet anybody from the ship for the rest of the day. They didn't realise how difficult it was going to be remembering each other's name! It was difficult enough to remember their own!

The next morning, Grace was awake early and by daybreak she was fully dressed. She was standing next to the bedroom window, looking out into the bay. There was only one pirate ship in view. Easily recognisable, compared to the usual smaller pirate ships, the *Empress* was anchored where Grace remembered. She still had mixed feelings about what Anne, no, Fiona, had said. After all, it did make some sense. Too many pirates did go on for too long. They rarely saw out their normal span of years. Many were killed in battle or drowned. Others were captured, tried, convicted of piracy and hung by the neck. Grace rubbed the soft skin around her own neck. She thought of Calico Jack and his crew. All dead now, so young. All hung by the neck at a public execution. The last thing they'd have heard was the noise of the baying crowd.

Grace remembered back to her and Fiona's prison cell, where they could hear the distant cheers from the crowd of onlookers as each man's turn came to be hanged. What good was their treasure to them now? Hidden away, probably buried on some Caribbean island. How long, how many years, decades, or even centuries, would pass before their hard-won treasure saw the light of day again?

"Anything happening yet?" Fiona was awake and sitting up in bed.

"No, but I don't think it'll be long."

"Bluey always said he liked to go early. Make the most of the daylight." Fiona emerged from her bed and slipped on her dressing gown. She walked over to stand next to Grace by the window. "It's a nice day, he'll want to take advantage of that."

People were arriving at the harbourside. Two boats were being loaded with fishing equipment.

"Looks like the anchor bein' raised," said Grace. "Won't be long now."

Fiona grabbed Grace's arm. The anchor finally stopped high up on the side of the hull and was secured into its usual position on the cat-head. The ship began turning slowly and the sails were unfurled from their fastenings on the masts. The large fighting frigate kept turning until all the women could see was its stern. Fiona focused her attention on the captain's cabin windows. A tear began to well up in her right eye and she squeezed Grace's arm even harder. Grace gently caressed Fiona's fingers. They both continued to watch as the ship headed out to sea.

"Goodbye, Bluey, my love," whispered Fiona, as the ship finally disappeared over the horizon, heading away to adventures new.

CHAPTER 14

After Bluey and the *Empress* had sailed away, Fiona and Grace left their bedroom and went down to the inn's bar. There they found fresh fruit being offered for breakfast. In this hot and sultry tropical climate, they didn't want anything more.

They ate in silence until Fiona finally said, "Do you fancy going to Charles Town? It's a long way away from here, but much safer. We can then start our new life well away from the Caribbean."

"I don't know anything about it, other than you grew up there."

"Charles Town was quite a buoyant town when I was there. Lots going on, new buildings and lots of people moving in. Besides, it's easier to get back to England from there. If that's what you'd eventually prefer."

"What about New Providence and 'eneagua... our treasure?"

"We need to check with some of the ships. But I'm sure both those places are on the way to South Carolina. Not sure we'd be able to get a ship from here all the way though. We'll probably need to check and see if there are any ships that'll take us to 'la bahía de Guantánamo', in south-east Cuba."

"Why Cuba? That's Spanish."

"Because that's where we're likely to find someone to take us on to Heneagua, and maybe Nassau too."

After breakfast they wandered to the harbour. The weather was warm and they breathed in the refreshing sea air. Three boats were currently moored. One, named the *Parrot,* was being unloaded. Grace walked across to the side of the boat and asked for the captain.

"That's me, lady. Can I be of 'elp?" The captain was about 50 years of age, with a deeply tanned and leathery skin.

"My friend and I," said Grace, using her right hand to shield her eyes from the sun. "Were wonderin' if you knew anyone who could take us to Guantánamo, in Cuba?"

"Cuba, you say." The captain rubbed his grey beard, whilst he thought about the question. "Best bet is José. His ship comes 'ere from Cuba once a week. Brings beef, sugar and the like. Due 'ere, day after tomorrow."

"José's ship, is it a merchant ship?"

"Yes, lady. Not a pirate ship!" The captain laughed and Grace smiled.

"But can 'e take passengers as well?"

"'As done before. Got a couple of cabins 'e uses. Guantánamo will take about, mmm... probably two days."

"Thank you. Oh, what's the name of the ship?"

The captain laughed. "You're not superstitious, I 'ope! It's called *Vital Spirit*! Apparently the Spanish believe it lives inside your body. Like a sort of soul, I think!"

Grace stared at the captain, she didn't know what to say.

"Be 'ere before mid-day," said the captain. "Normally 'e'll sail about then."

Grace said thank you again and walked back to Fiona. "Did you 'ear all that?"

Fiona replied, "Yes, two days' time."

"What we goin' to do till then?"

Fiona smiled. "We've changed our names. Now we need to change our past – come up with a new history! This should be fun!"

It was two days' later, just after ten o'clock, when Grace and Fiona arrived back at the harbourside. They easily spotted the *Vital Spirit* being unloaded. The ship had three masts with rolled-up sails and unusually high fore and aft structures. They reminded Grace of two small castles.

Two men were piling sacks and bags of goods onto a trailer after they'd been craned over from the ship. Once the trailer was full, the driver said "gee up" to his horse and the load was pulled away. As another horse and cart approached, Grace spoke to one of the men standing next to the ship.

"Can I speak to Captain José?"

"'Ablas, Capitan?"

"Sí, por favor."

The man turned away and shouted in Spanish up to two men standing at the side of the bulwark. Grace wasn't sure what he was saying, but she hoped he was trying to get her message to the captain.

"Sí," came the reply. One of the crewmen then disappeared.

Two minutes later a stout, well-dressed man came down the wooden gangplank. He had a smile on his face and a swagger in his step.

The man who Grace had been speaking to earlier pointed to her. The captain stepped off the gangplank and walked over to Grace and Fiona. His first words were, "Hola! I speak good in'gleesh."

Grace and Fiona both smiled. Grace said, "We've been told you take passengers to Cuba."

"Sí, sometimes. You two? Where you want to go?" asked the captain, flashing two gold front teeth.

"Guantánamo."

"Sí, I go dare. You want to go today?"

"Yes. We were told you have two passenger cabins. Are they available?"

"Sí. You want see?"

Both Grace and Fiona nodded their heads and Grace said, "Yes, please."

"Come. I show."

Captain José waved his hand and the two women followed him onto the gangplank.

The rest of the crewmen watched Grace and Fiona's every move as they stepped off the gangplank onto the ship. As they walked towards the ship's stern the captain explained that his vessel was a 'carrack' ship, a specialist for carrying cargo. "Very heavy and strong – easier to fend off attacks from pirates!"

"Pirates!" exclaimed Fiona. "Do you have pirates near Cuba?"

"Do not worry, our ship is far too big for dem. Dose 'gentlemen of fortune', dey prefer smaller, treasure-laden vessels. Dey leave us alone, most. Dey know, we deliver food to Léogâne. Come, let me show cabins."

The captain led them down a set of wooden steps to a short corridor. The women could see three doors ahead of them. The captain pointed to the end cabin and said that was his. He opened one side door and then another, explaining they would be sleeping in these cabins.

Grace and Fiona looked inside. They decided both cabins were clean and quite adequate for their two days' voyage. The two cabins were smaller than they'd been used to on the *Empress,* but as each just had one single bed, they were fine for what they needed.

They then agreed on a price for the transit and two days' accommodation. Captain José said he would send two of his crew to collect their bags.

Fifteen minutes later the two women left the ship and returned to the harbourside. They walked directly back to the inn, packed their remaining possessions into their bags and were ready to depart. Five minutes later, there was a knock on the door. The two crewmen had arrived and Grace pointed to their bags laying on the nearest bed. The first crewman nodded and the two men picked up the luggage and left the room.

Grace and Fiona made one final check that they'd not forgotten anything, and then left.

Fiona paid the bill and they made the short journey to the ship. For the first time in many moons they wouldn't be sailing on a pirate ship!

Hopefully, thought Grace, new and different sorts of adventures were about to begin!

CHAPTER 15

The *Vital Spirit* left port at the sound of two bells. Both Grace and Fiona were standing on the large aft deck and gazed back towards the harbour.

Once out of Saragoa Bay, the square-shaped main sails were set and the ship slowly turned. Finally it was repositioned for a northerly route. The weather was set fine, hot and sunny, a south-south-westerly steady breeze and a quiet sea. However, according to Captain José, a storm was possible later. For the moment, though, the *Vital Spirit* sailed on steadily, dipping her bow occasionally and creating a gentle spray on the side of the hull.

Once Captain José finished barking out his orders, the atmosphere on deck was more relaxed. He took the opportunity to join the ladies and said, "You lik'a dey sailin', ladies?"

As part of Grace and Fiona's 'rewriting' of their personal history, they decided it was important to reduce their sailing experiences to just a few months: only for essential travelling. Now was an opportunity for them to see the captain's reaction.

Fiona started by saying, "I've not been on many ships. I much prefer to be on dry land."

Grace continued the theme. "I've travelled more than my friend and prefer it when the sea's as calm as this. I don't like it when there's a storm. Sometimes I suffer from sickness."

"We'll probably get a storm dis afternoon. Shouldn't be long dis time of year. Not 'urricane season," replied the captain.

"Have you been sailing a long time?" asked Fiona. She thought a long conversation with José might give them some useful information.

"Around 30 years. Dey last ten, as capi'tan of dis ship."

"Do you sail further than the route between Cuba and Hispaniola?"

"Not very often. Always a demand for food in Léogâne. My younger brother, Diego, 'e's got 'is own ship. 'im sail wherever the customer wants to go."

"Is he in Guantánamo?" asked Fiona.

"Sí, 'e lives dare."

"We want to get to South Carolina. It's in the Thirteen British Colonies. That's where Grace's husband and children live. Do you think he would take us?"

"As I say, ladies, 'e go most places... for muchos dineros!" replied the captain, smiling and rubbing the fingers and thumb of his right hand.

"Will you introduce us when we get to Guantánamo?"

"Sí. No hay problema. Good man, Diego. 'E'l take you to your Carolina."

The three carried on talking until Captain José, looking up to the sky, said the storm would soon be here and he needed to give new orders to his men.

The two women went back to Fiona's cabin, sat down on the edge of the bed and waited for the storm. They'd both experienced storms whilst on board ships before, but this ship was smaller than the *Empress,* so they weren't sure how it would react.

"Were you 'appy with our story to our captain?" Grace asked. "D'you think 'e was convinced?"

"I didn't hear anything you said that he wouldn't believe."

Suddenly there was a bright white flash and, seconds later, a large clap of thunder. It made Fiona jump. Almost immediately heavy rain pounded the side of the cabin.

Grace smiled at Fiona's reaction to the thunder and then said, "What do you think of the captain's suggestion of 'im talking to his brother, Diego?"

"Sounds like a possibility. Depends on whether he's free."

"Do you really want to go back to South Carolina? You told me before that you couldn't wait to escape."

"I know, but then I was young and argued with my father a lot. I got married just to spite him. I don't think he would recognise me now."

Grace thought that he probably would. After just a few years would a father really not recognise his own daughter? "Whereabouts did you live?"

"We lived in the centre of Charles Town. It was expanding really fast when I was growing up and my father set up a law practice. His office was two streets away. I think he was doing really well. My mother was always quiet and looked after the house, plus me and my younger brother, David. David was born in Charles Town; he's seven years younger than me. My mother couldn't handle me. I suppose I was a bit wild! She left dealing with me to my father."

"But you fell out with your father!" said Grace, now holding on to the side of the bed. The ship was swaying more and the rain continued to batter the ship.

"We were always arguing and him telling me off. As I said, I only married James to get away. I certainly didn't love him. He was a sailor and told me about his sailing trips. It all sounded a lot better than the life I was having at home. Same really with Jack. They both told interesting stories. I'm probably too gullible when it comes to selecting my men."

Grace smiled. Aren't we all? she thought. "The sea's getting rougher."

"Mmm," said Fiona, but she wasn't really listening. She was wondering what had become of her family. Maybe I'll find out more when we arrive in Charles Town.

As the captain had predicted, the storm didn't last very long, and when it finally abated, Grace and Fiona left the cabin and went up the stairs and onto the main deck. The hot sunshine was shining strongly again, causing steam to rise from the wooden floor panels under their feet. They both walked carefully trying to avoid any possible slips, and then climbed more steps to the aft tower. They wanted to get some fresh air and look at the view. All they could see, however, was water, and, in the distance, big black clouds. No sign of land or any other ships.

Captain José and three of his crew were standing on the for'ard deck. The captain was pointing and giving orders to the crewmen.

Where the two women now stood they were catching a cooling sea breeze. Bracing and refreshing, it kept blowing their hair across their faces.

"It seems strange," said Grace, turning so she faced straight into the breeze, "but it's been so long since we've fought the enemy whilst sailin' on a pirate ship. I 'ope we've made the right decision."

Fiona pushed her hair back, holding it in place with her left hand. She turned her body to face her friend. "Maybe because I'm now a bit older and, hopefully, a little wiser, I don't miss it. It's all in the past. So are Jack and Bluey. After we've collected our treasure, I want that to be the end of my pirate's life."

"Let's just 'ope nobody's already found it."

Fiona closed her eyes and, once again, pushed back her hair. After a few seconds she said, "Heneagua is before New Providence. We still need to decide if we want to stop there first. That's where some of Jack's treasure is buried."

"Let's just see what Diego 'as to say about where, and 'ow far, 'e's prepared to take us. We can then make that decision."

CHAPTER 16

It was two days later when Grace and Fiona heard the cry, "Land ahoy!" Grace was already on the main deck staring up at the crow's nest when Fiona joined her.

"Looks like we're comin' to Cuba," said Grace, anxious to see a new island.

The two women climbed the steps towards the for'ard deck. In the distance they could see glimpses of land appearing just above the horizon.

"Our first view of Cuba," said Fiona, raising her right hand to shield her eyes from the blazing sun.

"¡Buenos días!" said a smiling Captain José, as he arrived at the top of the stairs. He walked over to join them. "Two hours and you'll see Guantánamo. Do you 'ave place to stay?"

"No," said Grace. "We thought we'd just find an inn."

"Guantánamo is small town," replied José. "Quite poor. De 'arbour's mainly used by Spanish merchants. Dare are two inns, but I wouldn't recommend either for you fine ladies."

Grace looked at the captain with some concern. "Where would you recommend?"

"Diego and 'is wife, dey 'ave rooms. Nice people too."

Grace and Fiona looked at each other. Both had a relieved expression on their faces. "That sounds much better," said Fiona, turning back to face the captain. "We'll then be able to discuss our sailing plans with Diego."

"Sí! I take you when we arrive at 'arbour. I now need supervise docking at quay," said José, before walking away to talk to the helmsman.

Grace and Fiona stood quietly and resumed looking ahead. Gradually, more land came into view. In the distance Fiona spotted the remains of a shipwreck close to the beach, It was sadly in a state of dilapidation. Large waves were crashing at its remains. It had once been a great vessel of three masts, but now it had laid so long exposed to the ravages of the sea and weather that the masts, and most of the surviving hull, were covered with webs of dripping green seaweed.

Grace was thinking about this man, Diego. She was curious about what they were going to find. Neither she nor Fiona had even met this man and now they might be putting their trust in him when they collected their treasure. Was this going to be a wise and sensible move?

As the ship edged closer to the quay, Fiona and Grace watched the activity below and listened to Captain José shouting out his orders. The ship turned slowly, its port side drifting towards its docking point. When there was about a two-metre gap between the ship and quay, crewmen threw the mooring ropes towards the awaiting handlers. The handlers grabbed the four rope ends and gradually pulled the ship towards the dock. Once satisfied the ship was in place, they tied the ropes around four old tree trunks. On board the ship the same ropes were pulled tight and fastened around the capstan. *Vital Spirit* was now moored. A few seconds later the gangplank was gently lowered down the side of the hull and secured.

There was a lot of shouting and activity as four crewmen ran down the gangplank. They immediately set up pulleys and more ropes for unloading the cargo. Already on the quayside were empty horse-drawn trailers waiting for cargo to be hoisted off the ship.

The two ladies now walked down the gangplank, stepped on to the quayside and waited for the captain and their luggage.

Although Guantánamo's harbour was not very large, there were another two ships already moored. Both were being loaded with cargo. Fiona looked across at the waterfront and its ramshackle range of shabby wooden buildings. She easily spotted one of the inns and could hear shouting and loud music. Maybe a good thing, she thought, that we're not staying there!

Five minutes later Captain José walked down the gangplank to join the ladies. He pointed to the inn and said, "Very noisy, much drink, music and wild women. No place for you pretty ladies." He then laughed and Fiona and Grace smiled. "My men bring bags. Come, I take you to meet Diego and Luisa."

José strode off across the quayside. Grace and Fiona had to walk briskly to keep up, hitching their skirts as they crossed the muddy street. They stepped onto a wooden boardwalk and arrived outside a wooden cabin a few minutes later.

Fiona and Grace both looked at the building, set back from the boardwalk. It was single storey, well maintained with a large veranda. Sitting on a rocking chair was a young woman peeling vegetables. A small girl was sitting on the floor, next to the woman's feet, playing with two cloth dolls.

"¡Hola, Luisa!" shouted José, as he pushed open the small wicker gate.

The woman immediately looked up and smiled. She put down her bowl of vegetables and wiped her hands on her apron. "Hello, José," Luisa replied in clear English. When José had climbed onto the veranda he gave Luisa a hug and a kiss on the cheek.

Grace and Fiona stood on the path and studied Luisa. Underneath her apron, she was dressed in a bright floral dress and her dark brown hair was pulled back behind her head and tied into a small bun.

"Meet mis amigas, Grace and Fiona. Dey lookin' for bed."

Fiona and Grace stepped on to the veranda and the three women smiled and shook hands.

"Diego?" asked José.

"He's at the quay, helping to load his ship. He should be back soon."

"I'm goin' back to quay now. I speak to 'im."

"Before you go, José, would you like a drink?"

"No, gracias. I 'ave beer with Diego."

At this, José said his goodbyes and promised Fiona and Grace that their luggage would arrive shortly. Both Grace and Fiona thanked José and waved as he walked away.

"I'm sure you two fine ladies would like a drink. I have some fresh lemon juice indoors."

Grace said that would be nice and Fiona nodded.

"You two sit there in the shade," said Luisa, pointing at two extra chairs. "I'll bring the drinks out here in a minute. Come, Mary, you can give me a hand."

The little girl stopped staring at the new guests and ran after her mother.

"Luisa's nice," whispered Fiona. "It's a nice house too."

"Mmm," said Grace. However, she was thinking to herself, yes, all okay... so far.

CHAPTER 17

Luisa returned to the veranda carrying a small tray containing four glasses of lemon juice with sugar water. Mary followed behind carrying a plate of biscuits.

For the next ten minutes the three ladies made light conversation until the drinks had been consumed. Luisa then led Grace and Fiona into the house and showed them two bedrooms. Both rooms were tidy and basically furnished, but certainly adequate for a short stay. As well as a bed and a wardrobe, each room had a bowl and jug of water for washing. The windows were open and the gentle breeze was helping to move the warm air.

Suddenly they heard a shout of "Hola!" The three ladies returned to the veranda, where two men from the ship were standing with Fiona and Grace's luggage. Luisa told the men where the luggage should go. Once this had been dealt with the men left the house and said, "Adiós!" Grace and Fiona smiled and replied with their own thanks.

It was just over an hour later when Diego arrived home. He'd met with José and they'd both been for a beer. José had explained to Diego about Fiona and Grace's plans to sail to South Carolina. Diego had said it was possible, "if the ladies are prepared to pay muchos dineros!"

Whilst Luisa made dinner, Grace, Fiona and Diego sat on the veranda with glasses of beer. The sun had set and the chirping frogs had begun their evening chatter. Grace and Fiona listened to Diego whilst he explained about his family and his ship. He told them he was much younger than his brother. José being the eldest of six children, Diego being the youngest.

Diego was tall, slim and dark skinned. Very tanned from working many years in the Caribbean sun. Cheerful and enterprising, he was keen to know more about the ladies' plans and ambitions.

Whilst on board José's ship, Grace and Fiona had discussed how much detail they would reveal to Diego on their first meeting. They'd finally agreed to only mention the furthest point of their journey. If Diego didn't want to sail all the way to Charles

Town, then there was no point mentioning Heneagua or New Providence. However, if Diego sounded more positive, then, and only then, would they decide how and when to mention their treasure… but, only after they'd decided Diego could be trusted!

Grace opened the conversation. "We want to go to Charles Town, in South Carolina. That's my 'ome and where me 'usband and children are. Fiona's a family friend and will be stayin' with us for a while, before she returns to Ireland."

When Diego looked across to Fiona, she smiled and nodded her agreement.

Grace continued. "We want to know if you'd take us to Charles Town, and if so, 'ow much it would cost?"

Diego's English was very good and he was confident speaking the language. "Yes, I can take you. I can do some business in the Bahamas on the way back. My ship, the *Luisa*, has just sailed to Jamaica. It won't be back for about a week. Is that a problem?"

Fiona looked at Grace and then shrugged her shoulders. Grace replied, "No, that's not a problem, as long as we can stay 'ere."

"My wife already says okay," replied Diego. "You are welcome."

Over the next few minutes, they discussed and eventually agreed on the cost of the trip. Diego explained a few more details about his ship. In particular he described the two cabins they'd be staying in.

Fiona and Grace listened and agreed the cabins sounded fine… small, but fine.

Over the next week, Fiona and Grace enjoyed their time and felt very relaxed. They helped Luisa with her chores and played games with Mary. They also went for walks around Guantánamo and frequently visited the harbour. There they watched the constant stream of activity. Ships and fishing boats came and went, transporting their cargo. Except for two short heavy downpours, the weather remained warm and sunny during the whole of their stay. Life was good… it all seemed a million miles away from the horrible gaol in Spanish Town, Jamaica.

Early each morning, Diego took the short walk to the quayside and helped with the loading and unloading of merchandise.

In such a small and busy harbour town, all the men pitched in to help each other. There was lots of banter and wisecracks before groups peeled off and went to one of the two local inns.

It was on the eighth day that Diego returned and told the ladies his ship had arrived and was moored in the harbour. They would set sail the following morning at four bells, forenoon.

That evening, Grace and Fiona packed their cases, ready for their early departure. They'd really enjoyed their stay with Diego's family and were ready to move on. Their next decision, however, was where the ship's first stop would be. Fiona wanted to go to Heneagua, to collect Calico Jack's treasure, but Grace was not yet convinced of Diego's trustworthiness.

The next morning the ladies boarded the *Luisa*. When they heard the sound of four bells ringing loudly, they left their cabins and walked onto the main deck. As the ship began to move, a small group of people on the quayside waved them away.

Grace and Fiona waved back, especially to Luisa and Mary, who had arrived specially to wave their goodbyes. Slowly the ship turned towards the wide open stretches of the sea. Grace and Fiona continued to watch until the town of Guantánamo faded from view. Captain Diego gave orders for the main sails to be set. The wind was much stronger here and the cream-coloured sails soon began to billow.

Both ladies continued to watch from the aft deck until all land had disappeared. Fiona clutched Grace's hand and gave it a tender squeeze. She wondered what the future was going to bring… and just hoped Grace would not regret her final decision to abandon her life as a pirate. Time would tell.

The *Luisa*, now out of Guantánamo Bay, was sailing in an easterly direction. It was heading towards the Windward Passage, a navigable channel situated between the south-easterly point of Cuba and the north-westerly tip of Hispaniola. From there, it would enter the seas just south of the Bahama Islands, before changing course again, to a northerly direction. The first island after that would be Heneagua… before which, the ladies had to agree on their big decision!

That evening, Grace and Fiona sat on the aft deck. The warm breeze had a fresher feel compared to the sun's earlier intense heat. They were discussing how they would approach Diego as they'd now agreed to go to Heneagua and try to find Calico Jack's buried treasure. Fiona said she could probably remember most of the details from Jack's map. They needed to stop at the only harbour on Heneagua.

After breakfast the next morning, Diego joined the ladies on the aft deck. Fiona decided to open the conversation. "I think I know where there might be buried pirate treasure on Heneagua."

Diego was startled. His eyes wide open with surprise. "You have una mapa!?"

"No," replied Fiona, "but I saw it once and can remember most of the details."

"You suggesting we go to Heneagua and see if we can find this treasure?"

"Yes," Grace replied. "We'd be prepared to give you a third of whatever we find. Three equal partners."

"But, what if I decide to take all this treasure?" said Diego, smiling. "Would you trust me not to do that?"

Fiona then responded with a serious look on her face. "We trust you, Diego, otherwise we wouldn't have mentioned anything about this treasure to you. We've also met your lovely wife, Luisa and pretty daughter, Mary."

Diego's smile disappeared and he rubbed his dark brown beard. "Why do you mention my wife and child?"

"Because they are lovely people," replied Fiona. "Far too young to be losing their husband and father when he gets his throat slit open!"

CHAPTER 18

Heneagua is the second largest island in the Bahamas and lies about 89 kilometres from the eastern tip of Cuba. Mostly flat with some sandy hills, it has several freshwater lakes which occupy nearly a quarter of the interior. The island's population is mostly made up of transient treasure hunters, less than 30 men for much of the time. Most live temporarily, in and around the harbour, but their searches, looking for buried treasure, take them all over the island.

It was just after eight bells on the following morning when the *Luisa* sailed towards the tiny harbour. There were two rowing boats currently moored, but no large ships within sight. Captain Diego was aware the waters were shallow around the Bahama islands so decided to drop anchor about a mile from shore. He instructed his crew to lower a longboat and nominated four of them to join him and the two ladies. Fiona declared they would need spades for digging in the sand.

Once everybody was aboard, plus spades and six empty casks for collecting fresh water, the longboat was rowed towards the shore. Despite it still being early morning, the air was already warm and humid, so the rowers were soon sweating and wiping their brows.

On the quayside three curious onlookers watched the longboat come closer. A large ship, the size of the *Luisa*, was not a regular occurrence close to these shores. They usually only appeared looking for fresh water, unless it was a pirate crew trying to hide their ill-gotten gains!

When the longboat finally docked, one of the curious onlookers walked over to join them. Diego explained they were looking for fresh water and the ladies wanted to walk and 'stretch their legs'. The casks were then unloaded and Quilly, one of the crewmen, was delegated to acquire the fresh water.

Fiona led the rest of their group along the dusty main street. Grace looked at the largely dilapidated buildings, which had originally been constructed as temporary timber shelters. Most were now in need of serious repair due to damage inflicted by passing hurricanes. A few minutes later they'd reached the last cabin on the right.

"Is this it?" asked Grace, somewhat surprised. The building was obviously unoccupied as it had lost most of its roof.

Fiona nodded. "We'll definitely know for sure when we walk around the back. Jack put a pile of stones in one of the corners."

Grace pushed at the part-opened wooden gate, which immediately fell to the ground. They all walked round to the back of the cabin where in the far left-hand corner was a pile of stones about two feet high.

"Is the treasure buried under the stones?" asked Diego.

"No," said Fiona, "that would be too obvious. Jack's map said they were buried eight paces diagonally back from the stones."

Diego stepped forward and paced out eight steps towards the cabin. After his last step he kicked a small hole in the powdery sand.

"You're much taller than Jack was, so maybe your steps are longer. Move back a little."

Diego took one step backwards and kicked another indent in the sand.

"Okay," said Fiona, "let's dig here. We only need to go down about three feet."

Diego called the three crewmen over and told them to dig. Having only two spades between them, they took it in turns. Initial digging was easy as the sand was dry and fine grained, but once they'd gone down to just below knee height, the sand was wet and much heavier to lift. A number of rocks and stones also needed to be removed.

Diego was wondering if this was the right place. Would Jack have covered his treasure with rocks and stones?

When the crewmen started to flag, Diego decided to replace them.

After a short time he was ready to give up, but, suddenly, he hit something that sounded like wood. Everyone gathered around the edge of the hole and stared down. Diego cleared the surrounding rocks and sand, eventually uncovering an old wooden box! The three crewmen slid back into the hole, lifted the heavy box and placed it next to where the ladies were standing. They then scrambled out. Diego was about to follow when he stepped on something hard. He crouched down and brushed some of the sand away. Partially hidden was a second wooden box, slightly bigger than the first one. He picked up his spade and began digging again. Eventually, this box was also pulled out onto the dry sand. Diego wondered if there might be any more boxes, so he dug a little deeper and sideways but with no success. He finally gave up and the crewmen pulled him out of the hole.

The group stared down at the two boxes. Diego was just about to smash at one of the locks with his spade when a man's voice came unexpectedly from behind them. "My guess is that's Calico Jack's treasure," the newcomer announced, pointing two flintlock pistols at the group. "We've been looking for that treasure for a while. Heard he was hanged some time back. Won't be needing his riches anymore."

Nobody spoke, they just stared back at the two guns.

The man continued, "Twenty of us have been coming here for a while. Pirates also come, bury their treasure and go. We get to recognise the faces. Lots of treasure's buried on this island. Pirates been coming for over a hundred years. Bury their valuables and then disappear. Some come back, but most don't!"

Another man now appeared from behind the dilapidated cabin. He also held a pistol.

The first man carried on, "Lots of treasure-laden ships have sunk on those reefs out there too." He pointed one of the guns towards the sea. "Spanish galleons, like the *Santa Rosa*, are stuffed with gold."

Diego finally decided to say something. "We've got 40 men on our ship and 20 guns. If we don't return before nightfall, they've got orders to flatten this town."

The man laughed. "No need for that, mi amigo, there's enough treasure hidden on this island for all of us! Nobody's going to steal your find. Tommy here has even brought you a cart to carry your boxes back to the quay. Let me introduce myself – I'm Alwyn."

Diego ignored the introduction. "Then why the weapons?"

"Didn't know how you'd all react when I arrived."

The ladies and the crewmen began to relax, but Diego was still on his guard, keeping his hand on the pistol tucked inside his belt.

Tommy slipped his flintlock away and pulled the cart so everyone could see it.

Alwyn also stowed his firearms and pointed to the cart. "There you are, gentlemen… and ladies. Please, just leave the cart on the quayside when you leave."

Diego still hadn't removed his hand from his gun, but told his crewmen to place the boxes on the cart. Diego and the ladies moved closer to where Alwyn and Tommy were standing.

The crewmen heaved the heavy boxes onto the cart. "Must be a lot of gold in there," one of them whispered.

"It's very good of you to help us," said Fiona. She tried to sound harmless and innocent. "Did you know Calico Jack?"

"Not really," responded Alwyn. "He and his crew only came to the island twice, whilst we were here, that is. Last time he buried his treasure overnight when everyone was asleep. We knew he'd buried it somewhere here, but, before dawn, there'd been a storm, so all traces of his activity had disappeared. He went back to his ship after the storm. Obviously you knew exactly where it was buried."

Fiona smiled back at Alwyn and said, "Yes, I did!"

Two of the crewmen pushed the loaded cart in the direction of the quay. The rest of the group followed a few steps behind.

"'Ave you found a lot of treasure on the island?" asked Grace.

"Now that would be really telling, my dear. Suffice to say, it's all been worth our while… so far.

"How are you going to get off the island?" asked Fiona.

"Our ship's due to collect us in about five days' time."

Five minutes later the group had arrived back at the quayside. Quilly was standing next to the longboat with the full water casks. The other three crewmen stepped forward and the casks, spades and two wooden boxes were loaded onto the boat.

Diego helped the ladies aboard. They all sat down and the men started to row back towards the ship.

On the quayside Alwyn and Tommy sat on the cart, watching the longboat heading back towards the ship.

Alwyn smiled. "Pity for them that we got to Jack's treasure first!"

Tommy laughed and then replied. "At least they've gone away with two boxes of souvenirs!"

CHAPTER 19

Once back on board the *Luisa*, Captain Diego shouted his orders. The anchor was raised and the first set of sails were unfurled. The ship slowly turned and headed in an easterly direction. Once past the end of Heneagua, the rest of the sails were unfurled and a new northerly direction was set.

Diego joined the ladies on the main deck, where they were standing next to the boxes.

"Ready to see our treasure, ladies?" said Diego. He'd picked up a heavy piece of wood.

Grace and Fiona were anxious to see what Calico Jack had left. They both nodded and smiled in anticipation.

A number of the crew were also curious and gathered on the for'ard and aft decks waiting to see the treasure.

With the piece of wood, Diego smashed down on the rusted lock of the larger box. The lock flew across the deck and Diego bent down and opened the lid. Staring down at the contents, he started to laugh.

The ladies wondered what was so funny. Grace bent down and fully pulled back the lid. To everyone's surprise, there were no jewels, no gold, not even pieces of silver… just a collection of stones and rocks!

A number of the crew stared and smiled. Fiona's eyes were wide open!

Diego, still laughing, now hit the lock on the smaller box. It too flew across the deck. This time Fiona was quick to bend down and throw open the lid. Again it contained rocks and stones. However, Fiona also spotted a brown leather pouch and lifted it out of the box. She could hear the clinking of coins.

Diego and Grace leaned closer as Fiona put her hand inside the bag and retrieved some silver coins and a handwritten note. She read out the written message:

Thanks for your treasure, Jack.
It will compensate me just fine.
Mind, I've left you 30 pieces of silver.
Quite appropriate I'd have thought.
A.

"What does that mean!?" said Grace. She snatched the note out of Fiona's hand and stared down at the words.

Fiona, as well as being disappointed, now looked confused.

Diego said, "That's from the Bible. Jesus was supposed to have been double-crossed by Judas. Judas was rewarded with 30 silver coins."

"What's that got to do with Jack!?" asked Fiona. She didn't understand the connection with the Bible.

"Sounds like a pirate's payback," replied Diego. "Jack obviously doubled-crossed someone in the past. You shouldn't trust pirates, ladies!" joked Diego, laughing again.

Both Grace and Fiona ignored Diego's comment. They were more concerned about where Jack's treasure had gone.

After a few seconds Fiona put the coins back into the bag and handed it to Diego. "Here, you can have these, a contribution towards the cost of our fare."

Diego took the bag and smiled. "Do you know any more buried treasure sites!?"

Later that evening, the ladies sat at their usual place on the aft deck. They were still angry, but enjoying the refreshing sea breeze.

"Well, I didn't expect that with Jack's treasure," said Fiona. "Obviously someone else knew about his maps."

"D'you think it was that Alwyn?" asked Grace. "You said the note was signed with an 'A'."

"Could've been, I guess. But he said he didn't know where the treasure was."

"Probably knew where it was all the time," replied Grace. She paused to think. "But if 'e did take the treasure, why leave the note and the coins? 'E said 'e knew Jack had been 'anged, so why address the note to a dead man?"

"Maybe he took the treasure before he knew Jack had been hanged. He wouldn't dig it up again, once he'd heard of Jack's death."

Grace leaned back so the warm breeze blew through her hair. She enjoyed this time of day the best. "What we goin' to do now?"

"Do you mean about our treasure?"

"Mmm, partly, but didn't you say Jack buried some of his treasure on New Providence?"

"That's right!" exclaimed Fiona. "On Hog Island. The opposite side of the island to where ours is buried."

"Can you still remember exactly where?"

"I think so. I'll need to think… but I'm sure I'll remember."

"Well why don't we go there first. If Jack's treasure's still there… and there's quite a lot, then maybe we can leave ours till another day."

Fiona thought about this. "Okay, and if we can't find Jack's secret place, or the treasure has already gone, we'll collect ours, instead."

"Sounds like we 'ave a plan!" replied Grace. "When we goin' to tell Diego?"

The next morning Grace and Fiona climbed the stairs to the for'ard deck. Diego was talking to two of his crewmen. When their conversation ended, Grace walked over to speak to him. "Captain, can we speak to you?"

Diego turned around and looked at the two ladies. "Good morning. I hope you both slept well and didn't have nightmares about your pirate's treasure!" he said, chuckling.

"No I didn't!" said a slightly frustrated and annoyed Grace. Fiona shook her head from side to side. "What we wanted to tell you," continued Grace, "is that Jack 'ad more than one secret 'idin' place for 'is treasure."

"Ah," responded Diego. "So you knew Jack, and now, you tell me, you know of another hiding place."

Fiona said, "I think I can remember it from his map of Hog Island. It's next to Nassau."

"I know Nassau. That's a pirate town. We wouldn't be welcome, or safe, going there."

"There's a lot you don't know about us, Diego," whispered Grace, "and I suggest it would be best for you, and probably us too, if it stayed like that. We know people in Nassau. We'll be safe… I promise!"

Diego looked at Grace and then to Fiona. He noticed the seriousness in both sets of eyes. Slowly he began to smile and then briefly laugh. "Okay, ladies, let's go and 'ave an adventure in Nassau. See what treasure we can find!"

CHAPTER 20

The *Luisa* followed a north-north-west course. Off the starboard side, the ship was now passing a number of small sand-fringed islands, none of which appeared to be inhabited. These islands were just a few of the many hundreds of isles and cays that make up the Bahamas archipelago. Off the port side the view was of the unbroken length of the eastern coast of Cuba. In the distance mountains shimmered through a haze due to the strong mid-day sun.

The sea was generally calm and the breeze was just fluttering the sails. Grace and Fiona were standing on the starboard side staring across the sapphire-blue-coloured waters. In the distance they could see more small islands, stretching away, like stepping stones, as far as the eye could see. Much closer to the ship they'd earlier been watching dolphins, the occasional shark and a green turtle. It was quiet, serene and peaceful… at least for the time being.

Diego walked across the deck to join the ladies. He pointed out to sea and said, "That island is the southernmost island of the 365 Exuma Cays."

Both Grace and Fiona looked in the direction Diego was pointing. They shielded their eyes from the bright sun and stared at the sand-fringed isle.

"It's so tranquil and peaceful out 'ere," replied Grace, taking a deep breath.

Diego smiled and replied, "We'll shortly be stopping at one of these cays. There's an old settlement I've been to several times before. We'll be collecting more fresh water."

Fiona nodded and then asked, "Does anyone live on these cays? They all seem to be uninhabited."

"No, nobody lives here now. Sometimes you get people stopping for water who maybe stay for a few days. The original people who lived here were the Lucayan natives… but that was many years ago. They were captured, taken away and forced into slavery."

"That's sad," said Fiona, with feeling.

"What about pirates?" asked Grace. "Do they sail these waters?"

Diego rubbed his beard and replied, "Pirates. Rarely now. They once used the deep water harbour, that's where we're going to stop. It's not on the main merchant routes so pirates would only stop to collect supplies of fresh water. The British Navy doesn't come this way either. That's why it's quiet."

Both Grace and Fiona nodded.

"I need to go and speak to my helmsman," said Diego. "We need to change course soon."

A few minutes later, the *Luisa* slowly turned and entered a narrow passage of water, gliding past two rock-and-sand-fringed islands. The sea had become noticeably choppier through this channel, but once the ship had exited and was back into open water, it turned towards port and resumed its north-north-west course.

Despite all their time on Calico Jack's ship, neither Fiona nor Grace could remember these waters. They didn't recognise this part of the Bahama islands at all. The area was so different compared to bustling Nassau and Eleuthera.

Two hours later the *Luisa* gently steered towards a much larger island. It was late afternoon and Captain Diego wanted to get the extra fresh water on board before nightfall. About 400 metres from the old harbour, the ship's anchor was dropped and a longboat lowered into the sea. Eight crewmen climbed aboard and sat surrounded by empty water casks. They rowed towards the shore.

Diego, Grace and Fiona were talking on the aft deck, when suddenly a young voice shouted from the crow's nest, "Ship ahoy!" Immediately Diego looked in the direction the boy was pointing and a number of the remaining crew ran to the side of the ship. There on the horizon was a large ship that looked, at first sight, to be a Spanish galleon. As it came closer, however, Grace and Fiona began to recognise it. It was the large fighting frigate, the *Empress*. Captain Bluey's ship!

Diego started to shout orders, but with eight crewmen away on the island, there was little he could do other than sit tight and hope the ship would carry on its way. However, his hopes were soon dashed when he saw the large frigate turn and head in their direction.

"Captain," said Grace. "I think we're okay. That's the *Empress*, Captain Bluey's ship."

"But it's a pirate ship!" exclaimed Diego. "I can see the black flag!"

"Can you raise a white flag and set up a winch? Fiona will go aboard."

Diego looked at Grace strangely and wondered what was going on? When he realised she was being very serious he ordered the white flag to be hoisted and the ship-to-ship winch and its ropes set up.

The *Empress* came closer and, at the sight of the white flag, started to slow down and gradually drifted to the side of the *Luisa*. It stopped about 20 metres away. Fiona and Grace stood next to the bulwark so they could be clearly seen from the *Empress*. They waved and Grace immediately recognised the quartermaster, Richard Easter. He obviously recognised them as he turned and shouted back across his own deck. A few seconds later Captain Bluey appeared at the side of the hull and looked across.

Captain Bluey cupped his hands around his mouth and shouted, "Anne!? Is that you?"

Fiona shouted her reply, "Yes. I'm coming across on the winch."

Fiona couldn't wait. She was desperate to see Bluey again.

Grace asked Diego if he would order his men to prepare the ropes on the 'long hook'. At the same time a similar pole with a hook was pushed out from the *Empress*. The pole from the *Luisa* was eased out across the water with a looped rope on the hook. As the two poles met, the looped rope was swapped and the poles drawn back. On the *Empress*, the rope was tied to the capstan and pulled tight. On the *Luisa*, a looped rope was attached to the linking rope and placed at the edge of the bulwark. The end of the rope was then wound around the *Luisa's* capstan and pulled tight. Fiona climbed onto the edge of the hull and, with

Grace's help, she sat on the large loop and tightly held on to the main rope. When she was finally settled, the *Luisa's* capstan was slowly unwound, resulting in the rope between the ships beginning to sag. This was the signal for the capstan on the *Empress* to be wound in and take up the slack. Steadily, Fiona was pulled across the water until eventually she was seized and helped down onto the main deck.

"Well, well, well," said Bluey. "What a nice surprise."

Fiona smiled, leaped up and gave the captain a big kiss. There were cheers from the rest of the crew.

Diego watched all the action and then said to Grace, "I don't know what's going on, but it's better than being attacked by that pirate ship."

Grace smiled. "As we said earlier, you really don't want to know any more."

Diego looked across to the island. There was no sign of the longboat. "It looks as though we're all going to be staying here tonight."

"I don't think Fiona will be in any 'urry to return," she replied. Privately she was feeling a little envious of her young friend.

Bluey and Fiona went to the captain's cabin. There Bluey poured two goblets of wine and Fiona summarised her time since she and Grace had left the *Empress* at Léogâne. What she excluded, however, was her and Grace's plans to collect Jack's treasure from Hog Island.

"Mmm," said Bluey, when Fiona had finished. "So you and Mary have changed your names?"

"And we've made up a new life history. As you know, we want to start new lives and decided the only way we could do that was to make Anne and Mary disappear… forever."

"Sorry, for shouting your old name across the water."

Fiona smiled. "I don't think anyone could hear, other than Grace and me."

Bluey stared at Fiona. He'd missed her and thought about her a lot since she'd left. He wondered how he could persuade her to stay. "Are you really sure South Carolina is where you want to live?"

Fiona sipped the last of her wine and Bluey immediately topped up her goblet. "No, and that's the truth. Both Grace and I don't really know where we'll go. Don't forget, we're still escaped prisoners… just trying to run away from being recaptured."

"Then why not come back. Come back to me, and my ship?"

Fiona smiled and leaned over to give and gave Bluey a kiss on his cheek. "My pirate life is over, Bluey. I've told you before. I couldn't come back here, even for you. Tomorrow, the next day, or whenever, you're going to be caught, convicted and hanged! Just like Jack. You think you're invincible, but Jack was caught… we all were! Mary, I mean Grace, and I, we were the lucky ones. I don't trust my luck for a second time."

Captain Bluey leaned back in his chair and took in a deep breath. He didn't want to lose his love a second time. "So what's so special about South Carolina?"

"Special? Nothing there's special. It's where I grew up," replied Fiona. She picked up her goblet and had another drink. "I don't want to go home to my family; I just want freedom, a chance of a new life. A husband and children. It's not South Carolina I want. It's just the place I'll start my new journey from. My new life!"

"Wow! Sounds like a whole new adventure you've got planned!"

"I hope so. I don't want the horror of rotting in a prison… or being strung up and executed on the gallows."

"What would you say if I joined you?"

"What…!? When?"

Bluey gulped the rest of his wine and topped up his goblet. The sun had disappeared from the cabin's stern windows, so he stood up and lit two candles. Fiona waited for his answer.

"I don't know."

"That's what you said before."

Bluey sat down again and looked deep into Fiona's dark brown eyes. "All I know is a pirate's life. I told you before, I ran away from home and eventually joined Captain Booth's pirate fleet when I was just 14. I spent so many hours in the crow's nest, I thought I should be laying eggs."

Fiona laughed.

Bluey smiled and continued. "I've worked hard, been on different pirate ships, fought battles, got many scars and much treasure. Buried it around the Caribbean. That's all I know, Anne. Being a pirate… a 'gentleman 'o fortune'. Over 20 years. I think I'd be too frightened to do anything else!"

Fiona stared at Bluey, he had a sad and almost child-like expression on his face. She could feel his heartache and anguish and desperately wanted to hold him close.

She stood up and slowly walked around the table, stopping next to Bluey. She leaned down, stared into his dark, almost black eyes and passionately kissed him on his lips.

Bluey immediately responded and stood up. He pulled her close and wrapped his arms around her.

After a few seconds Fiona pulled away and looked searchingly into her lover's face. How could she ever think of leaving this man!?

She gently grasped his right hand and led him towards the bedroom.

CHAPTER 21

As dawn broke the next morning, both ships were preparing to continue their journeys. Last evening, following Quartermaster Easter's orders, the *Empress* had moved and dropped anchor further away from the *Luisa*. Easter didn't want any potential collision during the night.

Both crews were now waiting for Fiona to return to Diego's ship. A longboat was lowered and Fiona stepped in and sat down. As the four crewmen rowed towards the *Luisa*, Fiona waved to Bluey. He waved back, but Fiona couldn't see the deep sadness on his face. She'd resisted his pleas... for a second time.

"Everything ready, Mr Easter?" asked Captain Bluey. It was back to work!

"Yes, Captain. All ready, once the longboat returns."

"Excellent." He took one final glance at Fiona as the longboat arrived at the side of the *Luisa*.

Fiona climbed aboard and heard Captain Diego shout, "Up anchor, we're ready to go."

Grace walked over to Fiona with a smile on her face. "Welcome back," she said gently. "Did you 'ave a great time?"

Fiona smiled. "Yes, it was lovely. Bluey and I... we had a long discussion."

"Tell me more!" Grace insisted. "At least you seem a lot 'appier this time."

Fiona relayed a summary of her and Bluey's time together. She finished by saying, "I refused him again... told him I wasn't going to rejoin his pirate ship. He says he can't see a life, for himself, away from his ship."

"Bit of a stalemate, then."

"Yes. However, I think we might have come up with a solution. More of an ultimatum from me actually!"

Captain Bluey watched from the aft deck, as the *Luisa* headed north. The *Empress* was heading due south. He wondered if Fiona's suggestion could really work. It certainly had possibilities.

"Captain?" Easter was standing next to him. "Are we still heading for Jamaica?"

Bluey was suddenly brought back to the job in hand. "Yes, Mr Easter. Our plans have not changed! Let's go! '¡Vamos!'" he shouted, excitedly.

It was another two days before the *Luisa* sailed into the waters surrounding New Providence. For most of the later part of the 17th century, the island had been controlled by pirates. Most feared of the many swashbucklers who had operated from New Providence was one Edward Teach, better known as the fearsome 'Blackbeard'!

Nassau was so called in 1695, after Governor Nicolas Trott rebuilt the town and added a fort. However, Fort Nassau was heavily damaged in a Spanish attack in 1700 and the colonists living there eventually abandoned the fort in 1703. After a further Spanish attack, and a French invasion, the island of New Providence was slowly abandoned by the authorities and Nassau became a pirate territory once again. By 1713, there were still well over a thousand pirates in Nassau. Two head pirates, Benjamin Hornigold and Thomas Barrow, controlled the whole of New Providence. Barrow even declared himself, 'Governor of Providence'. However, In 1717, King George, desperate to rid the Caribbean waters of pirates, offered a pardon to any pirate who volunteered to surrender over the next 12 months. As a result he sent a new governor, Woodes Rogers, who arrived in the Bahamas in 1718. He was charged with two tasks. Firstly, accepting the surrenders of pirates and issuing pardons, and secondly, hunting down any remaining pirates who refused the pardon. However, during this time, the Spanish threatened New Providence and a number of pirates decided to menace Rogers' authority. By 1721 Rogers was financially bankrupt and departed back to England. Very quickly Nassau returned to being the pirate capital of the Bahamas.

It was late afternoon when the *Luisa* moored at the port of Nassau. It was just a short distance across the narrow sea passage to Hog Island. Captain Diego announced to the crew that the ship would be moored for two days and each crew member would have one day's leave. He ordered the chief mate to decide who was going ashore and when.

Diego had other plans for himself and the two ladies. With the help of two trusted crew members, Sérgio and Ned, the second and third ship's mates, the group would, under the cover of nightfall, quietly slip away to recover Jack's treasure.

It was just after midnight when Sérgio and Ned rowed the longboat quietly towards the silhouette of Hog Island. Because of the almost full moon, it was reasonably easy to see the island's trees and scrub growing down to the water's edge.

When the longboat landed on a small sandy beach, Grace and Fiona stepped ashore whilst Diego, Sérgio and Ned pulled the longboat along the sand, hiding it behind a group of limestone rocks and thick shrub. Ned collected the two spades and Sérgio picked up a supply of water and two hessian sacks.

The group pushed their way through the undergrowth until they came to a sand-covered, rocky clearing.

"I'm looking for a copse of pine trees," announced Fiona. "There should be a group of about ten, all very close to each other."

"That might not be so easy," said Diego. "Hurricanes come through here. Some of the trees might have been blown down."

Fiona peered in the direction she thought was north. "They should be near a mangrove swamp, next to a lagoon on the north side."

Grace stood on a large rock, pointed and announced she could see a group of tall trees straight ahead.

The group moved forwards. It wasn't easy walking over sand, hidden rocks and through the thick scrub just by the light of the moon. However, they eventually found a clearing and a stretch of water leading down to the north coast.

"This must be the lagoon," said Fiona. Then, pointing ahead, "Look! Mangroves… and a copse of pine trees. That must be what we're looking for!"

Scrambling amongst the protruding roots of the mangrove trees, walking became much trickier. Nevertheless, they eventually arrived next to a cluster of pine trees.

"There's only eight trees here," said Diego.

Grace moved forward and pointed. "Look 'ere! There's two stumps, maybe, snapped by passin' 'urricanes."

"Where next?" asked Diego, wiping the sweat from his brow.

"One of the trees has a hole in the bark, about head height," said Fiona.

The group spread out and searched each tree.

Suddenly, Sérgio shouted out, "Aquí!"

All five now moved towards Sérgio. He was standing next to a man-made hole about the size of a human fist.

"Okay," said Fiona. She closed her eyes and tried to remember the rest of the map's details. After a few seconds, she said, "The treasure's buried about four steps directly behind this hole in the tree."

They all peered behind the tree, in line with the hole. There was just a thicket of low-growing scrub.

"Are you sure?" asked Grace. Even she was now doubting Fiona's memory.

Fiona closed her eyes again. The others just stared and waited.

"I'm still sure that's what the map said. The scrub could have easily grown since Jack buried his treasure."

"That's true," said Diego. "This sort of scrub grows quickly. Let's try."

Sérgio and Ned paced four steps directly behind the hole in the tree and started to thrash at the scrub. The scrub came away quickly as the roots weren't very deep. Once the site was cleared, Sérgio and Ned started to dig. After about ten minutes Diego and Grace took over. The sand was dry, fine grained and reasonably easy to move.

When they'd got down to about waist level, Grace hit something solid and wooden sounding. Ned and Sérgio helped Grace climb out of the hole, giving Diego more room on his own. He slowly removed the sand until, finally, the top of a hardwood box was revealed. Sérgio took Grace's spade and jumped back into the hole. Between him and Diego, they revealed more of the box. Diego pushed his spade under what he thought was the bottom of the box and it slowly moved.

Ned now slid into the hole and the three men grabbed the sides of the box and heaved it clear of the hole. It was heavy, but there was a definite sound of coins and metal rattling. Sérgio and Ned scrambled up the side whilst Diego tested the ground for any more boxes. After five minutes of fruitless effort he gave up and Ned gave him a hand climbing out of the hole.

They all stared at the box. It was bigger than either of the two boxes they'd discovered on Heneagua. Diego had learned his lesson from the previous failed treasure hunt. This time they wouldn't be carrying the box all the way back to the ship before opening it. Hence the decision to bring two sacks. He looked at the lock and decided a firm hit would probably break it.

Grace had already anticipated this moment and handed him what she thought was a branch suitable for the job.

Diego smiled and said, "Muchas gracias."

Everybody stepped back except for Diego. He then gave a great heave and smashed at the box. The lock gave way, without any problem, and slid into the hole. They all moved in closer and Fiona bent down to raise the lid. The moment of truth!

CHAPTER 22

Fiona threw back the box's lid and they stared at large quantities of doubloons, gold sovereigns, guineas, loose jewels and many 'pieces of eight'! A true treasure chest!

As they all cheered and laughed, Fiona lifted out handfuls of the riches, wanting to explore what else was inside the box. She spotted gold plates and several silver items. Some were studied with even more jewels! Necklaces, rings, bracelets and a silver coronet!

Diego took hold of the two sacks and gave one to Ned. He suggested it would be easier to transport the treasure back to the ship in them. The two ladies agreed and the box's contents were removed and placed into the sacks. The empty box was then kicked back into the hole and Sérgio and Ned covered it with the excavated sand and stones. Ten minutes later the ground had been returned to looking undisturbed except for the missing scrub.

Diego and Ned carried the treasure sacks over their shoulders. However, the group soon found the route more difficult as they struggled to find their earlier footprints in the sand. This was made more difficult when the moonlight was blocked by the occasional cloud. Nevertheless, they eventually found their way back to the beach and followed the shoreline until they returned to the longboat.

Five minutes later, the boat was pulled back into the sea and they clambered aboard. Being a low-lying island, New Providence didn't have any easy-to-identify points of reference, so it wasn't until they were halfway across the channel that the shapes of the moored ships came into view. Grace guided the four rowers towards the familiar structure of the *Luisa*.

As the longboat drifted silently to the side of the ship, Ned grabbed a rope hanging down the side of the hull. He leaped off the longboat, and, whilst still holding the rope, quietly clambered up the side of the ship. Once on board he secured two more ropes and threw the ends down to the longboat. Sérgio grabbed the ropes and, with the help of Diego, the two sacks were tied securely and raised. Fiona and Grace followed next. Finally, Diego and Sérgio were the last to climb aboard.

In Diego's absence, the ship's chief mate, 'Duggy' Stephens, was in charge and had organised the watch. He'd spotted the group and walked across the deck to join them.

"Ev'ning, Captin," said Duggy. "All quiet."

"Excellent," said Diego. "I want you, Sérgio and Ned to get the longboat aboard and then come to my cabin." Diego looked at the ladies. "We'll take these sacks."

The group followed the captain's orders and the longboat was raised and secured. They all then congregated in the captain's cabin.

Diego ordered Sérgio to close the door and stop anyone from entering. Diego then emptied the contents of the two sacks onto his large wooden table. There were gasps of astonishment.

"Right, Ned," said Diego, pulling Ned closer to the table. "You have the first pick, any five of the loose jewels." Ned stepped forward and picked up his selection.

"Go stand by the door, Ned. Sérgio, come and take your five." Sérgio came over and made his selection.

"Duggy, help yourself to five doubloons."

Duggy picked up five of the golden coins.

"Thank you, gentlemen," said Diego. "You may go now. Duggy, make sure we're not disturbed."

The three men left the cabin.

"Well, ladies, the treasure I've given to my officers are out of my one-third share." Diego selected some more items for himself and asked, "Would you be 'appy if I 'ad these?"

There was still lots of treasure on the table.

Fiona and Grace looked at each other and smiled. They were more than happy with Diego's suggestion. Finally, Fiona leaned over the table and pushed the coronet towards the captain. "Should we call this the balance of our fare to South Carolina?"

The captain laughed. "We have a deal!"

After replenishing stocks of food, wine, rum and fresh water, two days later, the *Luisa* left Nassau and headed back in a northerly direction.

As a result of acquiring Calico Jack's treasure, Grace and Fiona agreed they wouldn't need to hunt for their own buried treasure, this time. They'd decided it should remain hidden… a nest egg for sometime in the future!

Captain Diego informed the ladies that the next stop would be Grand Bahama, a quiet island with just a few inhabitants. After that, they would be heading through the Straits of Florida and into the Atlantic Ocean. He estimated they'd arrive in Charles Town, in about 10 to 12 days' time. "That is," he qualified, "if we don't meet up with any stormy weather… or get distracted by any more pirates!"

Fiona smiled and told Diego Captain Bluey would make sure the message got out that the *Luisa* was not to be touched!

Diego wondered, again, who these two women really were!

After the brief stop at Grand Bahama for fresh water, the *Luisa* continued to head north. Whilst the weather was still largely warm, a few cold showers made the temperature feel much cooler. Fiona and Grace had become used to the tropical conditions. When it rained in the Caribbean, it was usually warm rain, not these chilly showers. They were not looking forward to a colder climate, something they needed to consider when deciding on their final destination.

Two days' later, the weather took a turn for the worse. The *Luisa* was hit by a fierce storm moving up from the south. Diego suggested it was probably the tailwind of a hurricane, passing through the Caribbean. He ordered the sails to be furled up as the ship was travelling too fast. Two helmsmen were employed to control the wheel. Even then, they had to use ropes to help keep the ship on course. The casks of fresh water were firmly secured in the hold and anything else that was moveable was fastened down and made safe.

With the strong winds came more squally rain and wild seas. Diego told everyone not required on deck to go below and secure themselves. "Things are going to get exceptionally rough, before they get better!" he announced.

He also made the decision to head closer to the shore. The two helmsmen made their adjustments and the ship headed in a more westerly direction. However, this meant the winds battered the port side and the ship began to list towards starboard. The helmsmen tied themselves to the deck and the crew below were ordered to move to the port side to try to counterbalance the wind's strength. This had a positive effect and, eventually, Diego ordered the ship to recommence its north-north-westerly course. The helmsmen fought again to adjust the wheel and tie the ropes back onto the hull. The ship responded and had almost returned to its upright position.

Still crashing over high waves and battling the winds, the *Luisa* sailed on.

As the storm raged, Fiona and Grace were together in Fiona's cabin. They'd both experienced storms at sea in the past, but each storm always seemed to be worse than the previous one. This time they tied sheets together to make temporary ropes. These they tied around each other, their ankles and then to both ends of the bed. As the ship tossed and pitched they lurched sideways and backwards but mercifully the knotted sheets helped them stay on the bed. Grace was beginning to feel sick, but desperately tried to resist. Fiona was praying and wishing for the storm to finally abate! They both heard crashes, bangs and creaking of wood and prayed the ship would remain in one piece.

"I've decided I hate the sea," Fiona shouted, raising her voice above the storm. "The more I experience its ferocity and wild torment, its violence and cruelty, the more I know I just want to live on dry land!"

Now the ship was sailing closer to land, the buffeting and crashing began to ease. The wind was still strong, but it was far easier for the helmsmen to control the wheel.

When the wind finally moderated, the two helmsmen, who had been roped to the wheel for about five hours, were shattered and soaked to the skin. Diego called for two replacements, but, shortly after, only one man was required.

Grace and Fiona could sense the sea calming down, so they undid the knots and removed the sheets from themselves and the ends of the bed. Although bruised and weary, they were grateful they'd not incurred any serious injuries. They also hoped the ship had fared just as well.

CHAPTER 23

Captain Diego was exhausted and drained. He thought every muscle in his body ached. When the storm finally abated, he'd ordered Duggy to take charge and went back to his cabin for a change of clothes. After removing his white cotton shirt, he noticed lines of blood where he'd secured ropes around his waist, essential to stop him being swept overboard and to a certain death. He stripped completely, washed his wounds and then fell onto his bed. Within seconds he was fast asleep.

Duggy ordered a complete check of the ship. He wanted to know if there'd been any damage. Fortunately, the report back was for only minor repairs, so he told the carpenter to start work immediately.

After Fiona and Grace had tidied Fiona's cabin and returned the borrowed sheets from Grace's room, the two ladies went upstairs to get some fresh air. Once on deck they took deep breaths of the cool sea air and were pleased to be standing steady again. Over the past five hours the temperature had dropped significantly and both now shivered a little. However, neither wanted to go back to their cabins just yet. They walked over to Duggy Stephens.

"Quite a storm," said Grace. "Glad it's over."

"Been through worse," replied Duggy. "You ladies okay? You look cold."

"A mixture of shock and a change in temperature," replied Grace. "It's just good to get out of our cabins and breathe some fresh air."

"Plenty of that out 'ere!"

Grace smiled. "Yes there is. Where's the captain?"

"Went to get a change of clothes. Was out 'ere with the 'elms-men, for over five hours. Knackered and wet through. Looked like a drowned rat, he did!"

The ship's carpenter walked over to join them. He wanted Duggy to see some damage to the ship. Duggy excused himself to the ladies and the two men walked away.

Fiona looked a little concerned. "I hope the damage isn't serious."

"If it was, I think Duggy would've known before now. D'you 'ave any idea where we are?"

Fiona pondered on the question. She knew there was still a long way to go before Charles Town. "Probably Florida, that way." She pointed towards the west. "I think that's still owned by the Spanish."

"A long way to go, then?"

"Fraid so."

Over the next week, the weather was much calmer, although the air temperature dropped several degrees. Diego was pleased with the ship's progress and was standing on the aft deck, staring out to sea. It had been a long voyage, much longer than he was used to, but after acquiring his unexpected treasure, it was going to be a very profitable one. Yes, it had been an adventure, but he was now in a part of the world he hadn't been to before. He still enjoyed sailing and all its challenges, especially navigating his way to new harbours. Mind, he still couldn't make out his two passengers... Fiona and Grace. Was that really their names? Why did that pirate captain call out "Anne" to Fiona? Still, the women had warned him it wasn't in his best interests to know too much. Why would they say that? Did they have something... or lots, to hide? Fiona knew of two lots of buried treasure! How did she know their locations? Were these women wives of pirates... or even pirates themselves!? He'd heard about women pirates, but in reality, Fiona and Grace seemed far too petite and feminine to be murderers and thieves. Maybe, as the ladies said, it is better for me not to know... but, of course, that doesn't stop me wondering!

The following day, the sun was shining and there wasn't a cloud in the sky. The temperature, too, was much warmer, but not to the level of Caribbean temperatures. Fiona and Grace were sitting on the aft deck, relaxing and talking.

"What am I goin' to find when we get to Charles Town?" asked Grace. She was shielding her eyes from the glare of the sun.

"It's a town," responded Fiona. "The capital of South Carolina. A major port, lots going on and many new buildings. Quite a few people from Britain have moved there. Anyway, I've told you all this before."

"I know, but it's still goin' to be all new to me."

"You have to remember I was just a child when I lived there. I left when I was 16. Everything seemed very big back then. I'm sure I'm going to see it much differently when I return."

"Are you goin' to visit your parents and brother?"

"I don't think so. I'm not sure I'd be welcome."

"Time's a good 'ealer."

"Maybe. We'll see. But we've both got new names! How am I going to deal with that? I don't want to go back to being called Anne. That life's all gone."

Grace nodded her head. "Maybe we need to think about that."

Fiona wanted to change the subject and then remembered. "There used to be pirates in Charles Town!"

"What!? Really!" replied Grace. She looked at her friend with a surprised expression.

"Yes, Blackbeard… and his fleet! Just before I left Charles Town. Blackbeard arrived and joined up with some other pirates. They blockaded the port. Demanded a huge ransom!"

"Did the authorities pay?"

"I don't know. Probably, because the port was reopened shortly after. That's when James and I left for Nassau."

Grace's eyes lit up. "I wonder if there's any pirates now."

"I don't think so. I heard the British Navy had moved in. Anyway, we're trying to get away from pirates, not rejoin them!"

Grace's excitement suddenly deflated. "Even so, Blackbeard! I'd love to 'ave met 'im."

"Well he's dead now, anyway."

Might not be a bad place after all, thought Grace.

The following day, Diego and Duggy were checking their charts and making calculations. Diego decided to redirect the ship closer to the mainland so he could, hopefully, identify some navigational points for reference. He was particularly looking for islands or rivers, draining off from the land, or any other significant feature close to the coast.

Eventually Diego spotted two islands he could use in his calculations. He immediately instructed the helmsman to change direction, back towards starboard and then head due north.

Later that same day Diego spotted the ladies sitting in their usual spot on the aft deck. He walked over to join them. "Good afternoon, ladies," he announced. "First thing tomorrow we'll be sailing into the port of Charles Town. I suggest you get your bags packed!"

CHAPTER 24

It was an hour after daybreak when the *Luisa* departed the Atlantic Ocean. It was now sailing between two islands sheltering the harbour entrance to Charles Town. Grace and Fiona had been up early and were now excitedly staring ahead on the for'ard deck.

The ship slowly entered a wide inlet and headed towards a peninsula where the Ashley and Cooper rivers flowed either side of the town. Fiona and Grace could already hear lots of noise from all the activity in the port.

Fiona immediately recognised the harbour promontory and the two rivers. From this height, she could see further inland and realised how much the town had grown since she'd been away. She pointed to a large merchant ship being loaded with rice and Sea Island Cotton. "I bet that ship's going to Europe," she said, "maybe even Britain."

Grace nodded.

Amongst all the activity, Diego and Duggy were searching for a mooring point. Duggy finally pointed to a gap between two merchant ships and Diego told the helmsman to steer in that direction.

As the *Luisa* inched into position, ropes were thrown from the ship onto the dockside. Two dock workers immediately grabbed the ropes, pulled the ship towards the edge of the dock and secured the ropes against two mooring bollards.

Fiona and Grace watched all the action and listened to the banging, shouting and all the activities on the dock. They then watched as the ship's gangplank was slowly lowered and secured.

A minute later Diego came over to join them. "Well, ladies," he said. "It's adiós. Time to say goodbye. Come, I'll take you down the gangplank."

Fiona and Grace had already said their goodbyes to Duggy, Ned, Sérgio and the other crew members, so they followed the captain back across the main deck and down the gangplank. Their bags were already waiting for them on the quay.

Grace was first to speak, "Diego, thank you so much. It's been a pleasure and certainly an adventure." She smiled at him and then stood up on her toes, leaned forward and gave him a kiss on his cheek.

Diego smiled back and said, "It was a pleasure, ladies. Good luck with your plans for the future."

Fiona kissed Diego and said, "Adiós, mi amigo!"

Diego laughed at Fiona's Spanish pronunciation. He spotted Ned walking across the dock with another man pushing a wooden handcart. "Ah, Ned's coming with your transport man. He'll take you where you want to go."

"Are you leavin' straight away?" asked Grace.

"No. We'll get more food and water first. Probably leave later this afternoon."

"Well I hope you have a safe trip back", said Fiona. "Give our love to Luisa and Mary."

Ned introduced the ladies to the man with the handcart. The transport man told them his name was Simon. He appeared to be about 25 years of age, tall and strong, with a mop of blond hair.

Grace and Fiona held on to their smaller bags, containing their treasure, whilst Simon picked up the rest of their belongings and placed them on his cart.

Last goodbyes and waves to the crew were made, and then Grace and Fiona were on their way. They followed Simon, as he pushed his cart up the gradual slope.

Diego watched the ladies as they walked away. He smiled to himself and, not for the first time, wondered who these two women really were!

As the two ladies walked up the stone pathway, Grace looked across towards Fiona. They gave each other a nervous smile. When they'd reached the top of the slope, Fiona looked around. Did she recognise any buildings or features? She could certainly see a lot had changed.

Simon pushed the cart over to where a horse and open carriage had been tied to a post. He placed the cases immediately behind the driving seat and returned the handcart back to where three other carts had been placed. By the time he arrived back at the carriage, the ladies had already climbed aboard and were sitting together facing forwards.

Simon closed the small passenger door and asked them, "So, ladies, where can I take you?"

Grace told Simon they wanted to go to a nice inn. Quiet and well away from the noise of the port.

Simon thought for a moment and untied the horse reins from the post. He climbed up to the driver's position and replied, "That would be the Crown. Modern and quiet. Especially nice for two fine ladies."

"Okay," said Grace. She looked at Fiona. "Take us to the Crown."

The journey through the port was slow and tedious. Lots of horses and carts, hustle and bustle and men on foot carrying cargo, parcels and merchandise. However, once they'd passed the last of the rows of dockside warehouses, the streets became more defined by cobblestone surfaces. Horse-drawn passenger carriages were prominent and the thoroughfare was lined with painted weatherboard houses, shops and a few offices. Most of the buildings were constructed of timber, but a small number were built of red brick.

Grace observed that most of the pedestrians walking along the sidewalks and in and out of the shops and offices were smartly dressed.

Charles Town had grown wealthy through the export of rice and Sea Island Cotton. It was a base for many wealthy traders, merchants and landowners and appeared to be charming, attractive and prosperous. But underneath this facade were a number of issues. The large expansion of plantation agriculture had meant there was a big demand for African slaves. They'd become essential for the area's growth, development and prosperity. There was also the constant bickering and tensions between Britain and Spain. These confrontations were mainly over borders in the south, towards Florida. Nevertheless, sometimes these tensions intensified, resulting in Charles Town and its port seeing periodic conflicts and attacks from both land and sea.

Grace leaned forward and spoke loudly to Simon. "It looks very prosp'rus."

"Yes ma'am," replied Simon. "The port's very busy. Lots of wealthy merchants and landowners moved down 'ere from the north and Europe. Life's really improved. Pirates have gone and there's a lot more food. Still lots of problems with the Spanish, but that should be sorted by the British Navy soon."

At the corner of a narrow lane, Simon pulled on the reins and the horse stopped walking. "We're 'ere, ladies," he shouted, as he jumped down from his driver's seat.

Fiona and Grace looked up at the building. Like the surrounding properties, it looked modern, quiet and clean. Simon opened the carriage door and helped the ladies step down. They walked into the inn and were surprisingly impressed, much bigger and more opulent than they'd been used to. Simon followed, carrying their bags. He placed them beside Fiona. Grace smiled and handed him two silver coins. Immediately his eyes lit up. He nodded and thanked her very much.

Whilst Grace registered for two separate rooms, Fiona looked around the impressive expanse. Two well-dressed gentlemen passed by, doffing their top hats and giving her a smile. Mmm, she thought, things have definitely changed!

CHAPTER 25

Three days after settling into their new accommodation, Grace had explored their new surroundings and wandered around most of the town. She'd been into many of the shops and had bought a few new clothes and two pairs of shoes.

Fiona, meanwhile, was less adventurous. She certainly didn't want to bump into any of her family, not just yet, if ever! For most of the time she stayed close to the inn and well away from her father's office. Ideally, she'd hoped she might meet one of the gentlemen who had smiled at her when they first arrived. Unfortunately, that didn't happen.

The following evening they decided to have dinner at a cabaret that had recently opened two streets away from the inn. Grace had been told that, unlike the local taverns, the Paris Cabaret served food at tables, had nice linen tablecloths and provided drinks with the meal. Also different prices were advertised depending upon the customers' choice of dish.

Fiona was keen to try something different, so she agreed to join Grace at this new establishment. They arrived at the Paris Cabaret at 6.30pm with hopes of a nice meal in a pleasant and elegant environment.

The ladies were shown to a table at the side of the room. Grace spotted that most of the other tables were already occupied by couples and foursomes. Elegant chandeliers were hanging from the ornate creamy white ceiling and the flooring was laid in a smooth wooden parquet design. Neither Fiona nor Grace could remember eating in such an opulent diner before.

"Not like being next to a ship's galley," said Grace, as she picked up her menu.

Fiona smiled and whispered, "Shh! Give me this nice setting any time." She looked around the room and noticed that most people were all dressed in their finery. As well as eating, they were either talking or laughing. It was the sort of place she knew she was going to enjoy, even more so, if she'd been sharing it with Bluey!

After a few minutes they ordered their food and drinks, Fiona pointed to a far table where there was obviously a merry party going on. Grace glanced towards it and then looked at some of the other tables. She made comments about the clothes other women were wearing and the attractiveness, or otherwise, of their male partners. Except for two younger men sitting on their own, most of the diners seemed to be much older than her.

When their drinks were delivered, the ladies started to chat about each other's day's activities. Grace reported that she'd now seen most of the town and was finding 'normality' not very stimulating or even exciting.

Fiona was sympathetic and felt partly guilty. After all, it was she who had persuaded her to give up the pirate life and travel to South Carolina. She knew she didn't want to lose her friend, but Grace was certainly intelligent enough to make up her own mind.

"Don't you want to see your old 'ome?" asked Grace. She was keen to see where Fiona had grown up.

"I'm not sure," replied Fiona. "I've got no reason to go back. It wasn't a happy time for me. It's history, not Fiona Kelly's history, but Anne Cormac's old home."

Grace was just about to speak again when their food was delivered and a small band started to play. They were both hungry and concentrated on eating their meal and listening to the music.

When they'd finished, both women sat back and sipped their wine. They relaxed and continued to listen to the lively music.

"I really enjoyed that," said Grace, gently wiping her lips with a napkin.

"Yes, mine was lovely too," replied Fiona. "That's the best meal I've eaten since the dinner I had with Bluey." She sipped her wine and noticed an attractive man walking towards their table. She'd spotted him earlier looking across at Grace.

"Excuse me, ladies, but my friend and I were wondering... as you're both sitting here on your own, if you wanted to join us? We have a table for four over there." The young man was smartly dressed in a maroon velvet jacket, a white shirt and a flamboyant maroon silk cravat. He pointed to his colleague, who gave them a smile and a gentle wave.

Fiona looked at Grace and gave her a smile. "That's very kind of you, sir," said Grace. "We'll join you when we've finished our wine."

The gentleman smiled and nodded, then returned to his colleague.

"Why did you say that?" asked Fiona. "Didn't you like him?"

"We shouldn't give the impression we're easy and would jump at their very first request. Yes, 'e's very nice, but let's make 'em wait a few minutes."

It was actually five minutes later when Grace and Fiona finished their wine, paid their bill and walked over to join the two men. When the men spotted the ladies approaching they jumped to their feet and smiled. Grace and Fiona were offered the two vacant chairs and they sat down.

"Well, first things first," said the man who had visited their table. "My name's William Barrington and this is my friend, George. We're both from England. Just here for a few weeks on business."

Grace thought William looked attractive and focused her response on him. "I'm Grace and this is my friend Fiona." Grace waved her hand casually in Fiona's direction. "We arrived on Monday from Guantánamo, in Cuba."

"Cuba? Isn't that an exciting place?" asked William. "Lots of rum and cigars!" He laughed.

"I think that's Havana," replied Fiona. "Guantánamo's more of a fishing town, small and much quieter. We were only there for a few days."

"Travelling are you?"

"Yes, we left England some months ago," said Grace.

"What do your husbands have to say about that?" asked William. He was very keen to learn the answer.

"We're not married," said Grace, and looked directly at William to see his reaction.

William smiled back and then George said, "We have a full bottle of wine here." He pointed to the bottle. "Would you like a glass?"

Both Grace and Fiona said they would and George asked a passing waiter for two clean glasses.

For the rest of the evening the group chatted and found out a lot more about each other, although Grace and Fiona were keen to avoid answering too many questions about their past. Nevertheless, the ladies did discover that William and George were both in South Carolina to check up on their respective father's estates. Both properties were predominantly growing Sea Island Cotton and rice, while herds of cattle were being farmed for both meat and milk. George told them they were staying together on William's father's estate.

Grace and William were getting on very well, but Fiona, although friendly, was rather cool towards George. Her emotional desires were still solely for her Captain Bluey.

The evening ended when the group realised the music had stopped and they were the only customers remaining. William invited the ladies for a ride back to their inn in his carriage. They accepted, and when they exited the cabaret, a carriage, with two horses and its driver, was waiting just across the street.

It took only a few minutes for the carriage to transport the ladies back to the inn. Fiona stepped down and waited for Grace, who really didn't want to leave. William asked her if she would like to meet again. Grace smiled, placed her hand on his cheek and said, "Yes, I would. That would be very nice."

Over the next week, Grace and William met together most evenings. Sometimes William stayed with Grace at the inn, other times William took Grace back to the big house on his father's large estate. George and Fiona only met one more time. Fiona told George she didn't want to start a new relationship because there was already a man in her life that she loved, and he was currently working in the Bahamas.

All too soon, William announced that the ship he and George were travelling back to England on was due to leave Charles Town in two days' time. They were both expected in England to report back to their respective fathers. Their work on the estates was almost completed.

Grace's face fell from a happy picture to one of sadness. She realised another short period of happiness in her life was about to come to an end.

William, however, had different ideas. He was in love with Grace and didn't want to lose her. "I think we've had a wonderful time, Grace. I've really enjoyed your company and I'd hate for us to break up now. Would you consider coming back to England with me?"

Grace took a deep breath, raised her eyebrows, but tried to remain calm. From feeling deep sadness, she was now quietly ecstatic. She leaned forward towards William, smiled and gently kissed him on the cheek. "William, dear William. I've loved every moment we've been together. This is all rather a surprise... a big decision for me to consider. Can I give you my answer tomorrow evenin'?"

William was disappointed, but at least she hadn't said no! He'd just have to be patient and wait for her answer tomorrow... the eve of the ship's departure back to England.

CHAPTER 26

When Grace arrived back at the inn, she immediately went upstairs and knocked on Fiona's door. Fiona was in the process of getting ready for bed, but let her friend into her room, especially after seeing the huge smile on Grace's face.

"William wants me to go back to England with 'im," Grace announced. They sat down next to each other on the bed.

Fiona smiled. "I knew he would. On that first night at the Paris Cabaret he was staring at you nearly all evening. What have you told him?"

"I told 'im I'd give 'im me answer tomorrow evenin'. The ship sails to England the next day."

"Have you already decided?"

"Part of me says yes, I want to be with 'im. 'E's nice, attractive and comes from a wealthy family. But the other part of me says… well… it means saying goodbye to you."

"We knew this time would come sooner or later. It could have been the same with me and Bluey. I'm hoping that's still going to happen."

"You told me about your plans. Do you think they'll definitely 'appen?"

"Who knows. Bluey could have been killed or captured by now. Anyway, we're talking about you. You've been given another chance. No need to go back to pirating and wearing men's clothes. Mary's gone. The future's about Grace and her new man, William… and your big, new opportunity in England!"

Grace looked sadly at her friend. Tears began to trickle down both cheeks. "We've been through such a lot, you and me… and now look at us, rich, free and with a future… with two men we love. We're so lucky." Grace leaned over and she and Fiona embraced.

After a few seconds they pulled away. Fiona said, "I guess the answer's going to be yes."

Grace smiled and wiped the tears from her cheeks. "Yes, I think so!"

"Well in that case, and please, don't take this the wrong way, but we need to improve your speech a little."

"What d'you mean?" queried Grace.

"You say 'appy, when it should be happy or 'im instead of him. You say comin' instead of coming. Things like that. William and his family are well educated, you'll need to convince them you are too."

"I'm not sure I can do that."

"Of course you can. It's just practice. Let's try now and we'll carry on again tomorrow."

The following evening Grace met up with William again. This time at a tavern on the edge of Charles Town. It was much quieter and less raucous than similar establishments closer to the harbour. Grace was extremely nervous. She really wanted to show off her enunciation. She had been practising all day.

William waited anxiously to hear Grace's decision. Would she be returning to England with him tomorrow?

After they'd sat down, William ordered two glasses of white wine and stared at Grace.

Grace responded and looked solemnly into William's eyes. "William, I've thought long and 'ard, er, hard, about your offer and…" With a huge smile appearing on her face, she said, "I've decided to go back to England with you tomorrow."

"Oh wow! I thought you were going to turn me down!"

"Fiona and I talked about it for most of last night. She's got her plans for the future and… now, so do I."

William stood up, leaned across the table and gave Grace a long and tender kiss. After resuming his seat he placed his hands on Grace's and said, "I love you, Grace. I promise you… you'll not regret your decision."

Grace wondered if his comment would really come true. What would William do if he found out my true identity? "I love you too, William. I just hope your parents will accept me as well."

"Father will adore you! Mother, well, she's the difficult one, as I've said. She likes to know lots about my girlfriends. As I'm their only son she wants to make sure I'll be marrying well."

Oh dear, thought Grace, is that going to be a potential problem?

For the rest of the evening they chatted. William described where he lived, his future plans and his vision for Grace's involvement. However, Grace was still unsure about William's mother, and his parents' ambitions for him to eventually take over the responsibility for and management of, not only the family's estate in Berkshire… but their interests in South Carolina too. Was this a step too far?

Finally, at the end of the evening, Grace announced she needed to get back to the inn to pack her belongings, otherwise, she wouldn't be ready for the ship's departure. William said he would send his driver to collect her and her luggage at ten o'clock. He also mentioned he'd meet her at the ship, as he still had some last minute legal business to deal with.

The next morning, William's driver duly arrived at the Crown inn at ten o'clock. Between him, Fiona and Grace, they managed to get all Grace's belongings onto the carriage. The ladies then sat back in their seats and watched the activity in the streets. As the carriage proceeded towards the harbour, Grace had mixed feelings and emotions. Excitement, certainly, about a future with William, but also apprehension. Saying goodbye to her best friend, Fiona, was going to be an ordeal!

As the carriage passed the warehouses, the noise and activity slowly increased. Horses and trailers, handcarts and individuals were carrying goods and merchandise in every direction. People were calling and shouting whilst loading and unloading the ships.

When Grace spotted her ship, the *Venturer*, she could feel her heart pounding. This was it. Had she made the right decision?

The carriage came to a stop and the driver jumped down to secure his horse to a post, then collected a handcart. The two ladies had already stepped down from the carriage and were watching as the driver removed Grace's belongings and placed them on the cart.

"All ready, ladies?" asked the driver. Grace nodded and he started to push the cart down the gentle slope towards the dockside, where the *Venturer* was moored. People, bags and goods were already going on board.

Fiona and Grace nervously glanced at each other and followed the driver down the slope. Grace held Fiona's hand very tightly.

When the ladies arrived next to the *Venturer*, there was no sight of either William or George.

At the gangplank the driver stopped the handcart and two dock handlers lifted Grace's bags aboard the ship. The driver nodded his head, said goodbye and wished Grace a safe journey.

Grace smiled and thanked him. However, she was now anxiously looking all around. There was still no sign of William or George.

Fiona could see Grace was anxious. "He'll be along in a minute. Don't worry." She then spotted George walking down the slope. "Look, here's George."

George came across to join them. "William's been delayed," he said, a little breathless. "He's with his father's lawyer, Mr Cormac. He shouldn't be long. Both William's and my belongings are already on board. I'll check if all the bags have been put in the right cabins."

"My bags have been collected and taken on board," said Grace. She was looking up the slope, trying to spot William. "They're two brown leather cases and both have my name on a label."

"Okay. I'll make sure your bags are put in the correct cabin." George smiled at Fiona, said goodbye and walked towards the gangplank.

"Mr Cormac!" announced Fiona. "That's my father!"

Grace smiled. "What a coincidence!"

Suddenly Grace spotted William rushing down the slope. He immediately joined the ladies and gave Grace a kiss on her cheek. He was breathing heavily and struggled to say his words, "Phew! Sorry… I'm late. Legal people… have no comprehension of time. Anyway, I'm here now."

"I thought the ship would be leaving without you," said Grace, now smiling and somewhat relieved. "George has gone on board."

"Oh, okay. Good. Look, I'll leave you two to say your good-byes." William leaned across to Fiona and gave her a kiss on her cheek. "Lovely to have met you, Fiona. Please don't forget us."

"No, I promise, I won't," replied Fiona.

At this William smiled, left the ladies and rushed up the gangplank.

Grace looked at Fiona and they both had tears in their eyes. They embraced and hugged each other tightly.

"All aboard!" came a shout from on board the ship. It was the last call for all remaining passengers.

Several people pushed past Grace and Fiona to climb the gangplank as the two women were embracing. Slowly, they separated and Grace gave Fiona a note with the addresses of both William's home and his father's estate in England. Fiona folded it carefully and placed it into her purse.

"Final call," came the same voice again. Deckhands were standing next to the gangplank ready to pull it on board.

One final hug and Grace climbed up the gangplank and onto the ship. The gangplank was lifted and pulled aboard. The securing ropes were untied from the mooring bollards and hauled up.

Grace stood next to the bulwark and waved to her friend. Fiona responded as the ship slowly pulled away from the side of the dock. They both watched and continued to wave until Grace couldn't see Fiona anymore.

CHAPTER 27

When Grace had finally disappeared from her sight, Fiona wiped her eyes and trudged back up the slope. At the top she spotted Simon, standing next to his carriage. She hailed him over.

"You want to go back to the Crown, ma'am?" asked Simon. He could see Fiona was upset.

"Yes, please," she said, with a sad voice.

As Fiona climbed aboard, Simon held the carriage door open. "Just seen you wavin' your friend away on that there ship."

"Yes, she's going back to England."

"You'll miss her. You were good friends."

"Yes, I will. I really will."

Simon scrambled up to the driver's seat, grabbed and cracked the reins. Once he'd navigated his way through the harbour activity, it was only a few moments before they arrived outside the Crown. Fiona stepped down from the carriage and holding a silver coin she raised her hand towards Simon.

Simon smiled and looked down at Fiona's outstretched hand. "No need for that, ma'am. Your friend paid me 'andsomely last time."

Fiona smiled and lowered her arm. "Thank you for the ride."

"My pleasure, ma'am. Maybe I'll see you again sometime."

Fiona smiled again and entered the inn.

Simon cracked the reins and said to himself, "Sad but pretty lady, she is."

Fiona walked up the stairs to her room. She sat on the bed and contemplated what she was going to do now... without Grace.

After a few moments she thought about the coincidence of her father's name cropping up earlier. It made her think of her family. She would certainly like to meet her mother and brother again, but, of course, they would only remember her as a child... a 16-year-old juvenile named Anne! She wondered if they'd heard anything about her pirate life? Her conviction and the birth of her daughter? What would she say? What would be achieved... by going back!? Would it only result in more heartache? She'd already caused lots of that whilst she was growing up. Would she even be welcomed back!?

The *Venturer* had entered the choppy waters of the Atlantic Ocean. Grace was in her cabin unpacking her second case when there was a knock on the door. When she opened it, William had a big smile on his face. She immediately invited him in and closed the door. Now they had time for a proper lingering kiss.

After they'd pulled apart, William spotted Grace's clothes on the bed. "I can see you're settling in. Everything okay?"

"Yes, fine, so far – and the bed is big enough for two!"

William laughed. "We'll have to try it out and make sure, later. It was the only cabin left. George's and mine are both singles, so you've come out the best."

"I've been thinking about a comment you made last evening," said Grace, with a serious edge to her voice. She sat down on the side of the bed.

William could see the worried look on Grace's face, and sat down next to her. "Which comment are you talking about?" he asked. He was worried about what she might say.

"You said your mother may not like me!"

"I'm sure I didn't say those exact words. However, Mother is often… well, difficult. She is with most people."

Grace stared at her hands, resting together in the middle of her lap. "I've also been thinking about your father's estate and you being expected to take over. Surely your parents will want you to produce a male heir."

William pushed his left arm towards Grace and gently squeezed her right hand. "In an ideal world that would be true, but the estate hasn't followed a normal line of inheritance. My grandfather bought a small part of what is now the estate from a friend, who'd found himself in financial difficulties. Grandfather then, over time, purchased more acres. My father's eldest brother, Uncle Giles, he was destined to inherit, but, unfortunately, he died. Fell off a horse when he was out hunting. Then there was Uncle Harry, he was next in line. However, he'd already joined the British Navy and subsequently died when his ship crashed on rocks, somewhere near Jamaica. That left my father. He was the youngest of the three brothers, and obviously hadn't expected to inherit. Even now, some part of him wishes he never had. He had other plans and was well aware that running both estates came with lots of responsibilities. He once described it to me as 'a bit of a millstone around his neck'. About two years ago, I had a long discussion with him and quietly he told me that if I didn't fancy the job, he'd understand. I could sell everything if I wanted to. Mind, my sister's husband, Thomas, he's always been keen to take over... and he's certainly more interested to take it all on than I am."

"But your mother?"

"Mmm, yes. As I say, that's a little trickier. She married my father, I think, for the increased status and wealth it gave her. But, don't get me wrong, I'm sure she loves him and she's certainly been a good wife. However, Mother has always been the main voice on this issue. She wants the Barrington family's name to inherit and continue to run the two estates. As for me, well, I'm not so sure I want all that responsibility. I was due to marry about four years ago, but Mother's demands eventually frightened my fiancée away. Probably just as well now that I've met you."

Grace smiled. "Well I guess now I've got to prove your patience was worth it!"

William smiled and looked deep into Grace's eyes. "I know it will be."

Grace leaned forward and kissed William. She then pulled him back so they lay together on the bed. She kissed him again, this time more passionately, and started to unbutton his shirt.

It was two days after Grace had left Charles Town when Fiona marched out from the Crown. It was eight o'clock in the morning and she was on a mission. She vaguely remembered the direction and strode along several streets before coming to a stop at the corner with Beaufain Street. Across the road she recognised the old wooden structure of her former school. Three pupils were entering the building. She looked up and down the street, deciding she still recognised most of the neighbourhood. The area looked a little tidier, definitely a lot older, but otherwise most of the buildings appeared largely unchanged. She turned left and slowly walked along the new sidewalk, passing a row of detached wooden houses. Three properties along, there was a dark-blue-painted house, she recalled this was where her school friend Sheila Bailey had lived. She looked up at Sheila's bedroom window and wondered what had become of her. Next door was old Mr Taylor's house. She particularly remembered his horrible dog, always barking and would certainly savage you if it was given half a chance.

Not much further now, she thought.

Eventually, she stopped and looked over the road. There was the familiar frontage of Cormac House! The same old Irish-green-painted clapboards and the name plaque, screwed next to the front door. She then looked up to the small bedroom window on the top floor, all bare and unoccupied now. No sign of her old leprechaun curtains, or Jenny, her doll, who used to reside on the window shelf, watching all the people passing by below.

Fiona suddenly felt sad, miserable… and totally alone.

She was just about to walk away when the front door opened. Her father! She immediately recognised him when he stepped outside. He closed the green door behind him and looked up and down the street. He adjusted his hat and gave Fiona a cursory glance, before striding away. She remembered this was the direction he usually took to his office.

Fiona watched him march briskly along the street. He still had the same air of authority and confidence. Yes, that was her father alright. She smiled to herself and pondered whether or not to follow him. But what would she do when he finally entered his office?

About to walk away, she decided to take one last look, one final look, at her former home. Instantly she was alarmed. Looking out through the kitchen window, directly across to where she was standing, was a woman's face!

Was that her mother!?

Fiona panicked and rushed away, turning down the first street she came to. Hidden from sight, she stopped to catch her breath. Her breathing was heavy and her heart racing. She leaned back against the brick wall. After about a minute, she carefully peeked around the corner. She was still breathing heavily but, thankfully, the only person she could see was a man, driving a horse-drawn cart. It was slowly moving in her direction.

Fiona turned back and walked along the road. She just wanted to get away… now regretting her decision to return. She was angry with herself, this was her past life, Anne Cormac's life. Anne Cormac was dead!

Twenty minutes later, Fiona re-entered the Crown. She went straight up the stairs to her room and, after closing the door, threw herself onto the bed… and burst into tears.

CHAPTER 28

The *Venturer* entered the deep waters of Funchal harbour, on the south side of the island of Madeira. Originally claimed by Portuguese sailors in the service of Prince Henry the Navigator in 1419, Madeira was later settled by Portuguese fishermen and peasant farmers. However, following the increase of commercial treaties between England and Portugal, important English merchants started to settle on the Island and Madeira wines were developed by several English companies. Gradually, production and the quality increased and a small number of producers began to take control of the growing and important Madeira wine trade business. The unique fortified, sweet-tasting wine became very popular in European markets and on the other side of the Atlantic Ocean, especially in the Thirteen Colonies.

The island of Madeira also prospered due to its advantageous constant mild climate. Moneyed aristocracy, travellers and tourists visited the island, wanting to benefit from the climate's popular therapeutic and restorative effects. A number of the passengers on the *Venturer* were travelling to Madeira for these very purposes.

When the ship finally moored, about half the passengers disembarked with all of their belongings. Some were heading for the wineries to discuss business deals, others were heading for the inns and therapeutic experiences.

George was also leaving the ship. He had business dealings to conduct. His father was a major wine importer into England and South Carolina, and George had been charged with the task of negotiating new deals with a number of the major wine producers.

William and Grace followed George as he walked down the gangplank. Once on the dockside he called to a man sitting on an empty handcart. The man joined him and George pointed to his luggage. He told him where he was going to stay.

The man nodded and walked to the side of the ship, where he hoisted George's luggage onto his cart.

Grace said goodbye and wished George good luck with his trading. She then walked away to investigate the dockside shops.

William said goodbye and shook his friend's hand. He wished him well with his business dealings and promised to meet up again when George returned to England.

When the cart was loaded, George checked everything had been collected, then looked back at William and said, "Well, good luck with your mother, William. I think Grace is a lovely woman. You're a lucky man!"

William smiled and thanked his friend. "Yes, I am... and I'm going to make sure Mother doesn't ruin my relationship this time... not like she did with Elizabeth."

"As I say, good luck." George patted William on his shoulder, turned and followed the man pushing his handcart.

Whilst William continued to watch George until he was out of sight, new passengers were nudging past him to embark onto the *Venturer*. Their belongings, pushed in handcarts, were following close behind. William stepped out of their way and watched the activity on the dockside. He observed the loading of merchandise, in particular, the large cases of Madeira wine being carefully lowered into the ship's hold. Maybe that's something I ought to get into, he thought. Must have a word with George, when he gets home.

Four hours later William and Grace were back on the *Venturer*. They watched from the bulwark as the gangplank and mooring ropes were pulled back on board the ship. The *Venturer* then slowly moved away from the dock. After a few moments, Grace and William walked across the deck and climbed the stairs to the aft deck. There, they could watch the ship leave the harbour and catch the last of the day's rays of sunshine.

Grace stood close to William and rested her head on his shoulder. "Are you happy?" she asked, remembering to emphasise the 'h'. She had been practising her pronunciations every day, since her conversation with Fiona.

"Yes, of course," came William's instant reply. There was no hint of hesitation. "It's brilliant to be with you."

Grace smiled and snuggled up closer. "How long is George staying in Madeira?"

"Probably a week, I think. His father's quite a big wine importer, so he's got a number of deals to do."

"You're not involved. With Madeira wine, I mean?"

"No, not yet. But I gather there's a lot of money to be made, especially in the colonies. George told me the selling price in South Carolina is really high. He wants to try to export to some of the other colonies as well."

"If you didn't take over running the family estates, what would you like to do?"

"I don't really know. All I've ever known is working with Father. I quite enjoy it really, but I don't want all the responsibilities. Especially when things go wrong. The Sea Cotton, for example, is constantly devastated. Sometimes by the weather and sometimes by some sort of insect. I just report the problem back to Father. It's him who has the sleepless nights."

Grace smiled, then brought the discussion back to William. "Mmm, but you're still young. You could start a new career."

"I'm not that young – 32 is pretty old to be thinking of a new career. By the way, I don't know how old you are?"

Oh dear, thought Grace, I can't tell him the truth. "I was 29 just a few weeks ago."

"You look younger. Still age doesn't matter to me."

Grace smiled. If only he knew the truth! With his mother, that's going to be more of a problem. She's bound to know 29's a lie.

Fiona kept looking at the calendar and counting down the days. It was 20 more long and uncertain days before she knew for certain whether Bluey had kept his promise. What if he didn't turn up? What would she do then? Go to England… or Ireland? Start a new life on her own? Move up to New York, or Boston? She sighed. Must get well away from the Caribbean. Search and see where Grace is living… and then what? No, she didn't intend to burden Grace and William with her problems.

She desperately wanted her Bluey to turn up!

The shipping routes around Cornwall and the Isles of Scilly were known to be notoriously dangerous. Strong tidal currents, gale force winds, dense fog and submerged rocks were all potential hazards. Over the years, lots of ships had been lost trying to sail through this treacherous stretch of sea; resulting in crew, passengers and cargo never arriving at their final destination!

It was a wet and windy day when the *Venturer* sailed alongside this treacherous stretch of Cornwall. It was due to dock at the port of Bristol later that day. Whilst not a major storm, all the passengers were requested to stay in their cabins. Captain Duke wanted all his crew to concentrate on finding the safest route through these perilous waters.

William and Grace used the time to make sure they were fully packed and ready to disembark once the ship finally docked. They sat on Grace's double bed and waited for the captain's announcement.

The *Venturer* safely passed by the tiny island of Lundy and then turned in a starboard direction. By the time they'd arrived in Bridgwater Bay, the wind had eased.

Captain Duke gave orders for the ship to head north-east and enter the Severn Estuary. He was keen to keep good time, as sailing in these precarious waters was dependent on the tides. Miss the high tide and the ship could easily run aground.

It was almost dusk but land could now be seen from both sides of the ship. It wasn't long before the *Venturer* passed Portishead Battery Point and entered the mouth of the Avon river. Slowly the ship sailed into the deep water channel known as 'Saint Augustine's Reach', the heart of Bristol's docks. Here ships had time for goods and passengers to come and go, but every captain had to be conscious of the next full tide. The *Venturer* was no exception, so once the ship had finally moored, William, Grace and all the other passengers, complete with their belongings, were quick to disembark.

William found a carriage for hire and asked the driver to take them to a coaching inn where they could catch a stagecoach to take them onto Newbury in Berkshire. The driver thought for a moment and then said, "The Plough's yer best bet, sir. You'd then want a stagecoach 'twas goin' to London. That'll be tomorrow, now. Should stop at Newbr'y for fresh 'orses."

"The Plough it is then," said William, with a joyful voice. He helped Grace climb aboard and followed behind. Meanwhile the driver placed and secured their luggage behind the driver's seat.

It was dark when the coach arrived at the Plough. While William was checking in, he established that a stagecoach would be leaving for London at 10.45 the following morning.

Next morning when the stagecoach arrived at 10.30, there were already four people aboard. William and Grace joined them, sat down and nodded their greetings. Outside, the four horses were being fed and given fresh water to drink. The driver and a colleague placed William and Grace's luggage on the roof and strapped it down securely.

At 10.45 the stagecoach departed the coaching inn. Grace and William smiled at each other. They were on their way.

Grace gazed out of the window at the passing fields. It was a cool, dry, spring day and some trees were already displaying their new green leaves.

Grace's heart was now racing. Was it nerves or excitement? Either way, she'd soon be seeing the Silverwood House estate for the first time. Her new home!

CHAPTER 29

The four fellow passengers were friendly and chatted with both William and Grace. At Bath, however, they said their goodbyes and departed. During the break, to change the team of horses, two new passengers climbed aboard. A few minutes later the stagecoach was back on its way.

Grace was fascinated to see quaint villages, forests and lush green fields. Something she'd certainly missed whilst sailing the high seas. The two new passengers were less interested in conversation, so this gave Grace more time to watch the passing countryside. William, meanwhile, had dropped off to sleep and was resting his head on Grace's shoulder.

As the coach approached the outskirts of Marlborough, the driver pulled on the reins to slow down the horses. One of the wheels hit a large bump in the track. Immediately, William woke up. He looked out of the windows and asked, "Do you know where we are?"

Grace hadn't a clue, but the man sitting opposite said, "Just coming in to Marlborough. Next stop after that will be Newbury."

William nodded and rubbed his eyes. "Thank you," he replied. He turned to Grace. "Not far to go now."

Grace smiled, but was still feeling anxious. She was wondering about William's home, his mother, the estate and his father… all a new experience! Would she fit in, be welcomed or would William be challenged and asked, "What do you think you are doing!?"

At Newbury their coach stopped at another coaching inn. William climbed down and helped Grace to the ground. Whilst their luggage was being unfastened from the roof, William hired another carriage and informed the driver he wanted to go to the Silverwood House estate, near the village of Kingsclere. The driver doffed his cap and opened his carriage doors. Both Grace and William climbed in. Their luggage, now removed from the stagecoach, was transferred and secured onto the platform behind the driver's seat. He sat down and called on his horse to move on.

It was early evening when the carriage turned off a narrow country lane and entered the Silverwood House estate. After passing a red-brick gatehouse and a pair of black-painted ornate iron gates, Grace could now make out the silhouette of the large house. Three storeys high, across six bays of red brick, with ornate limestone dressings, the building looked amazingly impressive to Grace. She took a deep breath and continued to watch anxiously.

As the carriage approached a split in the gravel driveway, William leaned forward and called to the driver. "Turn right here, driver. We're not going to the big house."

"Reet ye are, sir," replied the driver and he guided the horse to follow the right-hand track.

William leaned towards Grace and said, "I live in the Dower House. It used to be my grandmother's home, on my father's side. The 'dowager', that's what my sister and I used to call her. She died about three years ago, that's when I moved in. It's just me and Jenkins."

"Who's Jenkins?" asked Grace, somewhat surprised that another person lived with William.

"Jenkins!? Well Jenkins is… er, Jenkins!

"That's no answer."

"Okay. Well, Jenkins looks after the Dower House. Been there forever. He must be 70, maybe older! Looked after my grandmother after my grandfather died. He basically runs the place. An absolute godsend. I leave everything to him."

"He lives in the Dower House?"

"Oh, gosh, yes. He's got his own area. I've never been in that part of the house. Look!"

William pointed across the sweeping parkland to a large building hoving into view. It was still partially hidden behind a copse of tall trees.

Grace's eyes followed to where William was pointing. Through the fading light she could just see a silhouette of a building. It looked similar in design to the main house, but slightly smaller.

"It looks really nice. You must love living there."

"Yes. It's very quiet… and large. At least it is for me on my own. You'll be able to put your feminine touch on it. A woman hasn't lived in the Dower House since Grandmother died, so a lot of the rooms are unused… and very dated. I really only use my bedroom and the kitchen."

"Didn't Elizabeth live there at all?"

"Good lord, no. She was only interested in the main house. Insisted on living with her parents until we were married."

Grace nodded, but her attention was focused solely on her new home!

Fiona, still based in Charles Town, was becoming more adventurous. She'd been shopping for new clothes and had made a new friend called Jean.

She'd first met Jean whilst they were both walking in a nearby park. Jean had been carrying a baby in a sling when two loose dogs began to annoy her. The dogs kept barking and jumping up. Fiona had been walking just a few paces behind and had rushed forwards to shoo the animals away. Both Jean and her baby were distressed, so Fiona persuaded Jean to sit down on a large fallen branch. Once Fiona was able to calm Jean, Jean was able to calm her baby.

They both chatted for some time. Fiona was particularly pleased to be talking with somebody about her own age. Jean explained that she didn't really know anybody in Charles Town. She and her husband, Jeremy, had been living here for only a handful of weeks. They'd moved to Charles Town, because Jeremy was working as an assistant to the new Provisional Royal Governor, Francis Nicholson, who had been appointed by King George. They should only be living here for about six months. At least, that's what Jeremy had been told.

Fiona told Jean about her 'new' life and explained she, too, was only living temporarily in Charles Town. She was waiting for her husband-to-be to leave his work in the Caribbean. They would then be moving on to somewhere new.

The two ladies agreed to meet up each day. Both enjoyed each other's company and Fiona liked Jean's daughter, Margaret.

Margaret reminded Fiona of what she'd lost in the Spanish Town prison. If she'd lived a life in 'more normal circumstances' her daughter would now be with her and her present life would have been so different.

When the weather was wet, Fiona and Jean would usually meet in the newly established Coffee House, on Broad Street. Despite its name, tea was still the most popular drink sold in the Coffee House. This establishment had become the main place for people to gather. Here they would meet to learn and discuss the news of the day, or just catch up with friends and discuss matters of mutual interest or concern. The ladies usually planned to meet at about eleven o'clock and stay for around two hours.

Today was a wet day and, when they met in the Coffee House, Fiona told Jean that, according to her calendar, it was tomorrow that she was due to rejoin her husband-to-be. She told Jean she was excited, but also anxious. She hadn't heard from Ben for quite some time and just hoped he'd remembered the date… and still had the same feelings for her!

Jean tried to uplift Fiona's mood by saying she and Jeremy sometimes had to have time away from each other. It just meant their time together was all that more special when he returned.

Fiona smiled and told Jean she wanted to carry on with their meetings, at least until one of them moved away from Charles Town.

Jean also wanted their meetings to continue, so she gave her friend an affectionate hug and said she hoped everything worked out fine tomorrow.

CHAPTER 30

Grace was staring at the red-brick building as the horse-drawn carriage pulled up outside the main entrance to the Dower House. William opened the carriage door and climbed down. He then turned and helped Grace do the same.

The main door was open, and, in the candlelight, Grace saw the silhouette of an old man in the doorway. He appeared to be dressed in a black butler's suit. Her nerves started to tingle.

The driver unloaded the luggage and placed it by the main door. William gave him some coins and he was quickly on his way.

"Good evening, Master William," said the old man. He glanced at Grace and then back to William. "Pleased to see you have returned safe and sound, sir."

"Thank you, Jenkins. Good to see you again," replied William. "I want you to meet my wife-to-be, Grace."

Grace looked at William with a surprised look on her face. Wife-to-be!

"Indeed, sir! Welcome to the Dower House and the Silverwood House estate, Miss Grace." He gave her a welcoming smile.

Grace gave Jenkins a friendly smile. "Thank you." She decided she liked this old gentleman.

William picked up two of the bags. "Let me get all this luggage into the hallway and then you can tell me what's been happening."

Jenkins held the door open. Grace picked up some of the smaller bags and placed them in the hall. William then collected the rest of the luggage.

Grace and William stood in the middle of the hall and waited whilst Jenkins closed the door. Grace looked around her new surroundings. Even by candlelight she thought it a wonderful room. Definitely dated decorations, but, a warm entrance, nevertheless… and a lovely rich plaster ceiling.

William, Grace and Jenkins then carried all their luggage upstairs to their bedrooms. Grace was shown to a lovely spacious room. The walls were covered with wallpaper depicting various tropical birds. It had a large double bed, its own bathroom, an open fireplace, two large wardrobes and an oak writing desk. All in all, thought Grace, a luxurious, charming and cosy room. She could get used to all this!

Once Jenkins had disappeared, William asked Grace, "What do you think?"

"It's lovely… and so grand. The wallpaper reminds me of the Caribbean."

"It used to be my grandmother's room. My room is further down the corridor."

"Where are Jenkins's rooms?"

"Oh he's not near us at all. He's on the ground floor, on the right as we came through the front door."

Grace walked over to William and gave him a big kiss. "This is so wonderful, William. Thank you."

William smiled and whispered, "For appearance's sake, it's better for you to have your own room. Mother will definitely quiz Jenkins."

Grace smiled. "You paint a picture of your mother as being some sort of ogre or dragon!"

William laughed. "Oh, she's not that bad, but she does have her own ideas and opinions of what's right and proper. Look, let me leave you to settle in and I'll pop downstairs and see what's for supper."

"Who does the cooking?"

"Mrs Bakewell usually pops over from the main house when I'm staying here and not eating with my parents. She normally assists the cook over there."

"She knew you were returning today?"

"Oh, yes. Jenkins would have given her the message. He knew my sailing dates and usually eats in the main house with the staff. Mrs Bakewell knows I've not got a great appetite so tends to cook simpler things for me. She knows the sort of food I like."

"I've got a lot to learn."

"After a week or so you'll soon get to know all the ropes. I'll see you in a bit."

William gave Grace a kiss on the cheek and left the room. Grace sat down on her new bed. Mmm, she thought. Know all the ropes! If William only knew where I'd first heard that expression!

Fiona was up early, she'd hardly slept during the night. She'd been thinking and worrying about Bluey. Would he turn up? What if he didn't? What would she do then? Her imagination had been running wild.

By 10.00am she was walking along the south side of Cumberland Street, heading towards the harbour. She was just passing the Powder Magazine building. It had been built even before Charles Town was named and had been used for storing gunpowder for many years.

However, it was not the gunpowder store Fiona wanted, it was the tavern, located just two properties further along on the same street. This was where Bluey had suggested they meet. It was the only building he could remember from his last visit to Charles Town, many years before.

When Fiona arrived, she looked through one of the windows, but there were only two men chatting and drinking. Neither were Bluey. She turned around and looked up and down the street. Except for an approaching horse-drawn cart, everything was peaceful and quiet. She watched as the cart stopped outside the gunpowder store. The driver jumped down, tied his horse to a post and entered the building.

Fiona looked through the tavern's window again and back up and down the street. It was still all very quiet… and no sign of her Bluey. She was still anxious and worrying whether he would arrive.

Two minutes later the driver reappeared from inside the gunpowder store, accompanied by a colleague dressed in worn leather overalls. They were rolling a small wooden barrel towards the cart: a powder keg, Fiona assumed. Gently they lifted it onto a pile of sacks and the driver roped it securely. They then walked back inside the building. Fiona was well aware that the powder keg was the primary method for storing and transporting large quantities of gunpowder. Whilst on board Calico Jack's ship, she had been told that gunpowder explosions were unique in their suddenness and unpredictability. Therefore she and her fellow sailors were always careful and gentle when storing and handling this dangerous black powder.

A minute later another keg was rolled out, lifted onto the sacks and secured by more ropes. Finally happy that the kegs would not move, the driver untied the horse, climbed back aboard the cart and picked up the reins. A gentle flick and the horse started to slowly pull the carriage away.

"Hello, Anne," whispered a voice from behind. Turning around, somewhat startled, Fiona looked straight into the person's face. The man was well dressed in a dark-green, fine-woollen, knee-length jacket, with matching waistcoat and breeches. His face was clean shaven and on top of his head was a long white wig and a dark-green tricorn hat.

"Bluey!? Is it you? Really you!?" said Fiona, still startled. She hardly recognised him!

"Expecting another man are you?"

Fiona leaped forward, threw her arms around his shoulders and kissed him passionately on the lips. After releasing him she stood back, smiled and looked at him from head to foot. "The beard's gone, the long black hair too… and where are the blue-coloured clothes?"

"Captain Bluey and Ben Thomas… they're history."

"What do you mean?"

"Captain Bluey's dead. Buried at sea. Lost overboard in a storm. Quartermaster Richard Easter, remember him?" Fiona nodded. "Well he's now captain of the *Empress*. Nobody's looking for me."

Fiona smiled and kissed Bluey again. "So what do I call you?"

"What do you think of Ben Wardley?"

"Mmm, sounds like a nice solid name. However, you've forgotten my name's now Fiona. Fiona Kelly."

"Oh yes, sorry. I forgot," said Ben, thinking about the name. "Yes, I can live with that… Fiona."

They walked away from the tavern arm in arm.

"When did you get here?" asked Fiona.

"Yesterday, late afternoon. I left the *Empress* in Cuba, three weeks ago. Had to do some business in Havana and then travelled, as a passenger, on the *Albion*."

Fiona nodded.

"Where's your friend Mary?" asked Ben.

"Of course, you wouldn't know. Mary's now called Grace and she's gone back to England with her new man, William!"

"New man! Really. When did this all happen?"

"About three weeks ago. She met him two weeks earlier, here in Charles Town. He was staying on business. Apparently, his father owns two large estates, one here and one in England."

"So you've been on your own for the past three weeks?"

"Only partly, I made a nice friend, called Jean. She's from England too. I'll take you to meet her tomorrow. Anyway, never mind Jean, I want to hear all your news."

CHAPTER 31

The next morning, Grace and William were walking over towards the main Silverwood House. Grace was extremely nervous and squeezing his hand. "I'm not looking forward to meeting your mother."

William needed to update his father with all the business news from South Carolina and he thought it would be a good time to introduce Grace to his parents. "Don't worry, everything's going to be fine." He gave Grace's hand a squeeze back.

Grace wasn't so confident, but she knew it had to be done, some time.

As they got closer, Grace could see the house was even bigger than she'd believed when she'd first seen its silhouette from the carriage the previous evening.

They stepped off the gravel driveway and climbed up the stone steps towards the front door. Benson, the butler, was already holding the door open. "Good morning, Mr William."

"Good morning, Benson. Father at home?"

"Yes, sir. He and your mother are both in the living room."

"Thank you. Please meet Grace, she's staying at the Dower House with me."

"Good morning, Miss Grace," said Benson, giving Grace a smile and a slight bow.

Grace gave Benson a nervous smile, "Good morning, Benson."

William and Grace proceeded towards the living room. However, Grace slowed down and then stopped. She took a deep breath and looked around the impressive, ornate and admirably decorated hallway.

William arrived at the living room door, but waited for Grace to catch up. He then opened the door and confidently entered. Grace followed close behind. She could feel her hands shaking with nerves.

"Ah, the traveller returns," said William's father. He stood up from a sofa, and walked towards his son. He was slightly taller than William, a little overweight, but with a definite twinkle in his dark-green eyes. "And I see you brought a new, and a very attractive female, friend!"

Grace looked anxiously from William's father to his mother, still sitting on the sofa. Her heart was pounding. She gave the man a small nervous smile.

William shook hands with his father, although his father couldn't take his eyes off Grace. "Yes, Father, please meet Grace… we hope to get married!"

"Indeed! Well, well, well," said his father, who took hold of Grace's hand and gave it a light kiss.

William's mother now stood up and walked over to give her son a welcoming kiss on the cheek. She then looked Grace over, from head to toe. "Welcome to Silverwood House, my dear."

A bit formal and starchy, thought Grace. Not as warm as William's father. She could still feel every nerve in her body trembling. She smiled and said, "Thank you. It's so good to finally meet you both." She was desperate to make a positive first impression.

"Well, William, my boy, I'm sure you have lots of news for me. Let's go to the library and leave these two ladies to get acquainted with each other." At this William's father grasped his son's shoulder and walked him towards the open door where they disappeared into the corridor.

"Well, Grace, come and sit over here. There's obviously a lot for us to discuss!"

Grace gave her another nervous smile. She walked over, smoothed down her long dress and sat next to William's mother. She stared at her and hoped she'd open the conversation. Now's the time I really need to concentrate on what I say, she thought, and also make sure I pronounce **all** my words correctly!

William's mother introduced herself. She said her name was Catherine and her husband's name was Edward. She then gave Grace a short potted history of the family, but also spent some of the time probing Grace's background. Whilst Grace was still feeling nervous, she was becoming more confident as she explained her 'newly invented' background. Nevertheless, she deliberately avoided being too specific, just in case she mentioned a name Catherine might know.

When a maid knocked on the door and brought in a tray of tea, the two men followed closely behind.

"Some problems with the cotton again," said Edward to his wife. "Damn bugs eating it. Need to talk to Godfrey, see if he's got a solution."

Catherine sympathetically smiled at her husband. There always seems to be problems in South Carolina, she thought.

Edward and William sat down on two separate sofas.

The maid poured out four cups of tea and then left. William stood up and asked Grace whether she wanted milk with her tea. Grace nodded. He passed her a cup and then added a small amount of milk from a silver jug. He then did the same for his mother, whilst Edward helped himself.

"Have you two had a nice talk?" asked William, sitting down with his own cup.

"Yes," said Grace more confidently now. "We now know each other much better."

Edward raised his eyebrows and looked at Catherine in a querying manner. Catherine smiled back and said, "Grace is a very nice young lady."

William raised his eyebrows and smiled. Grace blushed a little, but deep down she was extremely pleased… having achieved her first ambition!

Grace and William were invited, and both agreed, to stay for lunch. Later, when they walked back towards the Dower House, William said, "I don't know what you said to Mother, but she's not usually as friendly as that."

If only he and his mother knew the truth! thought Grace. "Mmm, she's not really the dragon I originally thought she might be!"

William laughed. "Father really likes you too. I knew he would. He loves a pretty face."

Grace grabbed William's hand and placed it against her cheek. I guess I'll have to keep up this pretence for quite some time yet, she thought to herself.

The next day, in Charles Town, Fiona took Ben along to her meeting with Jean. The usual introductions were made but after 20 minutes Ben made his excuses and left. He announced he had some business to attend to.

Jean smiled and told Fiona that Ben seemed like a really nice man. Definitely one worth waiting for!

Fiona explained that during the previous evening, she and Ben had discussed their future. They'd agreed it was time to move on, but were still pondering whether to go to Boston or New York.

"When's this all going to happen?" asked Jean. She was disappointed with this news, but pleased for Fiona.

"That's partly what Ben's business is about. He's going down to the harbour to find out which ships are travelling north over the next few days."

"Oh, wow. As soon as that?"

"Yes, neither of us want to stay here permanently. It was always going to be a temporary situation. Other than my friendship with you, I've got nothing to stay in Charles Town for." Fiona had definitely made up her mind that Anne Cormac's past was going to remain there… in her past! She was not going to visit her old home… or speak with her family.

"I can't say I blame you. I'll be pleased when Jeremy and I move back to England."

"I'll let you know what Ben finds out!"

Baby Margaret started to stir. She had been sleeping quietly in Jean's sling for the last hour. "Thank you." Jean stood up. "I think this young lady needs a feed. I'll see you tomorrow."

Fiona watched as Jean carried her baby out of the Coffee House. She hoped that one day, she and Ben would have a similar bundle to carry.

Fiona went back to the inn and tried to tidy up her room. In particular, she wanted to give her and Ben some extra space. The previous evening, Ben had moved all his belongings into Fiona's room. It was a bit of a squeeze, but they both hoped it would only be for a few days.

Just as she was finishing, Ben walked in. He told Fiona about the list of ships he'd managed to find out about… and their destinations. "We can go to Boston in two days' time, New York in five or Liverpool in nine."

"I want to leave as soon as possible, Ben. Let's go to Boston. I know we don't know anything about it, but, at least, it will give us a start."

The following day, Fiona said her tearful goodbyes to Jean and her baby. She paid the rest of her room bill and packed her belongings. Ben had kept most of his own clothes packed in his case from when he'd arrived just three days earlier.

Ben's business dealings in Charles Town had included discussions with two money traders. He wanted to convert his larger items of gold and silver to more easily transportable valuables. He'd recovered his hoard of treasure from two different sites in the Bahamas, but the treasure he'd buried in Cuba he'd decided to leave hidden… for another day.

Money trading in the Thirteen Colonies was now following the principles of the new banking systems recently established throughout Europe. Legalised money traders were slowly emerging and were keen to offer their services. Gold and silver were universally accepted as the usual basis for currency. This 'money' was also being accepted by merchants for their commercial trading and dealings too. The agreed standard of value was that one ounce of gold was equivalent to 15 ounces of silver. Silver coins could then be divided into smaller value coins based on their weight. The use of scales, to weigh a coin's exact weight, and thus establish a coin's true value, had now become an everyday item of use.

In Charles Town, since there were no locally minted coins, foreign coins like the Spanish dollar were widely used. The Spanish dollar, also known as 'pieces of eight', became the first international currency because of its uniform weight of silver and milling characteristics. Some countries even countermarked the Spanish dollar so it could be used as their local currency. With this uniformity, it became much more common practice for gold and silver to be securely deposited, for a fee. Paper bills of exchange were then issued by the money trader to the value of gold and silver left on deposit. It was Ben's intention to eventually get his newly acquired bills of exchange switched for doubloons and silver dollars in Boston, when needed. Other smaller size items of gold, silver and jewels he decided to carry about his person.

CHAPTER 32

Fiona and Ben stood quietly together on the aft deck of the *Swallow* as it sailed noiselessly out of Charles Town harbour. Ben had his arm around Fiona's shoulder as he assumed she was experiencing mixed emotions. They silently watched as the town disappeared behind the large harbour entrance rocks. The ship had now entered the waters of the Atlantic Ocean… and their new adventures were about to begin.

Fiona felt a mixture of excitement and sadness. Excitement about her new future with Ben, and living in a new part of the world, well away from the Caribbean Sea, but, sadness because she hadn't made contact with her parents and brother. However, as she'd kept reminding herself, to have done anything different could have easily jeopardised everything she and Grace had achieved so far. Anne Cormac and Anne Bonny, she kept telling herself, were no more. That was the safest decision.

A gust of cold Atlantic breeze suddenly made both Ben and Fiona shiver. Ben suggested they go back to their cabin, but Fiona told him to go ahead. She wanted a few minutes to herself. Ben walked away and Fiona looked back towards the harbour entrance. Charles Town was now hidden from view and she doubted there would ever be a time when she would return. Tears began to well up as she gently waved her hand… and emotionally whispered to herself, "Goodbye."

Grace was sitting next to the new writing desk in her bedroom. She was making a list of things she wanted to achieve over the next few weeks… and months!

Although as a child she'd not had a proper opportunity to learn to read and write, Mary Read, with Anne Bonny's help, during the quiet times on the *William* and *Empress*, had been determined to improve her education. Anne had told her repeatedly that it was important for her to be able to read and write, at least to a basic level. Mary practised diligently and still struggled with some of her reading, but with writing, she'd become much more confident.

When she'd finished writing her list, Grace sat back and looked through the window across the parkland towards the impressive Silverwood House. Her new life still felt like a dream. She was definitely happy, but then her thinking moved to how much she was missing Fiona. There was so much she wanted to tell her. She desperately wanted to inform her that William had proposed marriage and she had accepted – without a second's hesitation! Both William's parents seemed pleased, although his sister, Rosie, was a little harder to judge. Rosie probably sees me as a threat, she thought, especially to her and her husband's ambitions to take over the running of the two estates. After all, William had previously declared he wasn't keen on inheriting either of them. That, for the time being, was a challenge Grace needed to consider... and was determined to change!

Suddenly, tears began to well up in her eyes. She quickly wiped them away with a white cotton handkerchief. She promised herself that, one day, she'd definitely catch up with Fiona, again. After all, we've still got all our treasure buried in New Providence.

One day we'll both **have** to return to the Caribbean!

William was in the library at Silverwood House. He and his father were discussing some of the production issues at the South Carolina estate. Cotton and rice always seemed to be a problem, whilst there was also the perceived need for more African slaves to work in the fields. William found it difficult to discuss slave matters. He didn't agree with the policy, but knew the estate would collapse without their use.

Once father and son had completed all their business discussions, Edward said he wanted William to consider another matter.

William waited anxiously and wondered what his father was about to say. He hoped it was nothing to do with Grace, because he'd already made his mind up. Grace was far more important to him than either of the two estates.

"We had a discussion some time ago, William," began Edward. "About the inheritance of the two estates."

William nodded.

"Well, your mother and I have been talking and we think you might want to reconsider your decision."

William wasn't sure why his father had raised this issue. As far as he was concerned, nothing had altered. "What's changed, Father?"

"You getting married to Grace. You'll soon start a family and then there'll be your own children to consider."

"Children!" exclaimed William. "I'm not even married yet!"

"Only six weeks, my boy. Does Grace know about your feelings towards the estates?"

"Yes. I told her some time ago."

"What did she say?"

"Well, nothing really. I wasn't asking her for her thoughts on the matter."

"I see. Well maybe you should mention it again. Your mother thinks she would make the ideal wife to help you."

"It's Mother again. She's always interfering! Has she been talking to Grace?"

"Not about this, I'm sure. All I'm saying, William, is for you to think about it. I'm sure you'll have fresh thoughts after you've discussed it thoroughly with Grace."

"But what about Rosie? She and Thomas are much keener than I am."

"Never mind your sister. It's your decision, not hers."

William leaned back in his chair. He was annoyed and frustrated. Why was Mother putting pressure on him again? Had she really not spoken with Grace?

After dinner, that same evening, William decided to raise the matter with Grace. They were sitting together in the dining room at the Dower House. Eating in the dining room was just one of Grace's recent changes. She didn't think it was dignified or proper for them to eat in the kitchen as William had previously done while living there on his own. William was quite happy and relaxed about the idea. He was similarly relaxed and in support of a number of the other changes to the Dower House Grace had proposed.

"Have you spoken with my mother recently?" asked William.

Grace put her small glass of port back on the table. "We speak most days, William. You know that."

"Yes, I know. What I really mean is, has she discussed the future of the two estates with you?"

Grace slowly shook her head sideways and then answered, "No, I don't think so. Not directly or recently. If she did mention it, it was of an inconsequential nature. Why do you ask?"

William thought for a moment and, nervously, said, "Earlier today Father and I were discussing the future of the two estates."

Grace nodded and waited for William to say more. She'd wondered when Edward was going to raise the matter again.

"He mentioned that he and Mother had been talking about them."

"What was he saying?"

"That I should reconsider my decision about the inheritance. Now I'm marrying you, things have changed."

"What do you think?"

"I don't think anything has changed. I told you previously about my feelings towards the estates and you seemed happy with that."

"You didn't ask me what I thought. But, to be fair, it was too early in our relationship for me to make any sensible comment."

"Well, I'm asking you now. You'll soon be my wife and I like to think I'm doing the right thing."

"Your parents see you, being the only son, as having a responsibility, not only to the properties, but also to the many people who rely on the estates for their livelihood."

"But, that wouldn't change if Rose and Thomas took over running the estates!"

"I think your mother would prefer the name Barrington in charge, not Arnold, Thomas's surname."

"Mother thinks you would be good at helping me run the businesses. Would you be happy with that?"

"Of course! I'd be happy with whatever you decide."

William sat quietly for a few moments. "This is not what I'd planned for you and me."

"I think you once told me that inheriting the estates was not what your father planned for either. Sometimes life gets in the way of people's plans."

William poured himself another glass of port. He offered Grace a top-up, but she declined.

"I suppose I'd better think about my father's suggestion."

"Why don't you sleep on it, William. We can always discuss the matter again. In the meantime, I can try to help you overcome your fears and uncertainties."

"That would be really useful, Grace. It's so wonderful to have you in my life. You really understand me."

Grace smiled. "That's why I love you, William… and why we're getting married."

"Do you really think we could run the estates together?"

"I do. But if it's the South Carolina estate you're worried about, maybe Rosie and Thomas could be responsible for it. I'm sure your mother is more concerned with the inheritance of the Silverwood House estate."

"That's a good point! I've tended to look at both together… as one! Most of the problems, and my concerns, are certainly with the South Carolina estate. Maybe I could cope with just Silverwood House."

Grace smiled again. She had sown the seeds and now waited for the shoots of success! "As, I say, William, sleep on it and we can discuss it again… in the morning."

CHAPTER 33

The *Swallow* continued sailing north alongside the east coast of the Thirteen Colonies. It would soon reach the colony of Rhode Island where it would turn to the east. Then, after passing the islands of Martha's Vineyard and Nantucket, it would return to a northerly direction before sailing by the peculiar hook-shaped sandy peninsula of Cape Cod.

For the last few minutes, Ben and Fiona had been listening to a fellow passenger named Richard Blyth. He'd informed them that he lived in Boston and had arrived from England two years ago. He'd said he and his business partner, Alexander, had purchased four fishing ships to catch the large numbers of codfish that populated this part of the Atlantic Ocean.

"Is that where Cape Cod gets its name?" Fiona asked.

"Yes," Richard explained. "In 1602, an English lawyer called Bartholomew Gosnold came up with the name. He called it Cape Cod because of the large volumes of codfish thriving in these cold waters. Incidentally, Gosnold also named most of the islands around here. Martha's Vineyard was named after his infant daughter, who unfortunately died whilst she was still quite young."

"Oh that's sad," said Fiona with genuine feeling. "But, what a nice thought."

Ben then asked Richard about Boston. He wanted to know what it was like to live there as neither he nor Fiona knew much about the town. They understood it was established by the British and was largely very religious... but nothing else.

Richard thought for a moment and then said, "Boston is one of the oldest towns in the Thirteen Colonies. It was founded on the Shawmut Peninsula in 1630 by Puritan settlers from Boston in England, hence the name. Since then more religious people have arrived from England, Ireland and other parts of Europe. Their main ambition was to achieve a happier life, away from the religious persecutions they'd been suffering in their home lands.

Since 1700, many poor German farmers have migrated to this area. They tend to keep themselves to themselves and mainly still speak German. Most attend Lutheran churches and retain many of their own traditions, customs and foods. They're also keen to own farms and land. Some of the more enterprising ones have mastered the English language, which is necessary in Boston. Most business dealings and the legal system both use English. It's very difficult to develop your business unless you can speak it. Strangely, the Germans tolerate slavery, although, to be fair, few are rich enough to even own one slave!"

Fiona's concentration began to drift once the subject of slaves was raised. She hated the cruel and harsh treatment of black people as slaves. She remembered her friend, Black Pete, who'd managed to escape slavery. It had cost him the loss of most of his right leg. She and Grace knew they wouldn't be 'free' now without his help and kindness.

"The population in the Boston area was once growing very fast," continued Richard, "and the town was expanding rapidly. That is, until a sequence of smallpox outbreaks occurred after 1636. Then, just a few years ago, a further severe smallpox epidemic occurred, killing around another 850 people. About half the population of ten thousand caught the disease. Economically, Boston still hasn't recovered from these disasters. Other towns and cities in the colonies are growing at a much faster rate."

"Have we arrived at the wrong time?" asked Ben. He was concerned about his and Fiona's prospects in Boston… and, more importantly, their health! Would they need to move straight on to England… or somewhere else?

"Could have been worse," responded Richard. "The smallpox problem has largely disappeared. A lot of the businesses are concentrated around the harbour. Boston's oceanfront location has made it a busy and lively port. That's why I'm still here. Boston is mainly engaged in shipping and fishing. There's also a big whaling business centred around Nantucket."

Ben looked at Fiona with a questioning look, then turned back to Richard and asked, "We have some money and are hoping to invest in a new venture. Do you have any ideas, or suggestions, where there might be an opportunity?"

Richard pondered for a moment. "It's hard to say. The Puritans are a very powerful group… very influential. They've imposed a number of moral and religious orders and restrictions on every facet of Boston life. However, there is one opportunity you may want to consider. As I've said, there's lots of activity around the port, but the businesses aren't often very organised, especially when it comes to buyers and sellers trading with each other. I've just been to Charles Town to set up some deals for our fish to be exported there. But it's all time consuming, face to face. It would be much better if we had a middleman, an agent, or a broker, who could bring all this together. I know the farmers would like certainty with the price for their crops."

Ben looked at Fiona and both raised their eyebrows. They could see some possibilities.

In England, Grace had been helping William identify the areas he was most uncomfortable with concerning the prospect of inheriting the two Barrington estates. Both eventually concluded the South Carolina estate issues were by far the biggest challenge. William said he was particularly worried because it was so far away. Not just geographically, but it needed reliable management and continuous local supervision. There were also the ongoing problems with the cotton crops, and the rice prices were so unpredictable. And, of course, there was the underlying moral issue of slaves.

Grace suggested the only way the South Carolina business could be a success was if the owner was permanently on site. William, however, was categorical, he was never going to move and live in South Carolina. Grace told him she didn't want to return there either… temporarily or permanently.

However, Grace had the perfect solution!

When it came to the Silverwood House estate, the picture was completely different. Grace pointed out that none of the South Carolina problems existed here. Yes, there were some general challenges and issues that needed to be resolved, but nothing as major as in South Carolina.

Gradually William was realising it was definitely possible for him, with Grace's help, to run the Silverwood House estate… but, only if the South Carolina property was not included in his responsibilities.

Grace was privately elated with William's reaction, but she still had one more important proposition for him. She suggested he put this compromise solution to his mother and father.

William was hesitant. He couldn't see his father agreeing to splitting up the estates. However, when Grace suggested they should be the only terms on which he would accept the inheritance, William began to wonder. After a few moments, he smiled at Grace, and told her he would speak to his parents later that week.

Two days later, William had the meeting with his mother and father. He presented his compromise solution and explained his reasons for this new decision. In conclusion, he stated that this proposition was the only basis on which he would be prepared to take on the inheritance of the Silverwood House estate.

Once William had finished, his mother asked, "Does Grace support you with this decision?"

"Yes. Most definitely. Some of it was her idea! We've discussed everything together and, like me, she definitely doesn't want to go back to South Carolina… under any circumstances. However, she has convinced me that I could run the Silverwood House estate. The responsibilities here are so different, and certainly much more manageable. She's also very supportive and is looking forward to helping me run the estate… when the time comes!"

"Well, my boy," responded Edward. "That's an interesting proposal. Your mother and I will need to discuss your offer very seriously and consider all the points you've made."

CHAPTER 34

When Ben and Fiona disembarked from the *Swallow* at Boston harbour, they hailed a horse-drawn carriage. Ben asked the driver to take them to a nice, comfortable inn. As the carriage set off they looked out of the windows. The architecture was different to the properties they'd seen in Charles Town and most of the people strolling along the sidewalks were more formally dressed.

Ben pointed out of Fiona's window. "I think those people, dressed like that, must be the Puritans."

Fiona nodded, but was not very impressed. She didn't like the dull brown clothes and white bonnets the women were wearing.

A few minutes later the carriage pulled up outside a three-storey building. It was mostly covered by clapboard and painted in a dark grey colour. Above the entrance door the sign, Spread Eagle, was gently swaying on a metal frame.

The driver opened the carriage door for his passengers to get out. He then removed the luggage from the carriage's roof.

Ben and Fiona walked through the doorway. The driver followed, carrying part of their belongings. He placed them by Fiona and returned for the remaining bags.

Fiona looked around her. The expansive reception area seemed reasonably modern and clean, although a little dull. Ben registered their names and paid the driver with two silver coins.

An hour later, Ben and Fiona had unpacked their bags and decided to go for a walk. They strolled along a number of streets, looking again at the buildings and studying the local people and shops. After about 20 minutes, Fiona said, "It's much colder here than in Charles Town."

"Mmm," replied Ben. "I guess we'll need to wear our frock coats more often here. I'll get us a carriage." Ben hailed a passing horse-drawn carriage and told the driver to take them anywhere that new houses were being built. The driver flicked his cap and asked them to climb aboard.

When Ben and Fiona sat down, Fiona asked, "Why are we going to see if there are any new houses being built?"

"Thought we ought to at least have a look. They may be in a nice area."

Fiona was surprised, as they'd previously agreed to rent for a while before they made any decisions or commitments.

After about five minutes, the carriage stopped and the driver shouted, "Here we are, sir."

Ben leaned out of the window. He saw several large, detached clapboard houses. Two were still being constructed. "Come on," said Ben. "Let's take a closer look."

They climbed out of the carriage. Ben asked the driver to wait and passed him a silver coin. The driver thanked him and decided to give his horse a drink of water.

Ben and Fiona walked along the street looking at the properties.

Fiona was cold, but even she could see this was a really nice area. Very quiet, peaceful and… "Look at that view!" she exclaimed. She was looking past the houses down the hillside towards the coast.

"That's amazing," said Ben, excitedly. "You can see islands and ships. That's south-west." He pointed. "You'll be able to see the sun setting over there. I think we ought to come back tomorrow and have a proper look. Right now it's much too cold and we'll need to wear warmer clothes."

Ben and Fiona were up early the next morning and ordered a carriage driver to take them back to where they'd been the previous afternoon. This time they were better prepared and both wore thick frock coats and hats. They walked along the road again and, after passing where the two houses were being built, they found a wilderness containing small shrubs, long grasses and weeds.

They both quietly stared at the view.

"Nice view, isn't it," came a voice from behind. Ben and Fiona turned and saw a man with a hammer in his hand.

"It certainly is. Do you own this land?" asked Ben.

"Me and my brother, Amos," said the man. He was about Ben's age. "Interested in buying some of it?"

"Could be, depends how much you want for it."

"Me brother and me, we're building those two houses for ourselves." The man pointed to the two partly built houses. "Come and have a chat. Get out of this cold wind."

Two hours later Ben and Fiona had bought a parcel of land. They'd also negotiated for the builder to erect their new house as well. They were happy with what the two brothers were building for themselves and suggested only minor changes to the style and architecture.

In the carriage back to the Spread Eagle, Fiona burst into a laugh. Ben was bemused and asked what she was laughing about.

"You know, Ben, we were once pirates! Pirates don't live on dry land. We fight, we kill, we accumulate wealth at other people's expense. We plunder ships, we steal gold doubloons, pieces of eight and jewellery. We get caught and we are hanged by the neck. What are we doing buying property in a godforsaken place like Boston!?"

Ben laughed. "What you forget is that we're intelligent. We know when it's time to quit. We know that once our luck runs out, we'll be dangling from a gibbet. Yes, we would have had our adventures, but at what price? Lives cut short, buried treasure lost and worthless to us. Now it's a new life, well away from the Caribbean. Buying this property is just the start. We need to establish our new, long-term life together. We can transfer our ill-gotten gains into 'legal' assets. We'll sell the house when we want to move on. Boston, I agree, is not what I prefer, but it's safe. Nobody knows us here, or our backgrounds. We need to blend in, but, at the same time, hide away. Give us time to think about the future. Maybe Richard's comments were astute. Maybe there's a business opportunity for us here after all!"

Fiona looked at Ben and smiled. This was not the old Captain Bluey. It was the educated schoolboy speaking!

In the library at Silverwood House, Edward and Catherine were discussing William's proposition. Edward wanted the two estates to remain together, but Catherine said her son's suggestion made more sense. She was certainly more concerned with the future of the English estate than some inherited property in the New World, which, she knew, was just one problem after another.

Also, she was determined William should inherit the Silverwood House estate.

"What do you suggest we do with the South Carolina estate, then?" asked Edward. He was sure Rosie and Thomas wouldn't be prepared to move out and live there. After all, neither of them had even visited it!

"Personally, I'd try and sell it. Put the money to better use here in England. The estate in South Carolina is just a liability, a headache. It doesn't really make us any money. It probably costs us!"

Edward considered Catherine's comments and then thought about his daughter. "But, what about Rosie and Thomas? They still think they're going to inherit both estates."

"I'm not sure about Thomas," said Catherine with doubtful feeling. "As you know, he tells a good story but it's always William who travels to South Carolina for you… and that's despite William's reluctance. Have you ever asked Thomas to go there instead?"

Edward walked across the room and glanced at the large bookshelf, not really looking at the books. "You have a point. I've mentioned it to Thomas several times, but he always seems to have a reason why he can't go."

"But William always goes for you."

"I know. I had thought he was keen on the place and enjoyed travelling."

"Now there's Grace to consider. She's made it clear she's not interested in the South Carolina estate."

"I know. She's bright. Much better than some of William's previous women."

Catherine laughed. "That wouldn't be too difficult!"

Edward walked back and stood by Catherine. She was sitting on a sofa close to the warming log fire. "So, you think I should sell it?"

Catherine looked up at her husband. She had a devious smile and said, "Yes. But not just yet. Offer it to Thomas and see what he says. I would be very interested in his response… and probable excuse!"

CHAPTER 35

Ben spent several days visiting a number of the businesses in the harbour area. He wanted to find out if there really was a demand for a middleman. Most of the owners of the fishing ships, and a few of the export merchants, said they would be interested in supporting him. But only if he managed to bring buyers and sellers closer together. They also suggested they would like him to find alternative markets for their goods.

After a week of research, Ben concluded many of the local businesses were prospering, despite their trading difficulties, and were keen to expand their customer base.

Gradually a familiar picture was emerging and, after the ninth day, Ben discussed his findings with Fiona. She was impressed and agreed there was definitely an opportunity.

Ben smiled. "With a bit of luck and a lot of hard work, I'll be able to establish a good, legitimate business... and for us, a new and more traditional lifestyle."

Eventually it was agreed. Fiona would supervise the building of their new home and Ben would concentrate on their new – and legitimate – business adventure!

"What," said Ben, finally, with a smile on his face, "could possibly go wrong!?"

Grace's and William's wedding went smoothly. Grace did everything asked of her – even to the extent of wearing the family's traditional wedding dress, last worn by Catherine for her wedding to Edward. The weather had been kind and although there was deliberately only a small gathering of wedding guests, Grace was happy... she had finally married William... and was now a member of the aristocracy!

The next step, Grace pondered and smiled, was to succeed in her plans to eliminate the threat posed by Rosie and Thomas!

Edward eventually agreed to Catherine's suggestion of offering only the South Carolina estate to Rosie and Thomas.

A meeting was duly held and Edward told them William had changed his mind about inheriting the Silverwood House estate. He suggested their future now hinged on whether they would agree to move and live on the South Carolina estate. If they agreed, he promised to arrange for the transfer to be made in six months' time.

At first, both Rosie and Thomas gave the impression they were shocked at William's change of heart, but then, surprisingly, Thomas said he now saw the benefit and the opportunities of moving to South Carolina. His only demand was that they would not go unless the estate and all its properties were transferred immediately to their ownership.

Edward was astounded at how easily this meeting was going. He thought Thomas would have declined outright. Nevertheless, he readily agreed with Thomas's suggested compromise.

Now everything seemed to be perfect for everyone... or so it appeared!

It was only three weeks after Grace and William's wedding when Thomas and Rosie had packed all their belongings and were about to head off for Bristol, to embark on a new life in South Carolina. Rosie was still not totally convinced, but, as Thomas had been so keen, she went along with the idea. He promised that if they gave the opportunity a chance, for maybe one or two years, then if either of them didn't like it, they would sell the estate and return to England.

When the two carriages were ready to leave the Silverwood House estate, carrying Rosie, Thomas and all their belongings, the rest of the family, and some of the servants, were present to wave them away.

As the front carriage, carrying Rosie and Thomas, passed the waving group, it was Thomas who had a special scowl for Grace. Grace responded with one of her knowing smiles.

Nobody was aware of the earlier conversation between Grace and Thomas! This had occurred after Grace was supposedly looking for William, and had heard noises coming from the hay barn. On investigation, Grace had spotted Thomas with Maisie, one of the Silverwood House servants, enjoying sex on one of the hay carts. Grace made sure Thomas was aware of her presence, before she quietly and calmly walked away.

It was two days later when Thomas had spotted Grace walking alone between Silverwood House and the Dower House. He quickly ran over and started to plead with Grace not to tell his wife about what she had seen in the hay barn.

Grace stopped walking and smiled at Thomas. She told him she had no intention of telling anybody.

"Thank you, Grace. It was a mistake. I'm so pleased you understand."

"I understand completely, Thomas. If Rosie found out about your... er, indiscretion, should we say... well, your marriage would certainly be destroyed. You'd be thrown out on your ear by Edward and have to fend for yourself."

Thomas took a deep breath, closed his eyes and smiled at Grace. "Thank you," he said finally.

However, Grace wasn't finished. This was the opportunity she'd deliberately set up. "In return, Thomas, you can do me a favour."

"Anything, Grace. Anything."

Grace smiled again and said, "Sometime in the next few days Edward is going to offer you the chance to inherit the estate in South Carolina. This will mean you and Rosie leaving England to set up a new life... owning and running that estate."

"I don't want to go to the Thirteen Colonies. That's definitely not in our plans... and I know Rosie doesn't want to go there either."

"In that case I probably need to have a chat with Rosie." Grace started to walk away.

"Just a minute," pleaded Thomas. He was starting to panic. "You said you wouldn't speak to her."

Grace stopped walking and looked back at Thomas. "And I won't if you and her relocate to South Carolina. If you don't leave, then I'll make it my business to make sure you're both thrown off this property for good."

"You can't do that!" Thomas was fuming. His face was red and he was perspiring.

"Try me!" Grace's smile had now morphed into an angry stare. The last time Grace had the same sort of glare was in battle on Captain Bluey's ship.

Thomas was panicking and frightened. He knew he was in a difficult position. "But William's not interested in inheriting either of the estates. He said so… ages ago. Rosie and I are going to inherit… both estates. We plan to sell the South Carolina estate… certainly not relocate there!"

"Not any longer. William and I are going to inherit the Silverwood House estate. You and Rosie will have the South Carolina estate… all to yourselves."

"Anyway, that's not going to happen for ages. Not until Edward and Catherine die."

Grace's face had changed to a gentle smile. "Tell Edward you'll only take over in South Carolina if he agrees to an immediate transfer."

Thomas pondered this suggestion. "He's not going to do that… surely."

"He will. You need to speak to Rosie and tell her your new plans… before Edward does! You need to convince Rosie this is the best opportunity you and her will ever have… because, believe me… it is!"

"There's no other option?" Thomas was pleading but becoming resigned to the situation.

"Oh yes! I can have a nice chat with Rosie about your activities in the hay barn!"

Two days' after Thomas and Rosie had left for the Thirteen Colonies, William and Grace were walking back towards the Dower House. William said, "It's all a bit strange, Grace. I know for certain that neither Rosie nor Thomas were keen on the South Carolina estate. Rosie told me ages ago that when they inherited the two estates they would sell the South Carolina estate and give me some of the proceeds. I know Thomas was reluctant to even visit the place. That's why I always went for Father instead."

Grace put her hand around her husband's arm and squeezed it gently. "People change. With you agreeing to inherit the

Silverwood House estate, maybe they thought this was the next best option."

William was quiet for a moment, but then said, "I'm going to miss Rosie. We've always been close."

"Well, you've got me now, William."

William stopped walking and looked at Grace. He smiled and leaned down to give her a kiss. "Yes. Yes I have… and that's just wonderful!"

It was a day later when Grace called in at Silverwood House and spoke to Benson. She told him she wanted to speak to Maisie Tucker at the Dower House. Benson was a little surprised but said he would send her over immediately.

Ten minutes later, Grace was back in the Dower House and standing by the window in the sitting room. She was looking across towards Silverwood House and waiting for Maisie Tucker to appear. Five minutes later, Maisie came strolling across the pathway.

Grace had specially selected Maisie for her task. Young, pretty and voluptuous, she knew Thomas wouldn't be able to decline Maisie's invitation… and he hadn't! The time and date had been arranged and Maisie had passed on all the details to Grace.

Grace knew very well that men could be stupid and serious fools, when it came to easy sexual opportunities. Even more so, when an extremely attractive female like Maisie Tucker was involved.

Grace walked into the hallway and picked up a small velvet bag, then sauntered out to greet Maisie. They walked together across the grass and into the privacy of the garden behind the Dower House. Once happy they were alone, and couldn't be seen or overheard, Grace handed Maisie the velvet bag and gave her a smile.

Maisie smiled back and opened the bag. When she looked inside, her eyes lit up and she gave a short shriek. She picked out the four ruby stones Grace had promised her… five weeks ago!

CHAPTER 36

Two years later the lives of the two former lady pirates had changed considerably. They were now both absorbed in their new roles of being mothers and helping to run the family businesses.

Fiona was caring for her and Ben's 12-month-old son, Daniel, who was growing up fast, especially now he was toddling. Their newly built house in Boston had been completed six months ago and it had been Fiona's task to furnish and create their new home.

Ben, however, was spending more and more time at sea, travelling to England and mainland Europe, establishing trading connections and finding new markets for his merchant customers. The business was growing, but costs were still too high compared to income.

Fiona could see some of these issues. After being educated by Ben about the rules and systems of book-keeping, she was now handling the brokerage's paperwork and responsible for invoicing and collecting outstanding monies. As a result, she was more and more worried about the spiralling costs and the amount of time Ben was spending away from home.

She'd previously mentioned her concerns to Ben, but, as always, he took the optimistic view and told her that costs were always higher at the start of a business. He'd continued by saying they were still well protected by his 'savings' from his piracy days. Fiona, however, was not convinced and wondered if it was time to recover her share of the treasure from the Bahamas. She still had some of her share of Calico Jack's gold and silver that she and Grace had retrieved from Hog Island, but wondered how long that was going to last!

In England, Grace was not only attending to the needs of her ten-month-old son, Oliver, but was now solely responsible for running the Dower House. This was because of the recent sad death of Jenkins. In addition, she was purposely involved, and exacting more influence, in the day-to-day decisions being made on the Silverwood House estate. Indeed, due to Edward's serious illness, which had left him bed-ridden for the last two months, Grace and William had suddenly found themselves more directly responsible for the daily running of all the estate's business. This, despite the employment of the estate manager, Henry Commings, was still a big worry to William. Grace, however, just saw it as another opportunity, another timely step towards achieving her long-term ambition.

Nevertheless, even Grace was realising that to be able to spend more time with William, helping him to run the estate, she needed help to look after their demanding son. After discussing the situation with William, it was agreed that Grace and Catherine would interview some of the young women in the nearby village. Four girls were subsequently interviewed and finally, May, at 17 years of age, was seen by both women as the best and most sensible applicant. She was also willing to work flexible hours when necessary.

May and Oliver very quickly established a happy and contented relationship. As a result Grace decided to make the bedroom next to Oliver's room available for May. This would be used when May was required to stay overnight. Grace anticipated that these nights would probably coincide with the busy business days, such as market day or the build up to quarter days. May looked forward to these 'stop-over' nights, because in her parent's home she still had to share a bed with her two younger sisters.

As Grace became more and more directly involved with the estate business, it was decided to offer May full-time residence at the Dower House. May was overjoyed. Not only did she thoroughly enjoy looking after Oliver, but she could now visualise herself enjoying a more independent life… and a more opulent lifestyle!

During one of her now rare quiet afternoons, Grace decided to go for a walk in the grounds of the estate. There was a cooling westerly breeze and wispy white clouds were trailing across an otherwise clear blue sky. It was one of her favourite types of days. It also reminded her of her childhood, growing up in the countryside.

Back then she would secretly watch the wild birds and animals and enjoy the long summer days, the scent of wild flowers and the wonderful fresh air. Playing mostly on her own and usually dressed in her boy's clothes, she invented her own games. She particularly enjoyed counting and mentally recording all the different varieties of wild birds and their eggs she'd seen. Occasionally she was even allowed to ride one of the nearby farmer's old horses. She didn't know the horse's name, but she decided to call him Toby.

How interesting and wonderful, she thought, that life had now turned a full circle.

Wandering and enjoying the freedom of the open meadow, she knew this was her personal quality time. A rare opportunity to savour the peace and quiet. The best time to plan and think. Not only to reminisce about the few good times during her childhood, but also to ponder on possible solutions to issues that needed her attention on the estate. But, mostly, it was a time to think more about her plans and ambitions for herself and her son. Their two futures living on the Silverwood House estate.

Grace strode out across the large open grassland following one of the well-worn estate paths. Wilson, the head gamekeeper, had informed her that a few of the red and roe hinds had already produced their fawns. Grace was craving to see these young deer, especially as Wilson had told her some would be only a few days old.

Passing by a number of grazing sheep, she could see the extensive Kingston Wood in the distance. She knew the newborn fawns would be hiding in the long grass close to the wood. Nevertheless, she was hopeful she'd still be able to see at least one or two reasonably close too. Wilson had also suggested she should walk, as riding a horse could easily spook the herd.

Grace was temporarily distracted by a 'keey ya' call from somewhere up in the sky. Recalling the distinctive cry of a buzzard, she stopped walking and looked up. Placing her right hand just above her eyes, she instantly spotted the brown and white bird circling in the now clear blue sky. She watched quietly as the graceful bird appeared to be just floating in the air, its large wings stretched to their full span.

The buzzard was surveying the pasture below, looking for any sign of movement in the long grass. Suddenly the bird folded its wings and dived, landing no more than 20 yards ahead of Grace. It grabbed its prey and started to flap its brown wings, flying off in the direction of a large oak tree. Grace was engrossed watching the incident, knowing the captured rodent wouldn't have stood much of a chance against the buzzard's long and extremely sharp talons. The bird reminded her of some of her sword fighting days, where her opponents would have faced a similarly grue-some death. Only back then it was Mary Read, the lady pirate, whose sword was as swift and honed as any buzzard's razor-sharp talons. She smiled at the thought of her own well-earned prizes. However tasty the buzzard's meal was going to be, it wouldn't be comparable to her acquired treasure of gold, silver and jewels.

Grace began walking forward again, but thoughts of sword fighting were forcing her to reflect on some of her violent brawls and battles, both as a pirate and as a soldier. Yes, as a soldier in the army, where killing the enemy eased her feelings of hopeless-ness and despair. But then Tommy came into her life. He'd come to her rescue and the pains melted away. Until Tommy died, so unexpectedly, so young. Stolen from her life like everything else that had been either temporarily good or wonderful. Just short periods of happiness compared to the longer periods when the pain and anger returned. Too often she had felt cheated, bitter and miserable. Now with William, Oliver and the Silverwood House estate, her world had changed for the better. Finally happy, content and feeling a warming glow inside. No more anger, no more despair. She was determined nothing would ever happen that would bring back those dark, depressing and desperate times.

Grace continued towards the wood. In the distant field she could already see some of the deer. She'd have loved to share this wonderful moment with family or friends. Indeed, one friend she started to think about was Fiona. She wondered what had become of her. The last time they'd been together was hugging on the harbourside at Charles Town. Then it was their tearful waving goodbyes as she sailed away on the *Venturer*. She dearly hoped Fiona had now achieved her ambition of a new life with her Captain Bluey, living a happy 'normal' life. She remembered when Fiona told her all she wanted in the future was "a settled home, a husband and children… before it was all too late". She hoped her wishes had finally become a reality.

What would Fiona have thought if she knew Grace had already achieved these goals!? She smiled to herself and wondered if there would ever be an opportunity in the future, a chance, or a time when they would meet up again. She had so much good news to tell her dear friend… as well as her ambitions for the future!

Passing by a small collection of trees and bushes, Grace could see, about a hundred yards ahead, a herd of about 40 deer. She could easily identify the larger male stag with his new growing antlers still in velvet. She crept slowly and quietly, but knew the deer had already spotted her… and were wary. However, so far, they'd decided not to run away. She edged towards a cluster of trees and sat down on an old log. She could no longer see the deer, but, similarly, she hoped the deer could no longer detect her.

The cooling breeze was blowing from the animals' direction so she hoped they wouldn't pick up her scent. After a few moments she slowly stood up and peeked over a low-hanging branch. The deer were now eating the grass again and taking little notice of Grace's presence. Only the stag was still looking in her direction. Grace easily spotted five fawns close to their mothers and guessed they were probably just a few weeks old. One of the does wandered slowly towards the edge of the wood, just a few yards from where Grace was hiding. Here the grass was much longer. The doe stopped, looked around and then lowered her head into the grass. Five seconds later a very young fawn began to wobble as it tried to get up onto its feet. Eventually it staggered to the rear of its mother and hungrily fed on one of her teats. Grace could hardly breathe with excitement. After its feed the fawn dropped back into the long grass and disappeared from Grace's view. The mother bent her head back into the grass and, a few seconds later, slowly walked away to join the other nearby does.

Grace would have loved to share this lovely experience, but she knew William and his parents had seen it all before. He'd reminded her that these deer were not pets but part of the estate's supplies of venison!

After about ten minutes, Grace felt an ache in her back and decided to move. She'd been holding this same position for some time. Unfortunately, this brief rustle was enough to disturb some of the nearby deer and they, once again, stared in her direction. Time to go, she thought. She gave the herd one last look before turning and heading back along a different path.

Walking back towards the main house, Grace was thinking that next year, when she returned to see the young deer, she would bring Oliver. After all, the sooner he knew about the workings of the estate and his eventual responsibilities, the better.

CHAPTER 37

Fiona and Ben were eating dinner when Fiona asked a question she'd been churning over in her mind for some time. "When are you next going to England?"

"In about four weeks' time. Why?" replied Ben.

"I've been thinking about Grace and was wondering if I should go with you and visit her."

"You've not mentioned Grace for a long time. Why now?"

"It's been over three years since we last saw each other. I waved her away from Charles Town, just before you arrived. I'd like to tell her all our news and find out about her life with William and his family."

"Do you know where they live?"

"Grace gave me their address. Apparently, it's a large estate, somewhere in Berkshire. Do you know where Berkshire is?"

"Yes. It's to the west of London. I've never been there. However, I have some business in London, so we could go on to see Grace after that. But what about Daniel?"

"He'll go with us, of course. Grace will definitely want to see him. She doesn't even know of his existence. They may have children of their own by now."

"Okay. Let's make sure we collect all our outstanding accounts and we'll go together."

Fiona leaned over and gave Ben a kiss and an excited smile. "It's going to be wonderful, Ben. I can't wait to see her again. I've got such a lot to tell her."

In England, at the Silverwood House estate, Edward was not recovering from his illness, in fact he was deteriorating and losing weight. His doctor had tried removing some blood and diagnosed various herbal remedies, but nothing was working. William and Catherine began to fear the worst. Then one morning, at sunrise, when the young maid, Sarah, was delivering Edward's breakfast – plus his latest herbal concoction, she found him dead, lying in his bed. Sarah was shocked, but not surprised. She'd been told by Catherine that this could well happen… and very soon. Sarah calmly laid the food tray on the dressing table and went and knocked on Catherine's bedroom door. She announced tearfully, "I think the master's dead."

Catherine smiled sympathetically and they walked together along the landing to Edward's room. There Catherine could see Edward lying on his back, very still, quiet and not breathing. Sarah stood silently in the doorway, wiping her eyes.

"We need the doctor, Sarah. Will you take the tray back to the kitchen and tell Tom to fetch Doctor Brown? You'd better tell William as well."

"Yes, ma'am," said Sarah. She walked over to the dressing table, collected the tray and left the room.

Catherine sat on the side of the bed, looking down at her husband. She knew his death had been imminent, but it was still a shock and she felt so horribly sad. She held Edward's now cold hand and just stared at his face. His eyes were still wide open, staring at nothing, so she gently pulled down their lids. He looked asleep now. Nice memories started to flood into her mind and tears slowly trickled down her cheeks.

The rest of the morning was taken up with the doctor's visit and Catherine and William trying to console each other. Grace tried to be as helpful as possible, but she too was troubled and sad. She really liked Edward and knew he was fond of her as well.

Over the next week, the funeral was held and everyone on the Silverwood House estate were slowly accepting that they wouldn't be seeing the master again. William was particularly down and Grace took on the unenviable task of trying to help and console both him, and to a lesser extent, his mother. At the same time she was having to discuss the estate's needs with Henry Commings and Wilson. She was thankful that May was now living full time at the Dower House, taking care of Oliver.

About three weeks after Edward's death, life was slowly returning to some level of normality. Grace and William were spending more time at the main Silverwood House and having their dinner with Catherine. After each dinner they took the short walk back to the Dower House. By this time, May had usually put Oliver to bed, so the only time Grace and William would see him was briefly during breakfast.

Slowly Grace sowed the seeds with Catherine that it would be better for the running of the estate if she and William moved into the main house. However, it wasn't suggested that Catherine, in return, should move into the Dower House. That move, Grace decided, was not urgent, but would definitely have to happen reasonably soon.

It was a week later when Grace was working in the estate office, with Henry Commings and William, that she received a big surprise. Through the window, they all watched as a horse-drawn carriage approached along the driveway. When the coach stopped, at the front of the house, all three looked at each other in surprise. They were wondering who these people were as nobody was expecting visitors. They watched in silence as two adults alighted from the coach. A man and a woman, both well dressed, wearing smart and stylish clothes. Holding the woman's hand was a young boy.

Suddenly Grace gasped, stood up and ran out of the room. William and Henry stared at each other and wondered what was going on.

"I'd better follow her," announced William. "Looks like Grace may know these people."

Henry continued to watch events unfold through the window. He saw the man talking to the driver and then, suddenly, Grace ran across the gravel and gave the other woman a big hug. "Mmm," said Henry to himself. "I guess these two women do know each other after all!"

"Fiona!" yelled Grace, as she gave her friend a huge hug. After a few seconds, she released Fiona and stood back to look at her properly. "Wow! You're looking marvellous!"

"Hello, Grace. It's so wonderful to see you again. You're looking excellent yourself. I've got lots to tell you," replied Fiona, staring and smiling at Grace. They hugged again.

Finally Grace pulled out of the embrace and looked at the man standing and smiling next to them. Suddenly, she realised who he was. "Captain Bluey!" Grace exclaimed, and gave him a kiss on his cheek. She stepped back and looked at his clothes and clean-shaven face.

Ben looked around and then whispered, "It's Ben. Ben Wardley. I've changed my name… just like you."

"Sorry, er, Ben," whispered Grace in reply.

"Are you going to introduce me to your friends, Grace?" came William's voice as he strode towards them. However, William then recognised the woman, "Fiona! Well, well, well. So good to meet you again."

"So good to see you too, William. Let me introduce you to my husband, Ben."

The two men smiled and shook hands. "Good to meet you, Ben," said William.

"And you, William. Fiona's told me a lot about you."

"And who's this little man?" said Grace, squatting down to be nearer Daniel's level.

Daniel decided to be shy and hid behind his mother's long green skirt.

"This little rascal is Daniel," said Fiona proudly.

Grace tried to peek around the side of Fiona's skirt and said, "Hello Daniel." But this only meant he moved further behind his mother's skirt.

Grace stood up and looked at Fiona. "You both must stay… you've got to stay! I've got lots to tell you."

Fiona looked at Ben and he smiled back. Fiona then said, "That would be wonderful. Our ship sails to Boston in four days' time."

"Boston! Not Charles Town?"

"No," replied Fiona. She picked up Daniel, so Grace could get a closer look at him. "We've been in Boston for over two years."

"Is that all your luggage?" asked William, pointing to the bags on the back of the carriage.

"Yes," replied Ben. "Mostly Fiona and Daniel's. I tend to travel much lighter."

"Okay. Let's get it all inside the house."

The driver had been listening and immediately jumped down from his seat and scampered to the rear of the carriage.

As Grace led Fiona and Daniel across the driveway towards the front door, William and Ben took charge of the luggage, collecting it as the driver handed each bag down. Once all the bags were unloaded, Ben paid the driver the fare, plus an extra silver coin.

"Thank ye kindly, sir," said the driver. He climbed back up on the carriage, and drove away.

As William and Ben carried the bags towards Silverwood House's front door, Ben glanced at the impressive facade and thought, Not bad for a lady pirate!

Over the next two days Grace introduced Fiona to Catherine, Oliver and May. Daniel was also introduced to Oliver, who was excited to be playing with a new friend. With May supervising both boys, this gave the two mothers the ideal opportunity to update each other with all their news.

Ben and William got on well together. William explained the workings and challenges of the estate and Ben described his 'broker' business in Boston. The story he told William was that he'd decided to move on from working in his father's merchant business as he wanted his independence. No mention was made of his previous life as the captain of a pirate ship!

Ben and Fiona occupied Jenkins's former apartment in the Dower House. It had been refurbished and redecorated. An extra bed was moved into Oliver's room so Daniel could share with Oliver. May was able to sleep in her own room without any extra worry.

All dinners for the adults were taken in Silverwood House. It suited everybody, especially Catherine, who was enjoying all the extra attention and company.

On the third day of Ben and Fiona's visit, Grace suggested that she and Fiona go for a walk in the estate grounds. The weather was dry and warm, the previous day's hot sunshine had largely disappeared, the sun being hidden behind thick fluffy white clouds.

Once they were well away from any possibility of being overheard, Grace asked an important question, "Have you thought about our buried treasure?"

"Yes, I have. My share would come in very handy in Boston. Ben's business is doing well, but the expenses are still too high compared to our income. Ben's not worried, but I am. I've still got some of Jack's treasure, but it's not going to last us forever."

"You said Ben brought a lot of his treasure and money to Boston. Has that all gone?"

"No. But I'm not sure how much is left. As I say, Ben's not worried though."

"There's a lot on this estate that could be improved as well. It'd be less worrying if I knew my nest egg was closer to hand. Also I want Oliver, and any other children we may have, to go to a nice school. That all costs money too."

"Yes, but unfortunately our treasure's not just down the lane. It's thousands of miles away!"

"Any thoughts as to how we're going to get it!?"

Fiona stopped walking and looked around, checking nobody was close enough to hear. "I've been thinking about that. What do you think about this idea?"

Fiona explained her thoughts whilst Grace listened with a searching expression on her face. Once Fiona had finished, Grace thought quietly for a moment. "It could work. However, it's William I'd have to convince. I don't want him finding out about our pirate's treasure!"

CHAPTER 38

Two days after Fiona, Ben and Daniel had left the Silverwood House estate, Catherine arrived in the small formal garden at the rear of the main house. She was waiting for Grace. She'd made a decision and wanted to hear Grace's thoughts on the matter before she said anything to William.

Grace arrived on time and walked over to join her mother-in-law. The sun was warm and they sat on a wooden bench in a sheltered corner.

"Thank you for coming, Grace. I know you've got a lot of work on your hands," said Catherine.

Grace smiled. She wondered and waited. Catherine certainly looked very serious. What was she going to say?

"I've made a decision, Grace. I would like to take up residence in the Dower House and move out of Silverwood House. It's time for you and William to live here. It's all far too big for me on my own."

Grace was a little surprised, but quietly very pleased. "Are you sure? It's still your home. William and I would understand if you wanted to continue living here."

"No. Time moves on… and so must I. Silverwood House is a family home and it's time for a family to reside here again."

Grace smiled at Catherine again and gave her a gentle kiss on the cheek. "Thank you, Catherine. Have you mentioned this to William?"

"No. I wanted to tell you first. After all, you'll be the main overseer of the house. I'll leave it to you to tell William."

"When are you thinking of moving to the Dower House?"

"I want to have a look at the rooms first. I've not been in the building since Edward's mother died. I want to choose my bedroom and decide if anything needs changing or redecorating."

Grace nodded. "When do you want to have a look? Unfortunately, with Oliver there, not every room is always tidy."

Catherine laughed. "It's so nice to have a grandson I can see every day. A tidy home is not a cosy family home! Maybe I could visit at ten o'clock tomorrow morning."

Grace took a quick intake of breath. "Yes, that's fine," she said doubtfully. "I'll tell William this evening when he gets back from town. He was hoping to sell some sheep today."

"Of course. It's market day. I lose track nowadays, each day seems to be the same."

"You appeared to enjoy and get on well with my friends, Fiona and Ben."

"Yes, they're a very nice couple, and coming all the way from Boston to see you. They must be very special friends."

Grace wondered what Catherine would say if she told her the truth. "Yes, Fiona is a very special friend. She told me they might be moving to England soon. But it all depends on Ben's business. It would be wonderful if they lived much closer. Oliver and Daniel got on so well playing together."

Catherine smiled and got to her feet. "I've taken up quite enough of your time. I'll call at the Dower House at ten o'clock… tomorrow morning."

Grace stood up too. "I'll get May to tidy up a little. We don't want you falling over any of Oliver's toys!"

The two ladies smiled and then Catherine turned and started to walk away. Grace watched as she walked between the flower and vegetable beds before disappearing through a stone archway. Grace turned around and stared up at the red-brick facade of Silverwood House. Slowly a smile appeared on her face. Mmm, she thought, things are finally coming together!

When William arrived home, Grace was walking across the driveway towards the Dower House. She could tell William was in a good mood because he was smiling when he got down from his coach. He told her he and his two shepherds had sold all the sheep – and for a very good price!

"That's excellent news, William," said Grace, as they walked towards the Dower House. "Whilst you were away, Catherine told me she wants to move into the Dower House."

William suddenly stopped walking and looked at Grace. "Really!"

"Yes, she thinks it's time we moved into Silverwood House."

"I see. What did you say?"

"I told her I'd speak to you when you got back from the market. She thinks the house is too big for her on her own and it needs a family living there. Our family, William."

"I see. Do you want to live there?" asked William. He wasn't totally comfortable with the idea. He loved living in the Dower House.

"It's better that this all happens now. Catherine really wants to move out. She's coming to the Dower House tomorrow morning to decide on whether any of the existing decor needs to change."

"She's obviously made up her mind. I guess we don't really have much choice. I never thought I'd move into the main house. The original plan was for Rosie and Thomas to take over."

"Yes, well, that's all changed, William," said Grace, with a gentle smile on her face. "We're running the Silverwood House estate, not your sister and Thomas!"

Early the next morning, Grace and May had tidied up not only Oliver's room but also all the other rooms that were regularly used. Grace had told May what was going to happen. May was thrilled and couldn't wait to tell her family. She'd soon be living in the 'big house'!

At exactly ten o'clock, Catherine duly arrived. Grace had been watching her approach from the sitting room window.

When she heard Catherine climb the three steps to the front door, Grace took a deep breath and opened it. "Good morning, Catherine. Everything is ready for your inspection."

Catherine smiled and walked past Grace into the hallway. "You sound like a captain on a ship welcoming the admiral aboard!"

"Sorry," flustered Grace. "It's just that May and I, well, we've had a bit of a tidy up."

Catherine laughed. "In that case you'd better give me a tour. It's been so long since I last visited. I might get lost on my own!"

Grace smiled. "I told William last evening about your wishes. He was a little surprised, but is eager to support your decision."

"Excellent," responded Catherine. "I knew it would be better coming from you. William certainly listens to you."

Yes, he does, fortunately, thought Grace. "Where do you want to start?"

"Let's begin in the main reception rooms… and then work our way upstairs."

It was about two hours later when the two ladies arrived back in the hallway. After the tour of the house, Grace organised tea in the lounge. Catherine asked a number of questions, but was reserved with her reactions to the answers. Mostly nods of the head or just a "thank you".

Grace became a little worried and wondered what Catherine was actually thinking.

Finally at the point of departing, Catherine faced Grace in the hallway and said, "You have good taste, Grace. I like the redecorating you've had carried out. It all seems much fresher and less gloomy than when Edward's mother lived here. There's only one little bit I'll change. However, that won't stop me from moving in whenever it's convenient to you and William."

"Thank you, Catherine. Obviously I'll need to discuss it with William, but I'm certain he'll want to move just as quickly as you."

"Good. It will be nice to have a family living in Silverwood House again."

Grace looked at the floor and then tentatively said, "Yes, and the family will be a little larger soon too."

"What do you mean?" asked Catherine. "Are you expecting another child?"

Grace quietly smiled. "Please don't tell William. I'm going to tell him this evening."

"Well that's exciting news, Grace. Another reason for you and William to be moving to a much bigger property."

Yes, thought Grace. All very timely.

CHAPTER 39

On their ship travelling back to Boston, Ben and Fiona took the opportunity to discuss their future. Experiencing London and then the Silverwood House estate, Fiona was thrilled with her first ever trip to England. London was much more vibrant than Boston and she was excited at the possibility of moving there permanently.

Neither Ben nor Fiona were really happy, or felt settled, living in Boston. It had always been intended as a temporary stay, whilst they established a new 'normal life' and a legal business… well away from the Caribbean! Now was definitely the right time to be moving on.

Ben and Fiona were sitting in their cabin. Daniel was already fast asleep. "So, we're agreed," said Ben, looking directly at Fiona. "We're going to transfer my business base to London. Most of my contacts are there now anyway, so it makes sense. It's a much bigger market than Boston and our overheads will be lower. A lot less sailing for me as well."

"Yes," responded Fiona. She was feeling elated with the decision. "It's definitely the right time to be moving away from Boston. It's fulfilled its purpose and I won't be sorry to move. Boston, well, it's dull and too religious for me. The Puritans are too narrow-minded and they dominate everything that happens there."

"Okay. The first thing I need to do is to speak to Abraham, next door. He promised he'd be interested in buying our house if, and when, we eventually decided to move on. He knows all about the house, after all, it was him and his brother who built it!"

Fiona nodded. "Alternatively, we could always rent it out, but it would be difficult to manage from England."

"I agree. Abraham said he wanted to buy it, because he could rent it out himself. That's by far the best solution for us."

"But what happens if he doesn't offer a good price? We might be stuck with it."

"Abraham and his brother are fair people. I'm sure we'll be okay."

"I hope you're right." Fiona knew they would need to get a good price. Grace had told her that properties in London were very expensive!

Once Ben and Fiona had arrived home, Ben visited Abraham the very next morning. He explained that they wanted to sell their house as he, and Fiona, had decided it was time for them to move on. Although Abraham reaffirmed he was interested in buying the property, he told Ben that most of his capital was tied up in two new developments. He would have to discuss the matter with his brother.

Ben left Abraham's property a little disappointed and wondered if he should try to find a different buyer… but how would he go about doing that? When he told Fiona of his discussions with Abraham, she too wondered what they should do next.

"Did you manage to discuss a price?" asked Fiona.

"Yes. Abraham was quite happy to pay the price I suggested, but he needed to speak with his brother first."

"When are we going to know his answer?"

"He said he needed a few days."

"Alright. Should I start to pack a few of our belongings?"

Ben scratched his head. He had several opportunities already lined up in London that Fiona didn't know about. "Today's Tuesday. I'll give him till Friday. Maybe, if all goes well, we could start packing at the weekend. I'm just as keen to move as you."

On Friday, late afternoon, Fiona and Ben had a visit from Abraham. He announced he was bringing good news. "I've discussed the matter with my brother and we've both agreed that if you reduce your asking price by five percent then you've got a deal."

Ben and Fiona were anticipating such a move and had already agreed between themselves that they would be prepared to settle for their asking price less ten percent. So five percent was an excellent result.

Ben smiled and held out his hand. "Abraham, you have a deal."

Abraham smiled back and they shook hands. "That's good. Let's talk details."

Over the next hour, the three of them planned out the time-scales, the payment and what furniture and contents Ben and Fiona planned on leaving. As they agreed on each item, Fiona wrote them down to create a list that Ben and Abraham duly signed. This was their formal sale agreement. Finally, at the end of the meeting, Ben and Fiona shook Abraham's hand. It was all settled and agreed. Abraham promised the money in two weeks' time. At that point Ben and Fiona promised to vacate the house.

When Abraham finally left, Fiona and Ben gave each other a congratulatory hug. Ben said he would find out which ships were sailing to England, had availability and would be willing to transport the Wardley family to their new home.

It was two weeks and four days later when Ben, Fiona and Daniel boarded the merchant ship, *Pegasus*. As agreed with Abraham, the Wardley family duly vacated their house and temporarily moved into the Ship Inn, close to the harbour. That's where they had stayed for their last three nights of residence in Boston. Now they were waving Boston goodbye… for good! It had served its purpose, but now it was time to embark on a new life… and a new future living in England!

After unpacking their belongings in their cabin, Fiona and Ben stood together on the large aft deck. Ben held Daniel in his arms. It was a cold autumn day, but at least it was dry. They were all wrapped up in their frock coats and hats and watched as the town of Boston slowly disappeared from view. Neither of them spoke, but both were thinking the same thing. They were finally leaving their past behind and eagerly anticipating their new future in England!

CHAPTER 40

Over the previous four months a number of changes had happened at the Silverwood House estate. Catherine was now established in the Dower House where the decorators had been busy redecorating two rooms. Mrs Bakewell, the assistant cook at the main house, had also taken up permanent residence in the Dower House. Following the recent death of Mrs Bakewell's husband, Charlie, it was Catherine who suggested she move into the Dower House on a permanent basis. As well as being a competent cook, and especially since Edward had died, Mrs Bakewell had become a close friend of Catherine's and was now formally employed as a live-in 'lady's companion' as well.

Meanwhile, Grace, William, Oliver and May had all settled into the main house. Grace had immediately taken charge. She'd quickly changed three of the house personnel and personally supervised updating some of the main rooms. She continued to let William run the day-to-day business activities with the assistance of Henry Commings, the estate manager, and Wilson, the head gamekeeper. Nevertheless, she was kept updated with what was going on. Where she saw possible changes she made suggestions to William over dinner. William duly submitted these changes to Henry Commings the next day.

It was market day when William next met up with George Canning, his colleague from his travels to South Carolina. George's father had built up a large business in the European wine trade and, more recently, established business connections in the Thirteen Colonies for his Madeira wine. George was still undertaking a lot of travelling and negotiating contracts and deals.

The two men were sitting together in the King's Arms in the centre of Newbury. They had both completed their business dealings for the day and were now updating each other on recent events.

One recent development particularly interested William. George was explaining a new venture he wanted to tackle, and was giving William an early opportunity to invest. His proposition was for William to buy a share in a vineyard in Madeira. On his last visit to the island, as well as negotiating deals for his father, George had discovered that one of the better Madeira wine-producing companies was now for sale. He thought this was an excellent opportunity to establish a new business of his own and reduce his amount of personal travelling. He informed William he was looking for like-minded investors. He also mentioned it was his intention to move to Madeira permanently in order to manage the business.

After much discussion, William agreed the proposition was tempting, but the maximum he could invest, if he did so, was up to about ten percent of the vineyard's purchase price.

George had already achieved 85 percent commitment from other potential investors. However, he mentioned one complication; William shouldn't tell anybody about the deal because the company in Madeira had given George first option to buy and George was anxious not to alert potential competition. William agreed and said he would only mention it to Grace, nobody else.

George, however, told William not to even mention it to Grace!

On the coach ride back to Silverwood House estate, William stared out of the window. He was getting cold feet about the deal and wondered if he should be investing such a large amount of money away from the estate. Especially without getting Grace's, or indeed the estate's lawyer's, comments and opinion. That evening he decided he would tell Grace after all.

Over dinner, William explained his meeting with George and the details of the possible deal. Grace listened without interruption and when he'd finished she asked, "Have you actually committed this money, William?"

"Not formally, no. I've not signed any papers or shaken hands on the deal. I just told George, that, in principle, the deal sounded good and I would probably invest… but that I would also need some thinking time."

"I don't know anything about the Madeira wine trade. How much do you know?"

"Only what George has told me. His father makes a lot of money importing into Britain. He's trading to parts of Europe and the Thirteen Colonies as well."

"But you said this contract will just be with George. Why isn't his father involved?"

"George's father doesn't own any vineyards and George has always wanted to have a business of his own. He sees this as his first step. Do you think it would be a bad move?"

"I'm not sure, William. It's a lot of money which might be better used on this estate. But, of course, there's also some merit in spreading our risks."

"What do you think I should do?"

"I think we should sleep on it for tonight. Let's talk again in the morning."

William struggled to sleep that night. His mind continued to think about George's proposition. Although he hadn't previously been involved with George, business-wise, they had been good friends going all the way back to their school days. However, having hinted that he might invest in the scheme, William was concerned that if he backed out now he'd be letting his friend down. But Grace was right, would the money be better spent on the estate? Should he really mix friendship with business!? The estate did need the capital… and, after all, when the money was previously under his father's control, it was earmarked for the estate. He was fairly certain what his father would have said.

Grace too had a restless night. Partly she was uncomfortable with the baby now beginning to move about, and partly she was worried about William's possible new financial involvement with George. It sounded like an interesting investment, but Madeira was a long way away and what did George really know about managing a vineyard? At least if William's inheritance was invested solely in their estate then they'd have much better control of it.

Over breakfast the next morning, both William and Grace were still uncertain of the next move. William was annoyed with himself for telling Grace about the business proposition, especially in her current condition. The last thing he wanted was for her to have extra worries. But, at the same time, he knew Grace had a better head for business than he did, and he didn't want to throw away a large part of his inheritance.

Grace watched William as he ate his breakfast. She wasn't hungry herself and was still pondering on the dilemma. Maybe the investment was a good proposition, but, ideally, she wanted to be in control of their slowly dwindling capital. But how was she going to persuade William… without upsetting him?

Suddenly she felt the baby move and instinctively put her hand on her stomach.

William spotted Grace's movement. "Are you okay?"

Grace smiled back. "Yes… 'Little James', he's just wriggling about."

"Look, I've been thinking," responded William. "Now's not really the time to be giving you extra worries. I'll meet with George on market day, next week, and tell him the timing isn't right."

"Won't he be disappointed?" Grace was pleased with William's latest thinking.

"Yes, I'm sure he will… and I am too… a little, but, it's not the right time. My father wouldn't have considered it at all. He always said that all his time, money and effort, was for the benefit of the two estates. Mother, I'm sure, wouldn't be happy either."

Grace agreed. William was making a good decision, probably the right decision. She smiled at her husband and continued to stroke 'Little James'.

CHAPTER 41

The *Pegasus* entered the Thames estuary, heading towards the London docks. It was late morning and about an hour before high tide. There was a cold drizzle in the air, but the weather couldn't dampen Fiona and Ben's excitement. They'd already packed their four bags ready for disembarkment, and with Daniel wrapped up in Ben's arms, the three of them were watching the activity on the river from the ship's for'ard deck.

"I'm so happy, Ben," Fiona announced. "This is what I've been dreaming about since… well, a long time. I just know we've made the right decision and we're going to love living in England."

Ben smiled and looked at Fiona. He lowered his head and gave her a kiss. "I think you'll like London. It's inspiring and exhilarating… so different from Boston."

"I do hope so… but Boston was only ever a temporary stop. Now we can hold our heads up high… we're all legal and have a great opportunity. We've legitimate money from selling our house and you've got your lawful business here as well. No more hiding from the authorities."

"I've temporarily rented us a house in Cavendish Square. Lots of properties have recently been built in that area. People are moving there because the City and Westminster have become fully developed. Just give it a few months and I'm certain you'll get to know London properly. We can then decide where we'd like to live on a permanent basis."

"I like where Grace and William live… in the countryside. Maybe that's an option."

"Yes, I agree, but my work is still going to be mainly in and around the dockland area. It would mean a lot more travelling for me each day if we lived closer to Grace and William."

Fiona looked down at Daniel and smiled as he gave her a big yawn. Maybe when I've collected all my treasure from Hog Island, she thought, we can move to the countryside. We'd have enough money for Ben not to need to work!

The Wardley family stepped down from their carriage in Cavendish Square. Fiona looked around and noticed more new properties being erected in the distance. She looked at the recently completed house in front of her. It was a red-brick, four-storey, terraced townhouse, with ornate white-painted windows. Directly behind her she saw a circular area of land, mainly covered in grass, but with a few newly planted trees.

After the driver unloaded their bags, Ben paid their fare and waited anxiously for Fiona's reaction as she looked around. The carriage driver climbed back up to his driving position and cracked his whip. The horse moved forward, pulling the now empty carriage away.

"It's wonderful, Ben," said Fiona, looking up at the building and then down the street. "Nothing like I'd expected. Look at those windows, aren't they lovely?"

"We'll be the first people to live here. This street was completed three months ago. You wait here… I'll only be a few minutes. I've got to go to Number 4, to sign the papers and collect our keys."

"Okay," said Fiona, watching him stride along the pavement. She crouched down and spoke to Daniel, turning him so he was looking towards the house. "This is going to be your new home. It looks really big so I'm sure there'll be lots of rooms for you to play in and investigate." Daniel looked up at the building's facade. Fiona turned him around again so they were both facing the green open space. "Look at that lovely green park. You'll be able to play lots of games over there."

Daniel looked in the direction his mother was pointing. He nodded his head and smiled.

"Got the keys!" announced Ben, as he returned. He walked up the four steps and pushed one of the keys into the lock. Two turns and it was unlocked and he pushed open the door. "Come and have a look," he called. "I'll collect the bags."

Holding Daniel's hand, Fiona and Daniel made their way up the steps, passing through the doorway. Ahead was a narrow hall with wooden floors and a stairway straight ahead. She walked into the first room on the right.

"Everything okay?" shouted Ben, as he grabbed two of the four bags lying on the pavement. He placed them in the hall.

"Oh, Ben, it's wonderful."

Daniel escaped from his mother's grip and ran through to the next room.

"Glad you like it," Ben shouted from the hallway, before returning to collect the remaining two bags.

Fiona walked slowly into the middle of what was probably going to be the sitting room. It was already basically furnished, but still missing personal accessories. She looked around the room and was pleased the large bay window was letting in lots of light. The room definitely felt new, fresh and clean.

Ben placed the final two bags next to the others and closed the front door. He walked over to join Fiona.

"Oh, Ben, this is wonderful. I can't wait to see the rest of the house."

"Better than my cabin on the *Empress*?"

Fiona ignored the comment. The *Empress* was history. She looked at his smiling face, threw her arms around his neck and pulled his head down towards hers. She then gave him a heartfelt and lingering kiss.

As he'd promised to Grace, William met up with George on market day in Newbury. He was first to arrive in the King's Arms and purchased two flagons of beer. He walked to a table with two vacant chairs, placed the two flagons on the table, sat down and stared out of the window.

William was nervous and edgy. He knew he was going to be letting his friend down. How would George react? Would their friendship be over? He closed his eyes and tried to think of the right words to say.

Two minutes later George appeared, tapped William on his back and sat down. However, when he looked over at his friend, he was immediately concerned. William had an unhappy look on his face. "Wow, William, you look as though you're carrying the world on your shoulders. What's happened?"

William stared down at the top of his flagon of beer whilst he responded, "I'm sorry, George, but I'm not going to invest in your Madeira venture." He looked up and waited for George's disappointing response.

"That's okay," responded George, to William's surprise. "Since last week, I've found some more investors. Even my father wants a stake now."

"So, you're okay with my decision?" asked William, now slightly more relaxed.

"Yes, of course. Look, William, I've known you for years. After our conversation last week I was fairly sure you would come to this decision. Your world is with the Silverwood House estate. It always has been. I can understand that. As a good friend I thought I'd give you the chance to share in this opportunity. I've got more investors than I need, so someone else is going to be disappointed."

William took a deep breath of relief and picked up his flagon of beer. He downed a long draught and wiped his mouth on his coat's sleeve. He smiled at his friend and said, "I was worried I'd be letting you down, George. Stop you from finalising your investment."

"I wondered why you had such a sad expression. No, no problem at all. I'm sailing to Madeira in ten days' time… to complete the deal. I also want to see where I'll be living."

William took a long, relaxed sigh. "Well, I'm really pleased for you, George, I really am! I know you'll make a big success of this venture. Capital's tight for us at the moment, otherwise I'd definitely have invested with you. I know you'll not need it, but… the very best of luck!"

"Thank you, William. Thanks for your belief in me. I'll keep in touch and let you know how everything is progressing. I'm really excited, it's a great new challenge… something I've been looking forward to doing… for a long, long time."

William finished the rest of his beer and stood up. He patted George on his shoulder. "Drink up. Let me get you another beer. I want to toast your good health… and to your vineyard's success!"

CHAPTER 42

When William arrived home, he enthusiastically told Grace about his conversation with George. In response, Grace kissed him on the cheek. She was relieved. "So you weren't letting George down after all!"

"No. He says he's got more investors than he needs. Even his father, apparently, is going to invest."

Grace blew a sigh of relief. "Well, everything seems to have worked out fine."

"I know. I still think it might have been a good, long-term investment, but I realise now that our shorter-term needs are much greater at the moment."

Grace smiled. Yes, she thought, and Madeira was certainly never part of my long-term plans!

After a few seconds, William spoke again. "I nearly forgot. Whilst Wilson and I were at the market this morning, we discussed our venison with Charles Ferguson. He wants to take 50 of our deer… over the next six months. We've also got an increase on the price he paid last time. So that's going to pay for some of our bills."

Grace's expression suddenly changed to a more sorrowful one. She remembered back to the young fawns she'd seen hiding in the fields just a few weeks ago. She wondered if any of them would be part of the sale. Unconsciously she started to rub the bulge containing 'Little James'.

William could see what Grace was doing with her right hand. "Are you okay? In pain?" he asked.

"No. 'Little James', he's wriggling about again. Probably just keen and eager to see his new world."

"What if the baby's a girl? What should we call her?"

"Mmm, there's only a few weeks still to go. Maybe we'd better ask Oliver. After all, it was him who christened the baby 'James'. He definitely wants a baby brother!"

It was only three weeks later when Grace decided 'Little James' was on his way. Maisie had just entered the sitting room with a tray of tea. Immediately, Grace told Maisie to inform Catherine and ask Benson to get someone to fetch Mrs Bailey, the local woman who was usually called in for these events, urgently from the village. Grace sat back and started to take deep breaths.

Maisie placed the tea tray down onto the small table in front of Grace and rushed out of the room. She found Benson in the hallway and passed on Grace's message. She then told him she was going to the Dower House to tell 'madam'.

Ten minutes later, Catherine appeared and helped Grace to the nearby room where everything had been prepared for this moment. Grace lay on the temporary bed and Catherine mopped her brow with a damp cloth. Catherine noticed the contractions were occurring more frequently.

Twenty minutes later, Mrs Bailey appeared with her small leather bag.

William had been talking to Wilson when he was informed of the news. He arrived at the door and stared at all the activity. Catherine, however, quickly sent him away. "This is no time for a man to get in the way!" she shouted.

William looked across and gave Grace a smile, but Catherine pushed him into the hall and shut the door. William paced the floor and wondered what to do. Eventually he decided to go to the office. There he found Henry Commings writing a report.

"The baby's on its way," announced William. "Mother's just told me to go. Said I'd only be in the way."

"Come and sit down over here, sir," responded Henry as he stood to fetch another chair. "I'll get one of the servants to fetch you some tea, if you want."

William sat down on Henry's chair and stared out of the window. "Thanks, Henry, but I don't want any tea. Probably a whisky… but maybe it's a bit early."

"My wife, Jeannie, she's produced three lovely kids," said Henry, sitting down on the chair he'd just collected. "I got shooed off too when they were born. They told me I'd get under their feet! I asked them, 'Who do you think the baby's father is? It's me!' Didn't make any difference though. Still ordered me to leave!"

William looked away from staring through the window whilst Henry rambled on, but smiled once Henry had finished his story.

"What are you doing at the moment, Henry? Let's talk about business, it might take my mind off Grace and the baby."

For the next hour Henry explained what he was doing. William asked some questions, but his mind was only half concentrating. Finally, he decided to leave Henry in peace and wander outside to walk across the grounds. He needed some fresh air and time to think.

It was another two hours before he saw Maisie running across the field towards him. She was waving her hands in the air and shouting, "Sir, sir!"

William immediately changed direction towards her and walked much quicker. As they got closer, Maisie said, a little breathlessly. "Sir… sir… you've got a new baby… a baby boy, sir!"

William's eyes shot wide open. He had a huge smile on his face. He grabbed Maisie, and in the excitement gave her a hug and a big kiss on her cheek. Immediately regretting it, he quickly apologised.

"'Tis alright, sir," replied Maisie, smiling and a little embarrassed. "I know you're just a bit excited, sir. Special time 'tis."

"Yes, it is, Maisie. Thank you for bringing me the news. So, Oliver's got his young brother after all… he'll be pleased."

William and Maisie walked quickly back towards the house. William was desperate to see Grace… and his new son, 'Little James'.

William was finally allowed in the room to visit Grace and his new son. Grace was exhausted but very happy when she saw William arriving and carrying Oliver. Oliver just stared at his new brother and said, "Little James is really tiny."

Catherine, who was still sitting on a chair at the far side of the bed, smiled at her grandson's comment.

Grace was sitting up in her bed, holding her new baby. "You were about the same size when you were born," she told Oliver. Oliver just stared. Grace wondered what he was thinking.

Catherine stood up and walked around the bed towards William. She gave him a congratulatory kiss on the cheek and then took Oliver from his grasp. "Come on, young man, you must be hungry. It's nearly tea time."

Oliver smiled at his grandmother and was anxious to go.

"I'll call back later," said Catherine, and left the room. Oliver was asking her what they were going to have to eat.

William walked over and sat on the side of the bed. He peeked at his new son and then looked at Grace. "He's gorgeous. Are you okay?" he asked, with genuine feeling and concern.

Grace looked at her husband and smiled. "I'm happy. A little sore… and exhausted."

William gently leaned over and gave her a kiss. "They wouldn't let me in to see you. Mother said I'd only be in the way."

Grace laughed briefly and rested her hand on William's. "Can you put Little James in his cot, please?"

William stood up and walked over to pick up the wicker cot. He placed it on the table, next to the bed. He then carefully lifted the now sleeping baby from Grace's arms. He smiled and stared at him for a few seconds before gently placing him into the cot.

"Are we still going to call him James?" asked William, staring at his sleeping son.

"Oliver's decided that's what he's calling him, so maybe we should officially call him James."

"Sounds like a good idea."

"William?" said Grace with a tired-sounding voice. "I'd like to have some sleep now, please… if you don't mind?"

"No. No, of course. You must be totally exhausted. I'll call back later." William leaned over the bed and gave his wife another gentle kiss.

Grace smiled back and closed her eyes.

William looked at his son, one more time, before quietly leaving the room.

CHAPTER 43

Ben, Fiona and Daniel, had been living in their new house, in Cavendish Square, for just over one month. Fiona was loving the new selection of shops and buying extra items for the house. Ben, too, was enjoying their new home, although the distance to his business each day was longer than he'd expected. Nevertheless, once he arrived in the port area most of his clients were close by. He soon realised he could see more clients in a day than he could in Boston.

Up to now, all seemed to be going very well.

The first time Ben had travelled from Boston to London, he was staggered to see how hugely busy and congested the port area was… especially when compared to Boston, or even Charles Town. It was a massive expanse of land, stretching all the way along the River Thames at Billingsgate. After further visits he'd also noticed that all imported cargoes had to be delivered for inspection and assessment by Customs Officers, at the 'Legal Quays'. Here the ships were all regulated due to demand for space to load and unload their goods. The river was lined with continuous walls of wharves running for miles along both banks. Hundreds of ships were often moored alongside the quays, or simply anchored in the middle of the river.

Now he was based in London, Ben was learning about the history of the port area and the necessary 'tricks of the trade' that merchants use to get their goods safely onto dry land.

It was during one long and boozy lunch with one of his main clients, Clive Gilbert, that Ben was learning more about the history of London's port and its current situation.

Clive Gilbert, and his two partners, imported codfish, animal furs and skins from three of Ben's clients in Boston. He'd been trading in the port for over 20 years. "Do you know, Ben, there's been a port here since Roman times. As one of the oldest and most famous ports in Europe, it's proved crucial for national and international markets… a big contributor to the city's economic and financial growth and prosperity."

Ben nodded and sipped his beer. He was fascinated to hear how successful Britain's maritime trading had been. He was really keen to get a bigger slice of it for himself.

Clive continued, "Now, the Port of London, despite all the congestion you can see today, is still growing rapidly and this causes its own major problems. The authorities are restricting moorings to 1,500 vessels at any one time. Mind, that's still a squeeze, because it was originally only built for about 500 ships! Goods can remain for weeks in lighters before they can be dealt with. This obviously exposes them to attacks by both the weather and thieves! Well-organised groups of 'river thieves' can often attack the port in large numbers. We have to be always on our guard, or get our goods imported by another route."

"So, Clive, tell me. How do you get your fish into England then? Surely the ice melts with all these delays."

Clive looked around him and checked nobody could overhear him. Once satisfied he leaned forward and whispered, "We have our ways, Ben. I can't tell you specifically, but let's just say it's not all legal and above board! Also we're using some of the other ports around the country."

Ben was worried about Clive's comment. Clive's company was one of his major clients. He knew he couldn't personally cover any more ports in England.

"Besides," continued Clive, now sitting back in his chair. He took a sip of his beer. "We're thinking 'bout expanding... into other trades. Maybe this is something you can help us with?"

Ben sat up. He was suddenly interested again. "What other trades are you thinking of?"

"Have you met George Summers?"

"No," replied Ben. "Not yet, anyway."

"Okay. Well George is a big trader between here, Africa and the Thirteen Colonies. There's a big demand for goods to be exported from Europe to Africa. In return, slaves, gold, ivory and spices are traded in payment. The ships then travel across the Atlantic to the Caribbean and the Thirteen Colonies. There, the Africans are traded for sugar, tobacco, cotton, rice and other produce. These goods are then transported across to Europe."

"I see. So, you think you might be able to compete with George Summers?"

"No. That's not my intention. It was George's idea. He says there's a bigger demand than he can supply. So, Ben, the question is, are you interested in investing with me?"

Twenty-four hours later, Ben was sitting in the Cross Keys inn, waiting for Alexander, another of his business clients. He was still pondering Clive Gilbert's question: "Are you interested in investing with me?" Yes, Ben had told him immediately, but he'd now had time to think more about the logistics and capital outlay. Africa, the Caribbean and most of the Thirteen Colonies were areas he'd not been involved in trading with before. With the exception of Boston and its surrounding regions, Ben didn't have any clients in those areas. He'd mainly concentrated on the trade links between Boston and London. Did he really need to gamble his money on these new countries?

The previous evening, he'd mentioned the proposition to Fiona, but she'd listed her thoughts as to why she didn't really like the idea. Far too big for one person to try and handle. Too costly and too many issues in trying to deal with four trading centres... especially with the many different types of produce. And, finally, the moral issue of exploiting black slaves, which he knew she hated. She'd reminded Ben, not for the first time, how kind and helpful Black Pete had been to him in Jamaica. Certainly her and Grace's lives would have been a lot worse if Black Pete hadn't helped them escape from Spanish Town. She hoped slavery would soon be abolished forever!

Ben couldn't argue against most of Fiona's remarks, especially with regards to Black Pete. After all, without him, Ben and Fiona would never have met!

Yes, he did disagree with the principle of slave trading, but he also knew that lots of businesses would collapse without their availability. Collapsing businesses were no good for him... or indeed, most of his clients!

Ben had promised Clive his answer in two days' time, but, realistically, he was coming to the conclusion that this was far too big a business deal for him… and certainly, he didn't see the point of offending his wife.

"Hi, Ben." Alexander was standing in front of him, carrying two flagons of beer. "I noticed you sitting here, deep in thought, with an empty pot. Anyway, I've got you a fresh ale."

Ben looked up at his colleague and smiled when the new flagon was passed to him. "Thank you. Sorry, I was pondering a business proposition. How are you?"

"Yes, good, thanks. Well, to be honest, I do have a problem. It's to do with Christian Taylor, your client in Boston. He promised me 50 white bear skins and they've still not arrived."

"Christian's usually reliable. Give me a day or two. In the meantime, I'll see if they're stuck in port, probably haven't been released through customs yet."

Ben looked at Alexander, who was sipping his beer. He thought of his current problem with Clive Gilbert. Alexander is the sort of client I need – a small trader, one-to-one contract, Boston to England – not multi-produce, several traders, Africa and slave trading. No, that's all too big and complicated for me. The problem now is, how am I going to tell Clive… without potentially losing his fishing and animal fur trading business account!?

Suddenly there was a commotion outside in the street. Ben and Alexander stood up and walked to the window. A large crowd had gathered and were striding down the street. They were shouting and complaining about something.

"I wonder what's going on?" asked Ben, but more to himself than directly to Alexander.

"They'll be going to the hanging," explained Alexander, in a casual manner.

"What?!" exclaimed Ben. "A hanging?! What's that all about?"

"Oh it's all proper and legal. It's Jack Sheppard, 'Jack the lad', he's being hanged today."

"I've not heard that name. What's he done? Is he a murderer?"

"You've not heard about our infamous Jack!?. The lovable rogue! That's what some people call him. Admired by a few men and adored by lots of women. Come on, drink up, and I'll tell you the story as we walk along."

Ben drank the last of his beer and placed the empty flagon on the table. He followed Alexander out of the inn. The crowd had increased and the shouting was louder. It was an intimidating sight.

"Jack's being hanged in Oxford Road, that's where everyone's going," said Alexander, now having to raise his voice. They'd joined the throng and were being forcibly pushed along with the rest of the crowd.

"You were going to tell me what Jack had done." Ben also raised his voice. He was keen to know why so many people were interested in seeing this man hang.

Alexander explained, "Jack's a thief, a burglar and sometimes a pick-pocket. However, he's mainly remembered for defeating and embarrassing the authorities. He's escaped from at least three different prisons… even the fortress of Newgate! That prison's supposed to be the most secure in England."

Ben leaned towards his colleague, the noise was now intense and he was struggling to hear.

Alexander raised his voice even more. "Despite being hand-cuffed and shackled, he was still able to escape. That's why he's a bit of a hero to lots of people."

The crowd turned at the corner of the next street. Ben could already see that the route ahead was just as deep with people as their group. He wondered if they could go any further.

As the crowd began to bunch up, their walking became much slower, Alexander continued talking, "Jack's very agile, both in mind and body. Originally, he trained to be a carpenter, but also learned how to fit door locks and window bars, so decided to use these skills to suit his own ends. When he fitted door locks he kept a spare key. Then during the night he would quietly enter the property and steal valuables whilst the occupants were asleep. Similarly, he knew how bars were fitted to windows, so again, during the night, he would remove one or two bars, squeeze through the window and rob the owners whilst they were also asleep. Not content with that, he would refit the window bars before he left."

Ben laughed. "As you said before, quite a character. I'll make sure we employ an honest carpenter if we need any bars or locks fitting!"

The crowd turned into Oxford Road. It was obvious this was as far as they were going to go. Oxford Road was so congested there was nowhere left to walk.

Suddenly, there was a huge cheer. To their left, heading along the middle of the road towards them, was a cart, being pulled by a single black horse. In the back of the cart was a thin, small man, standing and waving to the crowd. He was handcuffed and shackled, but it appeared somebody had given him a bottle of brandy. He seemed determined to finish the whole bottle before he reached the gallows. At both sides and behind the cart were about 20 marching, uniformed guards.

As the cart slowly passed in front of them, even Ben and Alexander gave Jack a wave and an encouraging shout.

When the cart moved further along Oxford Road, more cheers rang out as Jack passed by. The crowd around Ben and Alexander began to disperse. There was nothing else for them to see and it was impossible to follow the cart.

Ben thought back to some of the hangings he'd seen in the Caribbean. Some legal, but many carried out by pirates! The common result of them all was a slow and torturous death! Although he'd only seen Jack Sheppard for a few seconds, he had a lot of sympathy for the man's ultimate fate.

He smiled and pondered, more a stroke of good fortune that it's his turn… and not mine!

As the two men turned around and began to retrace their steps, the crowd became much quieter. Their fun was over.

"End of an era," announced Alexander. He smiled and looked across at Ben. "Unless Jack can escape again… before he's hanged. I wouldn't put it past his abilities!"

Ben smiled back. "I'm not sure even Jack could escape past all those guards. Besides, that bottle of brandy will have had an effect."

Alexander laughed. "You know, Ben, London is the largest city in Europe. Through its port and merchant houses lots of goods and money have flowed for centuries. I reckon that's all going to continue… and well into the future. We know it's a great place to earn an honest living, but it's also the perfect place for a life of crime. Whilst the rich get richer and the poor stay poor, the Jack Sheppards of this world will still be around. Just like the countryside highwaymen and pirates at sea, there'll always be these types of criminals."

Ben just smiled… and agreed!

CHAPTER 44

Grace returned to working full time on the estate four months after James was born. Meanwhile, May was looking after both children, but Mrs Bates, from the village, was employed as a 'wet nurse' to feed baby James.

With the money saved from not investing in George's Madeira venture, more sheep and deer had been purchased. William and Wilson had been regular visitors to a number of markets and both were pleased with the quality of breeding sheep they'd obtained. William and Henry Commings had also visited Gloucester, where they'd agreed several contracts with buyers for selling their wool. Demand was still high for good quality fleeces, especially for the local cloth trade.

It was on a day when William and Henry were away again that Grace received a letter, personally addressed to her. Benson handed it to her, along with two business letters. He also told her the messenger had just delivered them and all three had been franked, sealed and paid for by the senders.

Since arriving at the Silverwood House estate, Grace had been secretly improving her limited ability to read and write. Despite Fiona helping her during quiet times on the pirate ships, Grace still felt guilty and restricted when it came to correspondence. She'd told William she'd experienced problems learning properly at school and now wanted to have a much better understanding. She especially wanted to help when it came to the workings of the estate. William could see the benefits for both him and the business, so he eagerly supported her ambitions. As a result Grace had obtained extra lessons at the Dower House, just after she and William were married. The local school teacher visited one evening every week.

After reading both the business letters, she placed them on the office desk. Neither were urgent so she left them for Henry Commings' attention. It was now that Grace focused her attention on the sealed and folded single sheet of paper. It had both her name and the estate's address written on the front. She wondered who could be writing to her. After all, this was the first personal letter she'd ever received!

Gently she ripped away the seal, unfolded the single sheet and read the following message:

10 Cavendish Square,
Marylebone,
London.
Dear Grace,
I hope you, William and Oliver are all keeping well. We are all very happy and well settled in our new home in London. I've written our address at the top of this letter.
It would be wonderful to see you again and I wondered if you would like to visit us for a few days to see where we live. I've got lots to tell you and discuss.
October is fine with us. Please do come, and bring William and Oliver too.
Let me know when you will be arriving.
With much love,
Fiona.

After reading the letter for a third time, Grace had a big smile on her face. Yes, of course, she said to herself, it would be wonderful to meet up again. As for things to discuss, she knew the letter was telling her that Fiona was ready to collect their buried treasure!

All she needed to do now was speak with William!

It was two evenings later when William arrived home from his business trip to Reading with Henry. As they were getting ready for bed, Grace told him about the invitation to stay with Fiona and Ben in London.

William agreed. It was an excellent idea. He was certainly in need of a break himself. He'd speak to Henry Commings the next morning and discuss which dates would be the most convenient.

So that was settled, they would all be going to London. Grace just needed now to tell William about her inheritance!

The following evening, over dinner, William and Grace were discussing the proposed trip to London. William had sorted out the dates with Henry Commings and how long they'd be away from Silverwood House. Grace was pleased and told William she would write to Fiona and tell her the dates. She'd also inform her about James and say she also wanted to bring May along too.

Finally, Grace had the big surprise for William!

"William," announced Grace. She took a deep breath. "I've got some more news."

William ate the last piece of meat and placed his cutlery down on his plate. He picked up his glass of red wine and looked across. "Yes?"

Grace had been thinking for several days about what she was going to say. The last thing she wanted to mention, or hint at, was buried treasure. She and Fiona had planned the proposed trip when she and Ben had stayed at Silverwood House estate. Now it was time to collect their rewards. She knew the story she was about to tell William was a lie, but she wanted to make it feel as believable as possible. After all, the venture she and Fiona were about to embark on was ultimately for the benefit of them both…and the Silverwood House estate.

"Whilst you were away last week," Grace continued. "I received a letter from a lawyer in London."

William's eyebrows suddenly shot up in surprise. He placed his glass back on the table and waited anxiously for Grace to continue.

"The letter told me my uncle Arthur had died and I was the sole beneficiary in his will."

"Well that's good news!" said William, somewhat relieved, but then suddenly realised what he'd just said. "I didn't mean your uncle dying was good news… well you know what I mean."

Grace smiled at William's embarrassment and carried on. "Well, actually, it is good news because, apparently, I'm due to inherit quite a lot of jewellery, gold and money!"

"Wow!" exclaimed William. However, he couldn't remember hearing about the existence of Grace's uncle Arthur before.

"Unfortunately there's a problem. All his possessions are in Jamaica and I have to go and collect them personally!" Grace knew that Jamaica was another lie, but she didn't want William to know anything about their trip to the Bahamas.

"Ah," responded William. He rubbed his chin. "That's more tricky. So you want me to go along with you?"

Grace was expecting this suggestion. This was the difficult bit. She hoped William would agree to her alternative idea. "The thing is, William. I don't know how long I'm likely to be away. It's obviously not possible to take Oliver and James and one of us needs to be in charge here. We can't just leave everything on the estate to Henry for such a long time, and you told me earlier that the next few weeks are going to be really busy."

"I don't want you to go to Jamaica on your own." William was worried.

"I was thinking of asking Fiona…" replied Grace. William couldn't see her fingers crossed under the table. "… when we visit them in London."

"What happens if she can't go?"

"I don't know," replied Grace. However, she already knew the answer, but she didn't want William to think otherwise at that moment. "I just hope she's going to agree."

CHAPTER 45

Grace, William, May and the children arrived in Cavendish Square late Thursday afternoon. After greetings, welcoming embraces, excited discussions about James and general updates from both families, everybody settled down for an enjoyable time.

Early the next morning William joined Ben on his trip to the London docks. He wanted to witness for himself all the lively activity Ben had described. Meanwhile, whilst Mary looked after the three children, Grace and Fiona took advantage of the unusually warm autumn day to go for a walk. In particular, they wanted the time to have a serious discussion.

"What did William say when you mentioned collecting your inheritance?" asked Fiona. This was the first opportunity the two women had to be alone.

"He was surprised and assumed he'd be going with me, but when I mentioned the children, the estate and that I didn't know how long I was going to be away, he became concerned. However, when I said I was going to ask you to join me, he appeared more relaxed. I'd already told him I'd be returning with a large amount of gold, money and jewellery that we could use for the estate's benefit."

"What happens to Oliver and James… whilst you're away?"

"That's not a problem," responded Grace. She had it all worked out. "As you've seen, James has just started eating solid food and May has been amazing with Oliver. Besides, Catherine thoroughly enjoys getting involved with her grandchildren. They'll both be fine. How did Ben react when you told him?"

"I told Ben, a few weeks ago, about us wanting to recover our treasure. Mind, I'd also told him in Boston that I still had some valuables buried in the Bahamas. It was when our finances were stretched, so he wasn't surprised at our plans. He said he'd organise cabins on a ship and arrange for two trusted colleagues to give us a hand. He also told me that the last of his own treasure is buried on Hog Island, so he suggested he join us and collect his valuables at the same time."

"Aren't you concerned about so many people knowing what we're doing?" Grace had already counted five people who were aware of their plans.

"Ben seems quite relaxed about it… and besides, we can't really do it all on our own."

No, thought Grace. That would be impossible… but nevertheless. She was nervous and worried. Too many people knowing… too much temptation!

Fiona could see Grace's expression change. She was obviously feeling uncomfortable about all this extra information. "In addition," Fiona continued, trying to lighten the mood, "we're much less likely to be attacked if we're protected by three burly men!"

Grace looked at Fiona and smiled. "I guess so. What about Daniel? Is he coming too?"

Fiona was a little anxious with her answer. "We have a friend, Constance, who looks after him when we're busy. She's the mother of Daniel's best friend, Archie. They live in the next street. Daniel has stayed overnight there before, but not for such a long break. He enjoys playing with Archie and his brother, Jack."

"Are you happy with that arrangement?"

"Not really," Fiona responded. She knew she would worry all the time she was away. "But it's the best we can do in the circumstances. Ben insisted on going with us. He's concerned about us travelling on our own. Besides, neither of us wanted Daniel to be subjected to such a long and hazardous trip. When we travelled from Boston to London, he was seasick several times."

Grace listened to Fiona but her mind was fretting about leaving her children. She knew they would be well looked after by May and Catherine, but it didn't stop her feeling guilty… or worrying all the time she was going to be away.

Fiona outlined the rest of the plans. "Ben's organised three cabins on a merchant ship, *Tigress*. The ship's itinerary means we'll eventually arrive in Hispaniola."

"Why Hispaniola?"

"The ship has cabins for five passengers. Otherwise it's carrying its usual cargo of wine bottles, cattle, textiles and clothes.

From Hispaniola, Ben thinks, it will be easy to find another ship to take us on to New Providence. He did try to get us on a ship going directly to one of the Bahama islands, but most merchant ships, because of the pirates, are giving the area a wide berth. The best he could do was the *Tigress*. Going to Hispaniola was the nearest he could manage."

Later that evening, whilst Grace and William were getting ready for bed, Grace explained that not only was Fiona accompanying her on her trip, but Ben was travelling with them as well.

"Oh," was William's reply.

"Apparently Ben has some business connections in Jamaica and thought it was a good opportunity to visit them. He'll be doing that whilst Fiona and I are collecting my inheritance."

Grace decided not to mention the extra two male passengers to William, but she did tell him the *Tigress* would be leaving London in just two days' time!

With the news that not only would Fiona be travelling, but Ben too, William was relieved. Nevertheless, he was still worried about the length of time Grace was going to be away… and the potential dangers and risks of sailing the high seas!

A worrying time for everyone!

That night, William lay awake and stared at the ceiling. He realised that when he, May and the children travelled back to Silverwood House tomorrow morning, Grace would be staying in London. It was going to be a sad and unhappy journey. He wouldn't be having the joy of his wife sitting at his side. Or, indeed, her company at Silverwood House, for probably, what? At least three months!

Ben had arranged for a carriage to take him, the ladies and their luggage to the Port of London. When they arrived, both women were surprised at the amount of noise and activity. Hundreds of ships and barges were being loaded and unloaded with all manner of merchandise. More vessels were anchored in the centre of the river, awaiting their turn to moor.

Grace just stared at what seemed to be an orderless and chaotic spectacle.

The *Tigress* was busy being loaded as well. The ladies watched as boxes, bags and crates were carried up the gangplank. Fiona was particularly amused to see cattle being craned over the side of the hull. She made Grace laugh when she joked, "I wonder which cabins these animals will be staying in!"

Two minutes later, Ben joined them, accompanied by two other men. He introduced Fiona and Grace to Leo and Josh. He explained that both men were employed by one of his clients as 'lightermen'. Both men were similar in build and appearance, strong and muscular with short black beards and straggly long hair.

After they'd all shook hands, Ben led the group up the gangplank and on board the ship.

Before Grace and Fiona went into their cabins, they stood at the side of the bulwark. They could just see over the surrounding warehouses and across towards the crowded city.

After a few minutes they gave each other a nervy and uneasy smile. Their new adventure was about to begin!

CHAPTER 46

When William arrived back at Silverwood House he was not in a good mood and demanded to speak to Henry Commings. He'd left May to deal with the children and Benson to supervise the unloading of the luggage. His priority was to find out what had been happening on the estate. He found Henry in the office quietly reading a report from Wilson, the gamekeeper. When Henry heard the door bang open, he stood up in surprise.

"Did you have a good trip, sir?" asked Henry, hesitantly. Still trying to recover from his master's noisy entrance.

"No, I didn't, Henry. What's been going on?"

Henry had not seen William this annoyed before. "Er, well, the new animals are settling in well and we've received another order of fleeces for the Merino and Leicester Longwool sheep. Also... we've taken delivery of another 100 head of red and fallow deer."

William stood and glared into Henry's face. After a few moments, he turned and started to walk back towards the door. "Right..., good," was his reply before storming out and banging the door closed.

Henry stared at the door. "What was that all about?" he said to himself.

Satisfied that Henry seemed to have everything under control, William headed towards the Dower House; he needed to tell his mother about Grace's absence. He was still angry about Grace's trip to Jamaica and now wished he'd insisted on going with her. However, realistically, he knew it couldn't work, one of them needed to be back at the estate. Nevertheless...

As William crossed the gravel path, he began to think about his father's comments all those years ago, when Edward told him of his feelings on learning he would inherit the two estates... and all their responsibilities. 'A millstone around the neck', were the words he'd used. William was now thinking the same way. Abruptly, he stopped walking. His mind was in turmoil. What would he do if Grace failed to return!? He shook his head in anguish… he couldn't comprehend a life without his wonderful wife.

When William entered the Dower House, he found his mother in the lounge. She was sitting on the sofa talking to her close friend, Mrs Bakewell, now the house cook and Catherine's live-in companion.

"Hello, William. What a nice surprise," announced Catherine, as William walked into the room. She immediately spotted the disturbed expression on William's face. "Grace not with you?"

"That's what I've come to talk to you about, Mother," said William, pacing up and down. Eventually, he sat down on the sofa next to her. He leaned over and gave his mother a gentle kiss on her cheek.

Mrs Bakewell spotted William's worried look and decided to leave mother and son on their own. She stood up and announced she'd make them a pot of tea.

Once Mrs Bakewell had left, William took a large breath and gave a long sigh. Catherine was immediately concerned. "There's not a problem between you and Grace, is there?"

"No. Nothing like that. It's, well, Grace has had to go away for a time. To Jamaica, to collect her inheritance."

Catherine was staggered. "Inheritance? Jamaica? What inheritance? You're not going with her!?"

William looked from his mother down to his hands. He then told Catherine about the letter Grace had received about the death of her uncle in Jamaica. "Fiona and Ben are going with her. Apparently, Ben has some business interests there and decided to go with them. Grace suggested it wasn't practical for both of us to go as there is still the estate and the children to take care of. She's going to be away for about three months."

"I see… and you're worried about her."

William looked up and stared into his mother's face. "Yes, I'm really worried. I don't want to lose her. It's a dangerous trip… but she says the inheritance is a small fortune… and it will set the estate up for good!"

"I'm sure Grace will be fine," said Catherine, trying to lift William out of his troubled and anxious mood. "It's only natural for you to worry. I always did when Edward had to travel away. Besides, if Fiona and Ben have gone with her… well, she'll be quite safe."

William nodded his head gently. "I'd hate for anything to happen. I'd never forgive myself for not going with her. Like Father warned me, the estate's becoming a millstone. Grace and Henry are the ones who really run it. I tend to do what Grace tells me. She's normally right… and Henry has a high opinion of her too."

Catherine was just about to speak again when Mrs Bakewell returned carrying a tray containing a pot of tea, two cups and saucers and a small jug of milk. She placed the tray on the nearby small table, smiled at Catherine and left the room.

Catherine started to pour two cups of tea. She pushed one over towards William and picked up her own. "Are you unhappy you've taken on the responsibility of this estate?"

"I'm not really sure, Mother. As you know, I never intended to inherit. Rosie and Thomas wanted to manage both estates. They were much keener than I was. But now they're in South Carolina."

"But you married Grace. Both your father and I knew she would be good for you and probably more successful with this estate… and so it's proved."

"I know." William paused, had a sip of his tea and said, "But what if Grace isn't here anymore? What are we going to do then?"

"William," Catherine spoke more firmly. "You shouldn't be so negative. Grace will be back… and very soon… you'll see. The best thing you can do is concentrate on the estate. May and I will look after the children."

Two days after the *Tigress* had left the Port of London it was sailing towards the Bay of Biscay. After that it would enter the Atlantic Ocean, where it would change course and sail south, keeping close to the west coast of Portugal.

The Bay of Biscay was often choppy and so it was today. A strong northerly wind was billowing the ship's three sails. Not the sort of introduction a first-time passenger would have enjoyed… but that didn't apply to former pirates, Grace, Fiona and Ben.

It was early evening and Grace was quietly lying on her bed. The ship was still rocking from side to side. She was already missing her children and William. She'd thought about them, both last evening, before she went to sleep, and again when she woke up this morning. All she really wanted to focus on for the next few weeks was collecting her treasure and returning home… safely. One last adventure, then back to Silverwood House. Back to being a mother and an organiser of both William and the estate. Her long-term plans all depended on this final trip being a huge success!

Once through the Bay of Biscay, the *Tigress* found calmer waters as it continued to head south past Spain and along the western coast of Portugal. Its planned first stop was to be Madeira. There it was scheduled to deliver empty wine bottles, the small herd of cattle and some of the textiles to Funchal. It would then take on board cases of Madeira wine and supplies of freshwater, fruit, vegetables and meat.

As the *Tigress* sailed past Cape St Vincent, the most south-westerly point of Portugal, the sea became, unusually for this stretch of water, much quieter and almost tranquil. The weather was also dry and much warmer.

Fiona and Grace were standing together on the large aft deck, located immediately above theirs and the captain's cabin. They'd earlier been chatting about the journey but were now just quietly staring at the trail of disturbed white water created by the passage of the ship.

When Fiona looked across at Grace she noticed a change to her friend's face. "You look worried, Grace. Are you okay?" she asked, although she had a good idea of what was troubling her.

"I keep thinking of William and the children. It's the first time I've been away since Oliver was born. I never realised I would be as maternal as this. My mother was never as caring about me," replied Grace. She was looking towards the horizon now and reflecting on the emptiness of the ocean. Just like her heart was feeling.

"I feel the same way about Daniel. Ben often disappears for days on business, but Daniel is the constant in my life."

"This has just got to be a success, Fiona," responded Grace. Her voice was much quieter and more serious. She turned to look directly at her friend. "I've never been as happy as I am now... with William, the children and the estate. I'm really worried something's going to go wrong... and change it all again. I only have good luck for short periods of time."

Fiona gave Grace a sympathetic smile and a gentle hug. After pulling away, she said, "This time it's all very different. The bad luck's over. You've got a lovely husband and two wonderful children. Nothing's going to change that."

Grace smiled back, but deep down she was still worried. What if the ship crashed or was attacked by pirates? Or she was finally arrested for her past crimes? All her future plans would come to nothing, come crashing down around her ears... and with them, the future of the Silverwood House estate!

The ladies stood looking at each other. Neither of them had anything more to say, but then Ben arrived. At least he was in a better mood. "Probably only another couple of days and we should arrive in Funchal," he announced.

"I've been there before," said Grace. Her voice sounded a little weary. "William and I called there on the way back from Charles Town. That's where George, William's best friend, lives."

Fiona immediately thought back to when they'd first met William and George in Charles Town. She knew George was a nice man... but it was Bluey she was in love with.

"Do you know where he lives?" asked Fiona. She wondered whether meeting with George would help Grace temporarily take her mind off William, her children and home.

"No." Grace looked down and rubbed her left hand, then twisted her wedding ring. "George wanted William to invest in his new venture there. He was buying a vineyard. I guess he now lives on that estate. I don't know the name, or where it is, though."

"So, William didn't invest?" asked Ben. He was watching Grace nervously twist her ring.

"No. We decided we needed all our money for the estate. We wanted to increase our stock of animals and renovate two of the outbuildings," said Grace. She remembered the difficulty they'd had coming to that final decision. "I'm sure the vineyard would have been a good long-term investment, but we didn't have any long-term investment money to spare. That's why it's so crucial I recover my treasure. I've got lots of plans for it… and lots to lose, if I don't get it back home safely."

CHAPTER 47

The *Tigress* moored at Funchal for just over 24 hours. Grace wondered if trying to find George was possible… or even a good idea, but in the end she decided there was nothing to be gained. After all, she didn't have anything to say to him. If William had been with her, she knew he would have jumped at the chance. After all, George was William's best friend, not hers. But William was not here, he was back home in England… a long way away from Funchal.

The next morning the *Tigress* set sail and headed south-west. This was the longest part of the voyage, straight across the Atlantic Ocean. Every sailor knew this was the most dangerous part of the trip. Here, the ocean was at its most unpredictable. High waves and gales, not to mention possible hurricanes once ships got closer to the Caribbean. This was where the weather could have its own devastating consequences. There was no emergency island whilst crossing this huge body of water, not until Bermuda, or the Bahama islands. If they were very lucky they may meet another ship sailing towards them… but there were no guarantees. This was neither the Caribbean nor the Mediterranean Sea. It was a huge and potentially terrifying expanse of water… and for a lot of sailors and their ships, the last place on earth they saw before disappearing into a deep watery grave!

It was several days after the *Tigress* had left Funchal when the weather took a turn for the worse. The rain lashed the deck, the wind ripped hard at the sails and powerful waves battered the ship from all sides. Grace, Fiona and Ben had experienced worse, but Leo and Josh were tied to their beds, trying not to injure themselves or falling over on the slippery floors. Captain Crawshaw had ordered crew members who were not currently needed on deck to go to their sleeping quarters and strap themselves into their hammocks. The usual watch was temporarily suspended and the men told to wait until they were called.

By early evening the rain had stopped and the wind, whilst still very strong, had finally started to ease. Earlier during the day the crew had swapped places three times and everyone was now feeling tired or exhausted. Captain Crawshaw called for Jack Taylor, the ship's sailing master, to come to his cabin. Taylor was the officer responsible for the ship's navigation and piloting. The captain wanted to know exactly where they were!

Once in the captain's cabin, Taylor and the captain examined several charts. Eventually, Taylor estimated where they might be. The ship had obviously been blown a long way off course, despite the helmsman's best endeavours to steer the ship in a south-westerly direction.

Taylor explained to the captain that as the clouds were now clearing he'd be able to get a better reading from using his mariner's compass in conjunction with the stars and the moon… probably in about two hours' time. The captain nodded and both men left the cabin. They climbed the stairs and went back onto the main deck.

In fact it was just over an hour later when Taylor announced the ship's new course. The helmsman immediately turned the wheel and the ship was now heading back south-west. The captain decided he needed to stop at St Georges, the capital of Bermuda. Here he would arrange for one of the ship's masts to be replaced and other minor damage to be repaired.

Captain Crawshaw knew it was potentially dangerous sailing in the waters around Bermuda. Besides the hidden dangerous reefs and storm force winds, there was still the outside chance of being attacked by pirates or privateers. However, since the British Navy had started to use Bermuda as a base, he calculated that most pirates would have fled and relocated to Nassau.

The *Tigress* limped slowly over the crystal clear waters towards the harbour of St Georges, a natural harbour located on the north-easternmost part of the Bermudan island chain. Taylor had navigated these waters several times before. His charts were constantly updated with the locations of the many dangerous reefs.

Due to its frequent storm-wracked conditions, the Bermuda archipelago had once been known as the 'Isle of Devils'.

The five passengers were now standing on the for'ard deck and watching as the ship inched its way towards the remaining empty dock. Three Bermudan sloops were already in separate dry docks, each in a different stage of construction.

Ben pointed at the three ships and explained, "These ships, when finished, will be Bermuda sloops. This type of sloop has been built here for many years. They've been specifically adapted and developed for sailing around these islands."

Josh and Leo were intrigued. They were used to the frenetic pace of activity at the London docks. This seemed much more relaxed and unhurried in comparison.

Once the *Tigress* was safely secured, the gangplank was lowered. All five passengers disembarked and started to appreciate dry land and regain their 'land legs'. They were also enjoying the warm sunshine and, whilst Ben, Josh and Leo watched preparations for the damaged mast to be removed, Fiona and Grace decided to explore the small town. Fiona, in particular, wanted to buy some thinner summer attire whilst Grace, who had never been keen on too many clothes, told Fiona she was quite happy with the collection she'd already got on board.

Minutes later the three men decided to leave the dock area and Josh pointed to a nearby inn. As they walked towards it, Ben wondered if he would recognise any of the local faces. He knew some former pirates now called Bermuda their home.

The men entered the inn and Ben ordered three flagons of ale. It was mid-afternoon and the inn was relatively quiet. Whilst the drinks were being poured, Ben looked around the bar area. There were only three other drinkers, older men, sitting at a nearby table playing cards. Ben didn't recognise their faces. He hoped they wouldn't recognise him either. Captain Bluey was no more, gone to 'Davy Jones's locker' some three years ago! Also absent now was the black beard, long black hair and trademark dark-blue coat. Today Ben was dressed in quite different attire. Dark-green knee-length coat, cream knee-breeches, white linen shirt with frills. His lower legs were adorned with silk stockings and black leather shoes with stacked heels. The whole ensemble was topped by a white shoulder-length full-bottomed wig and a matching green tricorn hat. Nothing like Captain Bluey had worn. Nothing like Captain Bluey at all!

Just as the three men picked up their flagons of ale and took their first sip, the entrance door burst open and four British Navy sailors marched in. The leader was dressed in a blue coat with gold laced buttons, the others in plainer blue coats and white waistcoats. All four had pistols in each hand... they were ready for any trouble! They spotted the two groups of drinkers and divided into two pairs. One pair walked towards Ben's group and the other towards the card players. Immediately everyone raised their hands... and held their breath.

The leader looked at Ben, Josh and Leo, very closely. The group stood still, alarmed and wondered what the hell was going on! Ben hadn't seen this face before and desperately hoped the leader didn't recognise his face either.

The leader stood back, sniffed disappointingly and walked over to the other group. There he made a similar inspection. Satisfied he hadn't found the person, or persons, he'd been looking for, the leader waved his arm indicating his group should leave the premises. They walked backwards towards the door and then out into the street. The door slammed behind them.

The three drinkers at the table started to relax and slowly lowered their hands. They began muttering amongst themselves. This was not an unusual incident.

Josh and Leo blew out sighs of relief and then took long swigs of their ale.

It was only Ben who had a self-satisfied smirk on his face.

CHAPTER 48

It was four days later when, after all the repairs had been completed, the *Tigress* finally left dock. Captain Crawshaw ordered the crew to set sail and the ship headed in a south-westerly direction. His plans were to aim towards Florida, but then, at the first sight of the mainland, alter course to due south… next and final stop, Hispaniola!

The weather was warm and the sea calm. A gentle breeze fluttered the sails. The five passengers were taking full advantage of the conditions and spending more time up on deck.

Ben and the ladies were currently standing on the for'ard deck, talking and taking in the view. Occasionally the beaklike snouts and curved grey fins of a pod of dolphins would break the surface of the water. This experience reminded Grace of the many days she'd spent sailing the Caribbean Sea. Now her life had changed completely and she just wanted to collect her buried treasure and get home… to William and her children!

For Josh and Leo this journey was a new and an exhilarating experience. Never before had either of them been fortunate enough to have ventured outside the confines of London. Now, sailing on such a large ship and visiting new foreign lands, it was all an exciting adventure. They were eagerly looking forward to the rest of the trip.

The warm breeze was both invigorating and refreshing… giving little indication of the change of weather conditions to come!

At Silverwood House estate, William, Henry and Wilson were sitting in the estate office, discussing the current situation and happenings on the estate. Without Grace's input, William was relying more and more on his two managers for their suggestions and guidance. Some of the more straightforward issues were already being carried out, but William was reluctant to make bigger and longer-term decisions, without his wife's input and agreement.

When the meeting finished, William decided to go for a walk. He headed towards the small lake where he often went to think in private. He wanted to try and work out the answers to the latest set of problems.

It was a cold day and the gentle wind was blowing from the north. William pulled up the collar of his frock coat and ambled across the meadow. Nearby, a large flock of Merino sheep watched his every step.

William was still worried and uncertain about his and his family's future. Like his father before him, he'd never anticipated being responsible for running the estate. He remembered back to when this situation changed, when he and Grace were due to be married. That was when his parents had spoken to him and told him of their change of mind. Previously it had all been agreed that Rosie and her husband, Thomas, would take over the Silverwood House estate. William would benefit financially from the sale of the South Carolina estate and seek a different path in life. But, suddenly, everything had changed. His sister and Thomas had surprised him when they'd announced they were going to live and work on the South Carolina estate. William couldn't understand this sudden change of heart, especially as he knew Thomas was always reluctant to travel to South Carolina… even for just a brief visit!

Why had they made this sudden and unforeseen decision?

William arrived at the side of the lake and sat down on an old fallen tree trunk. He looked out across the water and noticed the cold breeze was creating small ripples on the lake. In the distance a gaggle of geese were swimming serenely towards the far bank. They don't have my worries, he thought. All they have to do is eat and breed. Not like people who have to deal with the hundreds of problems of owning an estate. Many of which seem to arrive at the same time!

He thought again about Rosie and wondered how she was getting on in her new life. He'd not heard anything since she and Thomas had left England. Was she enjoying the new challenge, a new country, a new lifestyle? William reflected on his childhood, growing up with her. She'd always been a good friend. He was definitely missing her now. As for Thomas? Well that was a different matter. He certainly wasn't like George, or indeed, any other man he knew. No, I never really liked Thomas and the feeling was probably mutual. There was always something, a voice in the back of my mind, that kept saying, "Don't trust him." Was it because he seemed to be only interested in himself? He'd always find an excuse as to why he couldn't go to South Carolina, or, when there was a problem on the Silverwood House estate, he was never around to help out. Yes, he wanted all the benefits of the estates, but wasn't prepared to put himself out, especially, when extra work was required. What did Rosie really see in him?

He then remembered Grace saying something similar and telling him, "This would all have to change!" He didn't think too much about it at the time. He couldn't see how Grace would be able to change Thomas's behaviour. But things certainly did suddenly change! Was Grace responsible!?

William took a deep breath and wondered about Grace. Where was she? Was she well and safe? How long was she going to be away? He realised how dependent he'd become on his wife. How would he cope if she never came back!? He hated that possibility. The estate, the children… and him. They all depended on Grace being here!

CHAPTER 49

The *Tigress* was approaching mainland Florida. It was just before midnight and the sky was clear of clouds. The stars were numerous and shining bright. Below deck the five passengers, and most of the crew, were all asleep in their bunks and hammocks. Meanwhile, Captain Crawshaw and the ship's sailing master, Jack Taylor, were sitting at a large table in the captain's cabin. Taylor had just arrived after taking advantage of the clear night sky to update his calculations. Now, by candlelight, he and the captain were studying the ship's navigational charts and plotting the next phase of the journey.

Jack Taylor pointed to his drawings of the Bahamas archipelago. Made up of hundreds of mostly unoccupied islands and cays, navigation was dangerous sailing through these shallow waters. Taylor proposed heading due south and sailing much closer to the northern and west coast of Cuba. So it was agreed, the helmsmen would be given the new directions first thing in the morning.

For the next four days, the *Tigress* sailed serenely through the Straits of Florida and then entered the Santaren Channel. The weather had been fine and the temperature hot, the sun blazing down almost every day. However, at about 4.30pm on the fifth day, the warm breeze began to increase... and quickly turned into a very strong north-easterly wind. Black stormy clouds gathered on the horizon. Thirty minutes later the ship was pounded by the beginnings of a storm.

Captain Crawshaw stood on the aft deck, next to helmsman Robert Scott. He didn't like the way the weather was changing and wondered if the building storm was in fact the beginning of a hurricane.

Scott pointed to more heavy black clouds brewing from the direction of mainland Cuba. Captain Crawshaw nodded and immediately gave new orders.

They needed to find shelter... and fast!

Unfortunately, the *Tigress* never found emergency shelter or completed her journey to Hispaniola. During the subsequent violent hurricane conditions, the ship was blown a hundred miles off course. It had been driven at exceptional speeds by the wild winds and battering rain. So extreme was the weather that it was impossible for the crew to furl the sails in time. Four members of the crew had already been swept overboard trying to achieve this very task. The ship finally came to rest when she smashed into a long stretch of coral reef, adjacent to the tiny island of Pico, about 50 miles east of the Cuban mainland. The screams of passengers and crew were probably the first human sounds ever heard on this otherwise uninhabited paradise island. The high crashing waves constantly battered the ship, tossing it from side to side. Lurching and thrashing violently, it was a miracle the ship's hull didn't topple over completely.

By daybreak the winds had abated and the rain stopped. The live survivors clambered overboard and waded or swam to the nearby beach. From the original total of 23 crew and five passengers that had left Madeira, only five people dragged themselves onto the golden, powder-like sandy beach. Each person was severely bruised, battered and thought themselves incredibly fortunate to have survived such a horrifying and frightful ordeal. Three of the survivors were crew and two were passengers… one man and one woman!

None of the ship's officers had managed to survive. The three crew members were ordinary seamen, whose job it was to generally help with the work of the able seamen. Two of these 'men' were just teenagers, with less than two years' experience on board the *Tigress*!

By 9.30am, the blinding sun in the cloudless blue sky was already scorching. Its fierce rays were baking both the beach and the more exposed areas of the tiny island. Only a grove of about 20 palm trees gave any shade and respite from the hot tropical sun. Under these trees, hidden in the shade, were gathered the five dishevelled figures that had crawled and stumbled up the beach earlier that morning. Some were now laying exhausted, and hardly moving, others sat silent and were assessing their injuries.

The shattered *Tigress* was now motionless, imprisoned by the jagged coral reef, a graveyard for most of its former inhabitants. Only the aft section of the ship was still visible above the water. Gone were the three tall masts and much of the bow end of the hull. Nobody could deny the *Tigress* was a wreck. But at least it had managed to spare the lives of five, very lucky individuals!

Two weeks later the London newspaper, The *Daily Courant*, reported brief details of the hurricane's occurrence... and its devastating results.

In the early hours of July 10th, 1730, a violent hurricane hit the northern areas of Cuba. It lasted for almost two days. Casualties were considerable. Numerous buildings had been smashed to the ground and thousands of trees uprooted. Surrounding seas experienced waves of over 15 feet high. It was the worst hurricane recorded this year...

In London, few people were interested in such foreign news, except for the underwriters of Lloyds of London, who insured marine ships and their cargo. They eagerly wanted to know if any of their insured ships had 'disappeared', during these horrendous storms. They anxiously waited for further news.

The *Tigress* was due to arrive at the island of Hispaniola around July 20th, however, it was now August 28th and there hadn't been any further sightings of the ship. Three days a week Lloyd's of London printed its own newspaper, the *Lloyd's List*. In the Wednesday edition it recorded nine ships classified as 'missing'.

Listed at number 4 was the *Tigress*.

CHAPTER 50

On the 28th October 1730, at 11.30am, the captain of the merchant ship, *Spirit of the sea*, Captain Henderson, was sitting in the warm and comfortable offices at 16, Lombard Street. Located in the very heart of the financial City of London, these premises were the workplace of the marine insurers, Lloyd's of London. Henderson was explaining to three underwriters the details of a shipwreck that he and his crew had recently discovered.

"My ship and crew were heading for Jamaica," explained the captain. "As we were sailing through the Santaren Channel we were passing the tiny coral island of Pico. That's when young Nick, in the crow's nest, shouted that he could see a shipwreck on the starboard side. We sailed as close as we dared and then dropped anchor. The wreck appeared to be wedged on one of the coral reefs. The waters in this area are notoriously shallow so I didn't want our ship to become grounded. I ordered a longboat to be lowered and four of my crew went to investigate. The ship's aft was still proud of the water and appeared to be the only part of the hull not totally destroyed. I wondered if the ship had been a casualty of the hurricane in July. Twenty minutes later the longboat crew returned and reported the name on the ship's stern. The wreck was the remains of the merchant ship, *Tigress*!"

The three underwriters were listening to every word and making notes as Captain Henderson continued his story.

"I knew the captain of the *Tigress*, John Crawshaw, very well. We'd sailed on various voyages together before we had our own ships. I ordered another longboat to be lowered and four more of my crew and I rowed across to the island. I told the first longboat crew to go back to the wreckage and see if there were any people still possibly alive; although I was fairly doubtful after all this time that they'd find any. I also asked them to look for anything worth salvaging."

The underwriters kept scribbling their notes.

"My longboat crew rowed us up to the beach. We knew this island was unoccupied, but we were hoping to find anyone who might have survived. It's only a small island, so our search didn't take very long. We found four graves with crosses made from driftwood and palm leaves. Then Leading Seaman Potter called to me from under the cluster of palm trees. He'd found another body: a woman's body, but mostly a skeleton in rags. We could only identify her by the remains of her clothes. The wildlife had obviously been having a good meal! We buried the remains of this body next to the other four graves.

"We then collected the five casks of Madeira wine lying on the beach. They'd obviously drifted there from the wreck. Then we left the island in peace."

One of the underwriters had stopped writing and was slowly shaking his head.

Henderson continued, "When we got back to our ship the other longboat crew were already back on board. They reported there were only the remains of a few bodies to be seen. Sharks had probably taken the rest. They collected some of the other casks of Madeira wine and the ship's bell."

Captain Henderson lifted the bell from the floor and placed it on the desk immediately in front of him. Weighing about 50 lbs and made of solid bronze, it simply had the name *Tigress* and *1715* engraved upon it.

The three Lloyd's underwriters stood up and each shook the captain's hand. They thanked him for his report and the ship's bell.

Captain Henderson now left the building and strolled in the direction of the London docks. Before returning to his ship, however, he had one final task to complete.

An unenviable message to deliver.

He needed to call on Jean Crawshaw, Captain John Crawshaw's widow, who lived in the area of Tower Hill. He needed to inform her of the sad news. Henderson took a deep breath and tried to find the courage… and decide on the precise words he was about to say.

At least, he thought, Jean would now know how and where John had died. Other wives and families may never be as fortunate to know the fate of their own loved ones…

…or, indeed, the location of their final resting place!

www.ingramcontent.com/pod-product-compliance
Lightning Source LLC
Chambersburg PA
CBHW030817020726
47499CB00006B/1959